The Flea of Apollisian

by

Shane Moore

The Plea of Apollisian

A New Babel Books Release

381 High Point Drive

Holiday Shores, IL 62025

www.newbabelbooks.com

ISBN: 978-1-63196-018-5

Printed in the United States of America. Design by and © 2013 Kendall R. Hart

Other Abyss Walker Works

White Wraith—Origins

White Wraith—The Lock of Requ *Coming soon!*

White Wraith—Maelstrom Serpents *Coming soon!*

The Wererat's Tale—Book One: Of Rat's and Men

The Wererat's Tale—Book Two: Ring of the Nonul

The Wererat's Tale—Book Three: Collar of Perdition

The Abyss Walker series

The Trial of Innocence

Darrion-Quieness

Death of Kings

Birth of a Nation

Return of the Father

Swords and Plowshares—Patrick Tomlison *Coming soon!*

Other Abyss Walker Works

Dwarven Cookbook *Coming soon!*

Other Works by Shane Moore

"I am Villain" I, Hero magazine #2

Table of Contents

I dedicate this work to my long time friend and editor Sean Taylor. He is worth twice as much as I think he is and half of much as he thinks he is.

"Fools! The beginning and end shall be with the suspicion of an innocent child. Her actions alone will set the great wheel in motion that will bring about an eminent change in the existence of reality. This change will echo off the halls of Merioulus and cascade down into the depths of the Abyss!"

- Warning from the lips of the wicked great red dragon, Renagargus, just as he was set about his prison.

1 The Journey

Azure clouds floated slowly on the heavens of a perpetual twilight. Merioulus, the city of the gods, rested on a fog drifting among the great cumuli. A myriad of colors danced on the rivers and sparkled from jewel-encrusted buildings. The streets were lined with fertile gardens riddled with flowers. Narrow brick ways showcased marble statues and fountains, depicting the gods and goddesses in their glory. The water trickling from them filled great shimmering pools underneath.

Dicermadon, the mighty king of the gods, sat on his golden throne accented with gems. His bronze hand, bearing rings of every known metal, held up his weary head as he frowned. His creased face looked down on the world and at Panoleen. She had once been his love, if ever a god king could have one. He recalled how she looked at him with her soft, yet stern gaze. But now, another had captured the love contained in her beautiful eyes.

In anger, he slapped away a golden chalice that held his wine. The cup clanged as it bounced and skipped across the marble floor. Wine spilled out as it came to rest near the sandaled feet of Leska, the earth mother goddess. She stood in a light green dress that shined like an infinite sea of glimmering lights. Each tiny fold rippled like a wheat field in a light breeze. Her russet hair was long and straight, with flowers that also sprouted around her as she passed by. Leska picked up the chalice with her delicate fingers and casually walked to the jeweled throne to place within the god king's reach, where it slowly filled itself again. She turned to face Dicermadon, tilting her head with an alluring gaze. Her sparkling olive eyes showed admiration and respect.

"What troubles you, my great lord of lords?" Leska asked, her hand rubbing his knee to comfort him.

"Surely you're not troubled by Panoleen's new love?" In truth, she was jealous of her. Though she now held the god king's favor, his heart would always belong to Panoleen, the goddess of mercy before Dicermadon banished her from the heavens for frequenting with a mortal man. She'd been doomed to live a mortal's life on the realms. A fitting punishment, the god king had thought. She would age as the mortals did, and die. Since Panoleen was a Breedikai, an original god, she had no soul. Once she died, she would cease to exist. But what troubled Dicermadon, as well as Leska and all the other gods, was she had met a new lover and was soon to be wed. This lover had no way to fathom the depths of power dwelling within his bride to be. The entire pantheon of gods feared what would happen if they conceived a child, for despite all the power of the gods in Merioulus, not one could prophesize about the birth of her loins.

"She must be stopped!" Dicermadon smashed his chalice flat with his fist. Wine shot out in all directions, splashing himself and Leska.

She calmly wiped the wine away from her face and placed a comforting hand on his massive arm.

"We cannot, my mighty lord. It wouldn't be right. We do not interfere with–"

Dicermadon's booming voice interrupted her as he jerked his arm away from her. "Do not begin to tell me what I can and can't do, Leska! Let me remind you of your station! I am Dicermadon! Lord of lords! King of kings! God of gods!" His powerful visage glared at her while the arms of his throne cracked and splintered under his prodigious grasp.

Leska was knocked to the floor by the sheer power of his voice. Every tapestry, painting, and decoration rattled as his words echoed down the halls of Merioulus. All the gods throughout the city stopped what they were doing and looked toward the god king's chamber. Trembling, Leska raised her head and placed her hair over her ear with a finger. "But my lord, it is by your own decree that none of us who call ourselves good may intervene in the happenings of the mortal realm."

Dicermadon's expression softened and he smiled at Leska's bravery. "You are correct, my loyal servant. You often remind me of why you're the earth mother. Your wisdom of the realms is unchallenged by all. But I am Dicermadon, and my acumen is unmatched, even by you. I dare not interfere with Terrigan, but the evil gods hold no such decree. They'd be pleased to learn the identity of our fallen goddess, and it would seem the wench has lost her right to be shielded from their scrying eyes." Dicermadon smiled as the lesser gods in the chamber mumbled about the god king's proclamation to lift the veil of anonymity.

The double doors of the palace chambers burst open. Flunt strode into the chamber wearing a robe of molten lava that dripped and singed the floor as he walked. Fire danced around his eyes and hands. His hair was aflame like the bowels of Hell, and ripples of heat distorted the air around him. He bowed deeply in a genuine show of respect for Dicermadon. "My great king of gods, on Panoleen's behalf, I urge you to reconsider. I remember a time not so long ago, that your greatness held her in high favor. Certainly the approval of our lord of lords is not so fickle." The god rose after speaking. His molten cape flowed in an ethereal breeze as his defiant eyes of flame stared into Dicermadon's.

"Great Flunt," Dicermadon sat back in his throne and crossed his arms, "you're the last I would've thought to speak on behalf of our fallen harlot."

Other gods had gathered at the entrance. They gasped at the mention of Panoleen being a harlot and whispered amongst themselves.

Dicermadon waited for silence before he continued. "I don't need approval on this matter. Panoleen is no longer one of us. The goddess of mercy no longer exists! All that remains is a filthy wench who wishes to wed another mere mortal. Such a union cannot exist between a Breedikai and a man, and that fact alone is why the shield will be lifted."

There was a hush among the crowd; some shook their heads in disbelief. Dicermadon took a deep breath. "I care nothing for two pitiful mortals, or the happenings under their sun. Now leave me, all of you! I have no desire to discuss the matter further."

Flunt bellowed as he shook his bright orange finger at him. "You don't know what you're about to do, my king!"

Dicermadon erupted from his chair to tower over the god of fire. The sheer power of his presence forced Flunt to step back.

"I know of the prophecy!" Dicermadon boomed. "And that is why I will lift the veil. Panoleen's betrayal will not go unpunished!"

Flunt stared at his cold blue eyes and warned him. "There are many betrayals here, my king. I would be mindful that they all may be punished." He turned and strode out of the chamber.

Dicermadon's face wrinkled in anger as he thought, Your betrayal to my throne will be punished, my dear Flunt. Yours will be punished most of all!

As the crowd outside parted to allow Flunt to storm away, he grumbled to himself, "I may not have the power to stop the king, but I know someone who can delay Panoleen's exposure, even if only for a decade or two."

Chilling rain fell from a dark sky and pounded hard against the country home. Spouts of water gushed from the roof and drained into huge puddles. Davohn Ecnal sat in his old oaken chair and glared at the foolish note Lance had left. Smoke and ash from the roaring fireplace filled the small room. Crackling and popping, the fire matched the tune of the dreary evening. This journey Lance mentioned in his letter had better be over quickly. It had been many a night that he had waited up for his son. Davohn was a simple man from the southern reaches of Beykla, orphaned at a young age. He'd been taken in by a fur trader, learning the ways of trading hides and cutting wood. Though woodcutting kept him on the cusps of poverty, it was honest work and he enjoyed it. He'd married his childhood friend, Sonya, and had a son, Elijah, who helped around his small farm. Eleven years ago, both contracted brain fever and died. Davohn was crushed and withdrew from his friends and family, spending most of his time working or trying to stay busy. He later moved north from the small town of Portia for a few years before settling in Bureland.

There, he'd found and adopted an orphaned boy named Lancalion. Davohn called him Lance for short.

Davohn smiled as he recalled his many fond memories with Lance over the last few years. But though they had good times, he and Lance disagreed on several beliefs. Davohn despised the use of magic, save for the divine power of the priests or clerics. He felt magic was a tool only to be wielded by the godly, not by mere men, but Lance was more open-minded. A sign of the times, Davohn thought. The woodcutter had always known there was something unique about Lance from the day he found him wandering in the woods. Strange happenings followed the boy. Davohn figured the gods looked after him.

A flash of lightning followed by a thunderclap roused him from his doldrums. He focused on the front door to catch even the slightest glimpse of movement. His old eyes narrowed as they studied the door's every contour. Smiling warmly at its small nicks, he drifted back to the past. He fondly recalled the time he caught Lance tossing daggers into the wood, and how he scolded the boy of barely seven years as a result. Lance had argued that he needed to throw the daggers at the door because he didn't want to hurt the trees. Davohn tried repeatedly to explain that trees didn't have feelings. Lance argued that if a seed felt the sun, enabling it to grow upward instead of downward, then it was evident they had feelings. His poor son always had an innocent love for all things.

Davohn had surmised through talk from a few traveling merchants that Lance was born from a wealthy and politically powerful family far south of Beykla. The family, for whatever reason, had been mercilessly slaughtered. Some tales said it was by militia, while others said it was by orcs. The fact that they were cut down was never refuted. So Davohn avoided disclosing where he found Lance. He would hint the boy rode in on a merchant wagon, and no one ever questioned him about it. Orphan boys – or Ecnals, the surname for all orphans – were common, but a few years later, they were being killed throughout the kingdom. Davohn always feared the killers would come after him and Lance, but they lived unnoticed in their small town. Eventually, the murders subsided and the woodcutter forgot about them. As Lance aged, he spent countless hours in the city with who-knows-who, doing who-knows-what. The city dwellers weren't men of honor, much less men of goodness. They spent too much time drinking and partaking in escapades with women than they did helping the community.

A large knot of anger rose in Davohn's throat. That boy had lived with him since he was six, when they happened to cross on the trail. Just because his parents had been those of a high station in some city or country, did not mean he could fraternize with such ruffians. Davohn's anger subsided and he drifted back to his adopted son's childhood. Lance seldom, if ever, helped with the chores around the farm, let alone took the wood into the city. Lance always said woodcutting was the work of a simpleton, and he wouldn't subject himself to such peasant tasks. Davohn's heart pounded, reliving the ungrateful words of the boy. How dare he speak about honest work as if he was above it! It was at that moment he reached a resolve. That boy was going to learn some lessons tonight, Davohn thought to himself.

Lance pulled his thin sable cloak tighter around his face to keep out the driving rain. The long black robe, with many silver runes along the cuffs and collar, clung to his cold skin. The relentless rain pouring over his body managed to creep into small crevices of his cloak, soaking the precious robe. He shuddered as an ice-cold drop ran down the small of his back. Lance regretted having to wear the robe in such weather, but he needed to look noble, and being a woodcutter's son, he owned nothing else that remotely resembled nobility. He checked the leather pack hanging from his waist to ensure the water was only penetrating his cloak. He couldn't afford for his books to get wet. Lance was unsure of the magic in them. He knew they were called the Necromidus and that many believed them to be evil. The young man couldn't understand why someone would think magic was evil. A wicked man might use it, but that didn't make it inherently evil. No one ever claimed the knife that a murderer used as evil, only the man who wielded it. Lance surmised that if he wielded the magic in the four books, it wouldn't make him evil, either. He'd found them a few years ago on a dead body in the woods, miles from home. He kept the pack hidden until he learned to read well enough to understand its contents. Lance knew Davohn was unaware of his studies and the degree of his talents. He dared not risk trying out the pages at home because Davohn might find them. Lance knew how his adoptive father viewed magic, let alone from the Necromidus.

"It's the way of a lazy man to find strange energies to do honest work," Davohn had told him. The words had offended the boy profoundly. The Necromidus and the dark cloak he wore were the only two possessions he cared about. His mother had given him the sleek robe as a gift when he was about four years old. It was too big for him then, but she urged him to keep it close to his heart. She said it would save him one day when he was in a time of need. Somehow, using it against the rain in Bureland wasn't his idea of what she meant. Since he'd always possessed an unexplained talent for magic, and his mother was quite the accomplished wielder of arcane arts, Lance inferred that one day, he would do the same.

The mage drifted deeper into his thoughts,

remembering how his mother would give him a "sparkly kiss," as she called it, whenever she put him to bed. She would blow him a kiss, and gold glittering powder would dance across the room until it hit him on the cheek. He could feel the warmth of her lips when the energy touched him. She would then turn and close the door, leaving him in a beautiful dark bliss.

Darkness. Lance's memory shifted to a bleaker time. He recalled the day the men in polished bronze- colored armor and red silk capes, nothing like the Nalirian armor, barged into his home and spoke to his mother. Lance cowered in the corner of the other room. He heard his mother scream, then cry as she thudded limp to the floor. There was a man speaking softly as he tried to console her, and then he heard more men thunder into the house. Their armored boots softened as they stepped on the large red silk rug depicting a sword through a bright yellow crown – his father had earned it from a duke for his meritorious service in a far northern country. The next words Lance heard were enraged spell casting. The smell of burnt energies and scorched flesh overpowered the house, followed by silence.

Soon after, Lance heard a man's deep voice commanding soldiers to search every inch of the house until the boy was found. Lance clutched the small backpack containing the robe his mother had given him. Shaking uncontrollably, he moved his finger in a waving motion and chanted a few simple words. Hundreds of thin red weaves of magical energy shimmered around him. Once finished with the small shining net, he faded from view into the corner of the room. He had never tested his magic on people before, only animals in the forest. He hoped against hope that it would work against these soldiers. After a short time, the scary men left the house with his mother. He heard banging against the doors and windows of his home, and the muffled voices of the soldiers laughed and joked outside. He dismissed the spell and made his way through the house. There was a burnt smell hanging in the air, and he could hear the crackle and pop of a fire that roared louder and louder. As Lance made his way to his home's common room, he found his mother dead on the floor. Her face was badly burned from what appeared to be magical fire. Several pages of strange writing were scattered around her crumpled form. Lance never bothered to see what the papers were; he simply ran. He fled to the basement and snuck through a narrow passage that his mother had showed him in case a day like that ever came.

Lance made his way through the tunnel and into the forest. He glanced back only once, and he cried himself to sleep for the next few weeks over the image of his mother, dead on the floor, and the raging inferno he once called home.

Lance wandered through the forest as he traveled to the North and found refuge in an orphan house. There, he was given the orphan surname of Ecnal, though he seldom felt at home and often ran away. He moved from house to house, maybe six in all, until he ended up with Davohn, a woodcutter who had also been an orphan. Lance remembered how he was forced to work outside, hauling manure and other despicable jobs. Yet, for some reason, he found a liking to the gruff simple man. Lance soon grew to appreciate Davohn for all he'd given him, but he didn't like his laborious choice in life. Lance laughed as he recalled how he would use some of his magic, unknowing to Davohn, to tease him. He once caused Davohn's axe to be repelled from his grasp as he chopped wood. As Davohn raised the axe over his head,

Lance would form several clear weaves of magical energy to form between Davohn's palms and the handle. The axe would then fly from his grasp, sometimes thirty feet. The spells were simple to him, sometimes consisting of a few score of magical strands.

Davohn would look surprised and study his hands as if sweaty palms were the answer. Despite his uncertainty, he'd notice Lance's amusement, so he allowed it to continue, like a game to make the orphan smile.

When Lance was eleven, Davohn took him to Bureland, a tiny hamlet north of their farm. He was delivering wood to the Inn of Aldon. There was a common room there where many men gathered to eat, drink, and rent rooms. While inside, a drunken man tried to incite a fight with Davohn. Lance noticed that his adoptive father wasn't sticking up for himself, and the man was saying awful things.

Lance focused on the man's head, sending out a fine, tightly-woven net of brown magical strands. They enveloped the ruffian's head, and then nothing but belches were coming from his mouth. The more the man tried to speak, the more it embarrassed him, and soon everyone was laughing while he ran from the bar. Davohn and a few other patrons were afraid of what happened. For a long time, many thought the woodcutter to be some kind of wicked warlock. Lance could always see the energies around him. He could summon clear ones from inside himself, or manipulate others flowing in the world around him. Lance figured that each color had a specific purpose, but he seldom gave them much thought. He used only what he needed.

Lance was awakened from his daydream by a raspy voice. The cold wind, rain, and shadows of night were soon around him again.

"Here ya go, man," the man said with a twitching upper lip. "These weren't easy to come by. There isn't much here. I hope they're enough."

Lance regarded the dark man. He was probably thirty years old, missing all but one of his front teeth, and was unshaven. He had a scar across his nose and to his eye; both twitched as Lance eyed the brown leather pouch.

"About my money..." The man glanced around nervously.

Lance held his hands out palms up, gesturing to the weather. "Well, I can't very well pull them out in this rain, now, can I?"

The scarred man shifted uneasily as water dripped from the hood of his cloak. His one tooth jutted out from his lips as he spoke: "I'm not going anywhere without my money or these papers."

Lance held up the pouch. He concentrated and sent

hundreds of tiny red strands around and then into it. He felt the magic pour from his fingers and stretch deep into the pouch, changing the papers from detailed reports to ink portraits of him. Lance continued to hold it without speaking until the invisible energy left his hand.

The man grabbed it, oblivious to the spell, and pulled lightly. "Look, just open it a little." He looked around them again. "I'll shield it with my cloak. If they look like the ones you want, you give me my money!"

"Forget it," Lance replied. "You've stolen nothing to help me. Take this gold for your silence, these worthless papers, and be gone." He placed a leather coin purse in the man's hands before turning and walking away.

The man took a few steps after him. "You're going to pay me for nothing?" He dangled the fat coin purse in the air.

Lance turned to look at him in the slowing rain. "I didn't specify what exact papers I wanted. It isn't your fault you have no talent for recognizing anything of value."

The man began to argue the insult, but the gold in his hand held his tongue fast. "What do you want me to do with this?" He waved the pouch, his wet arm glistening in the light from one of many covered lanterns that lit the muddy streets of Bureland.

Lance shrugged as he walked and shouted, "I wouldn't get caught disposing of them around here."

The man watched Lance for a bit before hurrying away. Lance ducked behind a building and watched him run toward the Inn of Aldon. Sludge splashed up on the thief's breeches and he held his wet cloak tight. He looked around as he neared the two-story inn, and then, smiling with the gold and the leather case in hand, he went inside.

The inn was an average establishment, but the most prevalent in about two day's ride. Many adventurers, merchants, and other travelers stayed there. It had the reputation of being adequate for the well-to-do, but the common room was rough enough to attract unsavory characters. Gambling was expected there, and if one was lucky, a few serving wenches gave more than a smile.

Lance considered his plan and sighed. He was worried it wouldn't work, but he figured the guards might be dumb enough to fall for it. The wizard plopped in the mud next to a tree where he'd spoken to the thief, spreading a small amount of wet earth on the bottom of his cloak, and a smaller amount on his robe. He stood and surveyed himself, making sure even the tiniest amount of muck was in place. Once satisfied, Lance strolled toward the inn.

Two men stalked forward with no attempt to get out of the rain, or to keep the autumn shower from soaking them. They eyed the streets and alleys suspiciously as if expecting an attack. Water beaded and ran off of their well-oiled, russet leather armor with small, rounded metal studs protruding from the chests and backs. Lance guessed they took great pride in caring for their equipment. Their swords hung loose but confident at their sides. Having grown up in Bureland, Lance recognized them as city militia, as feared as they were respected. They often fought brigands and stray orcs who happened near or into the city limits. It was certainly unwise for a commoner to cross swords with them.

Lance took one final deep breath to calm himself before running to the men, pretending to hold his robe and cloak to avert them from becoming any more wet or muddy. He spoke to the larger of the two men, who hadn't shaved in a few days and wore a snug-fitting leather cap. This coif, or leather cap, was worn by all city militia across Beykla, not just in Bureland.

"What brings you out here in this nasty weather, noble sir?" The militiaman asked as he regarded

Lance. The flexing of his jaw muscles caused the coif to move.

Lance tried to appear scared and shaken as though he'd endured a terrible ordeal. "I was accosted by a vile ruffian, good sir! What else would bring a man of my stature out in this driving rain?" Lance wiped away water from his face and flung it at the ground as if disgusted.

The militiamen's faces were cold and unyielding, and

Lance was having a hard time gauging if they believed him.

"And what did this vile ruffian look like?" the larger man chided.

Lance continued, undaunted. "He was a horrid creature with a scar from his nose to his eye. He had one tooth, and oh, his breath! It was more revolting than his ragged appearance." He pointed to the inn. "He ran in there, the vermin! He took a pouch from me, a leather pouch. It had portraits that I paid an artist to render of myself. He also took my coin purse! I had one gold crown and twenty-six pieces of silver in it."

The large guard whistled between his teeth and leaned forward to look Lance in the eye. "That's a lot of silver to be carrying around."

As Lance looked into his eyes, he grew more impatient. This guard was trying to be difficult. Lance started again and spoke with spite and authority, "I am aware of that, sir. I should have had more gold and less silver as to keep my purse from bulging, but this is irrelevant. I demand that you do your civic duty: go into that inn and retrieve my belongings!"

Lance prayed the angry ruse would make them think he was truly a noble. He didn't have any social standing, but had studied the arrogant, whiny behavior of the occasional noble visiting Bureland.

The guard frowned and raised his voice to match Lance's. "And how are we to know the gold is yours, sir? Are you going to say you'll recognize it?" Rain and spit sprayed from his mouth. "Wait, I know. Your gold is yellow and will look like a small round sun!"

The ruse must have been failing, but Lance had to at least salvage the package. He'd waited too long to learn this information to be thwarted by a simple guard's inferiority complex. So Lance began again.

"I'm sorry, sir. This whole ordeal has been very traumatizing for me. I understand if you can't return my money, but please get my portraits! They are worth more than any amount of gold."

"Well, it serves you–"

The smaller guard cut him off. "We'll return your money and your leather case. Please excuse Harold's rudeness. This is his first night on the job." He raised an eyebrow at the other. "And he isn't performing as well as I'd hoped."

The larger militiaman frowned in contempt, but accepted the criticism for fear of further reprimand later.

Lance followed the guards as they stormed toward the inn, changing his gait to large strides to keep up with them. The large one had a scowl of determined anger across his face. Lance was glad he was following the big man, instead of the big man following him. The rain had eased for the moment, yet water still poured from the guttering and trickled into the swollen ditches. Though the Inn of Aldon was two stories, the majority of Bureland's buildings were one, their angled roofs made of either wood or clay, layered as they pitched downward to prevent the heavy Beyklan rains from seeping in. The buildings were primarily wood, with some made of stone, such as the inn.

As they neared, Lance fidgeted his hand in his pocket nervously. If the scheme didn't work, not only would he have lost those papers – and his coins – he might find himself in prison for hiring the rogue.

However, Lance hoped the thief would be just as interested in staying out of prison.

As the trio walked into the inn's common room, they were blasted by the smell of ale, smoke and body odor. It seemed as if the stench itself was repulsed and trying to escape. The room was large, holding about ten or twelve tables. The bar was at the south end near the door they'd come in. Dull, rusted lanterns hung from the low rafters, illuminating the room. Serving wenches hustled about, filling and refilling drinks, ensuring each patron had as much ale as their coin purses would allow. A large wooden staircase on the north wall extended from the busy room into a black hallway.

Across the room, Lance saw the rogue playing cards

with eight other rough-looking men. They were using an oak table that looked as if a few more could sit comfortably. The men ranged from large and tall to short and fat, and all carried weapons of some kind.

Lance swallowed hard and pulled his hands from his pockets. He hung his cloak on the brass hook by the door and ran his fingers through his course black hair. The warmth of the inn, though pungent, felt splendid compared to the weather outside.

The innkeeper was an average-sized balding man with a potbelly, who shouted angrily at the militia soldiers. "What's the idea, you two? Hang your cloaks up. I don't pay my wenches so they can follow you around, mopping up the water you string about!" He advanced toward them.

The smaller guard drew his sword, and the sound of the steel halted every conversation in the room. Regardless of the activity being conducted, business or pleasure, all men turned to looked at them. When the thief's eyes met those of the city militia, he jumped up, knocking his chair over behind him. He paused for a moment to find an exit, and then ran between tables to make his way across the east wall. Chairs and wenches were pushed over as he rushed toward the stairs. The larger guard dashed after him through the center of the room, while the smaller guard returned his sword to its scabbard and hurried along the west wall.

The thief paused as he reached the north wall, drawing a small thin sword and waiting while the big guard rushed at him.

The guard drew his mammoth sword as he approached. The polished blade was twice as long as the thief's, reflecting the room's light like a mirror. The militiaman's face tightened and his knuckles turned white. A foot shot out from a chair near him. The boot hooked his foot and he fell headlong to the floor. The room erupted in laughter.

The thief darted for the stairs again with sword in hand. The smaller guard turned to cut him off, hopping over a second foot as he ran past. He'd closed the distance to the thief and now only a single table stood between him and the stairs. The rogue glared at Lance as he leaped onto the table with his sword held high. Flagons of ale and plates of food scattered across the table, spilling as he ran across it.

The patrons who were amused before were now angry, shouting curses and waving their fists.

Lance focused his mind on the inner power swirling within him. He often linked it with the feeling of a hand when not in use. He knew it was there, waiting for his command. Lance called on it and sent out scores of thin wisps that only he could see. He created a weave that fell on the thief's hand. The rogue was bringing his sword down in a killing thrust at the guard, when the magical weave jerked it from his grasp. The militiaman waved his blade to deflect a strike that didn't come.

The thief didn't miss a stride after losing his weapon. He jumped from the table, over the small guard, and landed on the stairs. The outlaw took the steps two at a time as the guard labored after him, then abandoned the chase and returned. He approached the table to snatch the rogue's coin purse and leather case that was left behind. One of the men at the table started to protest, but the guard's glare silenced him. He tossed the purse and the package at Lance's feet and both guards started to leave.

"That one will most likely skip town, but keep an eye out, anyway," the smaller guard said to Lance as they stepped into the night.

All eyes turned to Lance as he casually picked up his things, then removed his cloak from the hook before walking out of the inn. Sounds from the common room resumed as Lance strolled away.

The street smelled of fresh rain, washing away the usual stench of local cattle that hung in the air. Though the rain had stopped and the stars were peeking between cloud breaks, the buildings and trees still dripped steadily. Lance was wet and a little shook up, but no worse for wear. I managed to get the leather pouch and my coins back, and none too soon, he thought. The spell that turned the papers into portraits wouldn't have lasted much longer. Remembering the glamour he'd cast on the leather case, Lance peered into it, making sure everything was still there, and then he checked the coin purse. The small leather bag was heavier than before. It seemed the rogue had not only scored a few extra coin while playing cards, he must have added his own coins, as well. He smiled at his good fortune. He'd managed to get these mysterious papers for free, to make the thief an outlaw, and prevented the rogue from being linked to him if the documents were noticed stolen. Lance would have preferred to have the thief arrested, but all in all, he considered it a successful endeavor.

Lance hurried to the eastern edge of town. He didn't want the thief catching him if he'd managed to elude the guards. Lance had exhausted most of his energy and didn't have the focus to control any more weaves, so another altercation could prove deadly.

He glanced around the village as he ran past a group of small wooden houses. He studied each one carefully, trying to recognize Jude's house, his only friend. Jude was unskilled in magic. In fact, he was skilled at very little, save for cleaving a man in two with a sword or axe. He was nearly a foot taller than Lance and twice as wide. Lance recalled how he'd saved him from a group of smaller men who were angry at him for taking their money in a game of cards. By hurling a few spells to spook them, Lance defused the encounter. Jude always claimed that Lance had in fact saved the group, and after Lance saw him fight later, he believed him.

He hurried past other houses littering the edge of town in a disarray of streets and alleys, and came to the shack Jude lived in. The wooden walls were eroded away and candlelight glowed from underneath. Rainwater dripped from the roof and into Lance's hair. He ducked under the small eave to keep it from seeping under his cloak to his neck. Lance never understood why his friend lived in such indigent conditions. As a swordsman, he made more than enough money to afford a better home, or at least one with guttering and sturdy walls.

Lance rapped his delicate knuckles on the door. He looked at them, not so much as a callus or scar, yet he knew they were deadly.

The door swung open and the smell of biscuits wafted from inside. Lance turned and met the silhouette of the man mid-chest.

The looming figure spoke with a deep, powerful voice, "Are you going to come in, my friend, or stare wide-eyed at your pretty little hands as if you wish to bed them?"

Lance extended his hand, and the man took it firmly in a warm greeting.

"Perhaps I have already had my wicked way with my pretty hands," Lance said with a nefarious smile.

Jude recoiled as he piously wiped his hand on his trousers and shook his head. "Come in out of the weather before it washes the guile from you. It would be difficult for me to recognize you then."

Lance stepped inside. There were many leaks in the ceiling dripping into pans and buckets. There was an old crumbling fireplace on the far wall with only embers burning. Frail rafters held up the ceiling, and a lantern sat on a thick stump that was brought in to act as a table. A large wooden chair, streaked with dark stains and splintered at its base, sat next to the stump. Jude bid him to sit in it as he pulled a rickety chair out for himself. Lance obeyed, but only after examining the chair to ensure he wouldn't soil or tear his cloak.

"So what, may I ask, is the reason for the visit of my humble castle?" Jude offered a tentative smile, gesturing wide with his muscular arms.

Lance smiled in turn and tossed the leather case onto the table. Jude pulled it closer and looked it over before opening its heavy decorated flaps. Lance was always careful with Jude. Though he appeared to be just a big man whose talents lie with his sword, Lance learned that Jude was able to read. This alone was a rare talent that could get him a much better job than digging trenches. Therefore, Lance had decided he was a valuable friend, and not one to underestimate.

Jude looked at the case's three sheets of strange writing and asked without looking up, "When did you get this?"

Lance paused before he answered. "I have known you a long time, my friend. If I were to guess, I'd say you not only know when I got it, but whether I have looked at it or not."

Jude took a sip from his flagon and swallowed slowly. He wiped his mouth with his sleeve before responding. "Well, I'd say because the outside of the case is wet, and seemingly valuable to you, you got it tonight while you were outdoors. Since your hands are wet, and these pages are not, I would also guess you haven't looked at them." Jude studied Lance's face. "Have I passed your test?"

Lance shifted uneasily. "What makes you think I'm testing you?"

"You've been testing me for almost a year, I'd say. Are we finished with these games or are you going to tell me what you have up your sleeve?" Jude folded his massive arms under his thick-barreled chest.

"I'm hiding nothing up my sleeves, other than my arms of course... and a small adventure."

"Lance, your so-called adventures usually involve trouble; a lot of trouble." He tried to appear uninterested.

"So what you're saying is that you're afraid of a little adventure?"

"No, what I'm saying is that whenever you're involved, there's no such thing as a 'little' adventure. A lot of trouble would be the correct description." Jude pushed away the leather case. "I have a lot going for me here. It may not seem like much to you, but it's all I have. Furthermore I–"

Lance interrupted in a soft, solemn voice. "I think when my parents were killed, they were looking for me instead."

Jude looked at him, astonished. "What do you mean? I thought your parents died from a sickness, and gave you up to protect you from it?"

This was what Lance had always wanted to believe. He didn't want to face the possibility that his parents were slain at the hands of the magistrate. He wanted to believe they loved him so much, they gave him up to protect him from a plague sweeping across Terrigan like a scourge. As Lance aged, the lie was easier to tell, as if the more he spoke it, the more it came to be true. Oh, how Lance wished it were true. He wished for anything but the truth, so that he didn't have to hear the screams of his mother, so the guilt of hiding as she was slain would be washed away. Instead, it always reared its ugly head to snap at him. Lance sighed deeply, letting his shoulders slump as he looked up from tired eyes. "Jude, my parents were killed when I was six. My father was hung from my swinging tree outside my home, and my mother was burned by the very magical fire that she so often commanded. The men who did this were looking for me, but I hid by using my own magic until they were gone. Then I ran as fast as I could."

Jude growled at the mention of Lance's foul magic. He knew his friend used it, though the extent of his ability was unknown to him. Jude hated magic. It was something mysterious and dangerous, best left to the gods. He'd heard stories of how the strongest of warriors were defeated by an old man in a robe because of magic. The old man had no armor, no sword, no way of defending himself, save for that which was unseen. Men were burned to a crisp without any fire nearby, and others were turned to solid stone. Jude wanted to speak up, to tell his friend of how magic was trouble, but he felt the pain in Lance's voice and let him finish.

"The goddess of mercy must have been watching out for me that day, because I wandered through the woods, surviving on what little I could find. I bounced from orphanage to orphanage until one day I met a man in a wagon. He was a woodcutter and was taking small trees he had felled into town. He said I could ride with him as long as I didn't fly away. I've always dreamed of creating a magical weave thick enough to allow someone to ride with the clouds. I learned later, much to my disappointment, that Davohn didn't have any idea about magic, so I kept my secret. I told him my parents were killed from a sickness and I ran away to keep from my Aunt Nancy. I told him she was awfully mean to small children, and that I wasn't even sure where she lived, since I had traveled for many months. But after a while, I believe he figured out there was no sickness."

Jude studied Lance's face. He had rarely seen him so open and honest. Yet Lance was known for his flair at storytelling.

Jude had seen him tell a bold-faced lie to a bar patron, and somehow the man believed it. Not only believed it, Jude thought, but had gone to the grave believing it. It was Lance meddling with that damnable dark power, but Jude realized that was who Lance was, and if he was to accept him as a friend, he would have to accept his magic, also. But he didn't have to like it.

"Lance, I thought you had a better grasp on religion. There is no goddess of mercy... Is there?"

Lance smiled at his friend's query. He loved to talk, to teach. "Well, my mother taught me that some gods were forgotten by men, that they were cast from the heavens. She said the goddess of mercy was one of those gods."

Jude shook his head and sat back in his chair. He raised his fingers to the bridge of his nose and grimaced. "So what do you wish of me, Lance?" His question lingered in the air as he waited for a response.

"Well, I need a swordsman. I was hoping you could be that for me. As I swing the blade of energies and knowledge, you swing the blade of steel. Of that blade, I know nothing." Lance hoped the admittance of inferiority would spur Jude into agreement.

"Lance, I've known you most of my life. You cannot afford my sword, and I can't afford to go without income."

Lance glanced down and forced a forlorn look on his face. "What's the minimum amount per week you would charge for your sword?"

"I think one gold piece a week would cover my expenses." Jude hated to disappoint his friend, but needed to keep him from going on some foolhardy journey. He thought this was the best way. Jude reasoned that he would appear as if he wanted to go but was unable to. This, in turn, would keep Lance from going while saving their friendship at the same time. He knew that once Lance had it in his head to do something, he was more than determined to get it done. He was resourceful, too.... Then Jude realized it was too late: he had been tricked.

A small leather bag overloaded with coins landed on the stump. The coins clanged against one another as the bag came to rest in front of Jude.

"Well then, swordsman, I'll pay you two gold pieces a week. Double the amount you asked for and you will find ten weeks worth of pay in the purse. I'll see you in the morning." Lance rose from the table.

Jude stared at the coin purse in disbelief. As Lance left, Jude cautiously opened it. Dozens of bright gold coins spilled out. Jude sat blankly staring at the glittering pile. This was more money than he'd eve seen in his life. He just hoped he would live long enough to spend it.

"Do the ends justify the means? Often this wisdom comes to light in life. If it has not, it will. There will come a time when you must ask yourself if the results of the methods you use to achieve a task are worth the end result. I wanted justice for my parents and was willing to break the law to find it. I don't know if the thief killed anyone to get those parchments. I don't know who he stole from, or if he stole at all. Is that wrong? I could easily say I paid him to retrieve the parchments. The methods he used are beyond my control, but were they?

"I was wrong for hiring Grascon to steal them. Had he not, I might have never been set upon the path I would unintentionally walk. But had I not, would I have walked down any path, or would I have become a victim like the Ecnals before me? A great person in time, lost to senseless murder. Of these things, I will never know.

"Do the ends justify the means? I guess it is a question best answered by those who suffer the means."

- Lancalion Levendis Lampara

2 The Plot of Kings

Hector De Scoran, the king of Nalir, sat rigidly against his golden throne. The tips of his armored hands clicked impatiently against the arm rail as he studied the ancient text:

"A day shall come to pass when the mother of mercy shall bear child. This child will be like no other, for gods and men alike will seek to vanquish him. The hate from the hells dwells within his mind, as compassion for the meek guides his heart. If allowed to live, this child will bear the false testimony of the gods, as he ascends the throne of righteousness while working the magic of evil. The evils of the realms will oppose him, but they will be crushed asunder as the scorpion under an anvil of fire, for he shall command evil and good alike unto his ascension..."

The king's scholars had studied this dusty tome of prophecies for years with minor success. Hector slammed it shut, furious that a two-bit thief had managed to steal a copy not two months ago. He had no idea why the rogue would be interested in it, but doubted he'd be able to use it. It took his scholars years to decipher a single sentence.

No matter, he had tortured and killed the watch who failed to capture the rogue, which pleased him a little.

Hector glanced around his room, deep in thought. Light flickered from the candles and shadows danced across the floor. On the far end of the room, two gigantic marble pillars lined an ornately carved door of thick, polished oak. Its hinges were crafted from cultured brass, and the supports were encrusted with a plethora of jewels. The chamber was magnificent, lined with tapestries depicting great battles and places of beauty, yet it provided no solace for his frustration.

As Hector rose from his throne, the leather under his armor plates creaked and popped. The king stretched his weary arms before sweeping back his long blue silk cape. The candlelight revealed his shoulder armor with an intricate design in the shape of a silver scorpion. For centuries, the arachnid had been a symbol of the kingdom's power and strength. As Hector ran his fingers across the raised design, recalling the words of his father and his father's father. "This is our kingdom, my son, do not be the one who allows a single grain of sand to be claimed by another." He would obey, regardless of the measures or sacrifices required.

The chamber door opened, interrupting his moment of vanity. A man in leather armor hurried to the throne, knelt to one knee, and lowered his head, never daring to look up. "My lord, I bear a message from the scouts."

"Speak!" Hector glared down at the messenger as if to strike him dead at any moment.

"My lord, there are two men traveling north from Bureland toward Central City. One is a large man, armored in chain and the other appears to be without armor or sword. He wears the house symbol of Ecnal."

Ecnal, Hector thought. Ecnal was no house of nobility. In fact, Ecnal was, or at least very nearly, wiped out by his own hand. The only surviving members that Hector was aware of were a woodcutter and some old women, and no woman of Ecnal would be of mercy or virtue. The house was an orphanage that took in children from rapes, deaths, and prostitutes. He had originally feared the prophesied child was an Ecnal, but after many years of having them slain, he decided it was improbable.

The dark king lowered his voice as he spoke, "And why, messenger, is this information valuable to me? We wiped out all the Ecnals years ago. I doubt this man is one."

"In my lord's infinite wisdom, I will never know its true value, but I was told the cloaked one does carry a Necromidus."

Hector's face tightened as he pondered it. The

Necromidus is a rare collection of books containing the basic incantations of Necromancy. All four tomes are essential for progression in that field.

"You have done well, messenger." Hector arched an eyebrow. "What is your name?"

He shifted nervously on the floor. "Optis... Optis Midigan, my lord."

"You've done well, Optis. Continue to serve me competently, and you shall be rewarded."

Optis's palms, wet with perspiration, were pressed firmly to the cold marble. He was worried when Soran had picked him to deliver the message, but it was turning out to be a blessing in disguise. He tried to hide his pleasure, though his widening grin betrayed his glee. "Yes, my lord. How may I serve you on this day?"

"You shall return to Soran with the orders I'm about to write. However, if the letter's seal is broken…" He held up an ivory scroll case. "...I will be very displeased."

Optis looked up at the case. It was covered in carvings and symbols, and was about a foot long. Optis nearly fainted in panic as his mind raced about his fate if something happened to it. He puffed his chest out proudly. "Only in my death shall another disturb the letter."

The king's eyes narrowed, causing the messenger to withdraw. "Optis, I urge you to ensure the letter is not disturbed, even in your death. For the icy fingers of my vengeance extend far beyond the realms of the living."

Fear gripped Optis; scarcely able to speak, he let out a meek response, "Yes, my lord." He was aware the king had arcane power far greater than most that walked Terrigan.

Hector opened the long ivory tube. His thick fingers stretched in to retrieve a parchment and he placed it on the podium before him. Dabbing an exotic quill into an inkwell, he wrote:

"Soran,

Once again, you prove your worth. Even though you haven't identified the child the prophecies speak of, you have found someone, and at the very least, something, and that interests me. The council of seven still works to unravel the prophecies, and sometimes I am forced to motivate them. Sometimes I motivate them for sheer enjoyment. I await your loyal service to my crown, Hector."

He dabbed his wax seal on the message and stepped down toward Optis. The messenger still shook from the king's proclamation of punishment after death, and cowered as Hector placed the letter in his knapsack. "Your task has been set, messenger. Do your duty."

Optis quietly stood, turned, and strode toward the door, straining to keep from breaking his hurried walk into a full run. When the sound of the chamber door clicking shut echoed across the room, Hector returned to his throne and re-opened the ancient text. "...When the mother of mercy shall bear child...." Hector frowned. Who is the mother of mercy? Did she already give birth? Why was she called the mother of mercy? All of these questions confounded the dark king.

Hector gently closed the tome and stepped down from his throne. He glided across the marble floor to a small door against the north wall. The old wood creaked as he opened it, revealing a large stone balcony lined with potted trees and beautiful oak tables and chairs. Tapestries depicting the black scorpion with an azure background hung from the walls. Ivy vines reached out over the edge and down the side of the castle. Moonlight poured into the throne room and the sound of the night breeze blowing through the trees' leaves resonated across the balcony. Blue silk curtains hanging from the railing casually danced in the wind.

Hector sat at one of the tables and opened the text again. He read awhile and in frustration, slammed

it shut. The sages were certain his kingdom was the one named as the scorpion, though they admitted having no idea who or what the anvil of fire was. He glanced out over his kingdom. He could see lush trees for about six miles and after that were hundreds of miles of deadly swamps. He felt trapped for the first time in his life. Before, the swamps isolated him from invaders and served as a perfect defense, keeping his kingdom from ever being conquered. But now... he took a deep breath. Now it seemed to serve as a cage, holding him until this anvil of fire arrived.

Hector stood up from the table, tucked the heavy tome under his arm and made his way back through his throne room to his bedchamber. He closed the door, locked it and sat on the corner of his giant bed. He placed the book on a stand and removed his armor. He was so exhausted, he let the steel lay where it fell and climbed into bed. The silk pillows enveloped him and he struggled to keep awake. At least I know it is a male child that is born, he thought before drifting off into a deep sleep.

Davohn sat in his chair; how he loved the green velvety fabric that lined the seat. He remembered how Lance worked most of a summer doing extra jobs at the library to buy him something nice for his birthday.

There was a distant rumble of thunder and a rising breeze whispered through the leaves of the large trees around the house. Davohn quickly forgot about the approaching rain and ran his fingers down the smooth contour of the armrest that his woodcutting axe leaned against. The dark polished oak had served him on many a day as he thought of work, play, or anything demanding more than passing reflection. The brief shower had let up an hour ago, though it seemed a heavier rain was soon to arrive. Lance would have no excuse for not coming home. The rains would have provided an explanation, but he should have been back before it started. Yet, now there was a brief dry spell and the fool boy still wasn't home. Anger tore through him as he recalled all the times in the past Lance had come home late, or the night he didn't come home at all. Though Davohn was angry, he remembered when Lance was a small child. The boy was always independent. Even at age six, when Davohn had found him, Lance had been alone in the wilderness for more than a month. The boy clutched a small leather backpack that he refused to let out of his sight. Davohn had always wondered what was in the pack, but respected Lance's right to keep it secret. The woodcutter thought it had something to do with Lance's ability to survive as long as he did. Any other child would have been eaten by a wild animal or something far worse. The deep woods of Beykla were known to hold many creatures that were not quite man or beast. They would have made short work of him, yet the boy confidently strolled up that day. He was hungry and dirty, but no worse for wear. Davohn pondered if the gods were keeping a watchful eye on him.

The woodcutter rose from his seat, slowly stretched his tired muscles, and walked into the kitchen. It wasn't a large home by any means, but it was more than adequate for him and Lance. Since Davohn was an orphan, he felt the Ecnal surname would serve him well. There were many others like him, so no matter where he went in the world, he might find a brother or sister. Since he presumed Lance was an orphan, Davohn hoped the name Ecnal might give him a greater sense of family.

He retrieved a wooden flagon from the cupboard and poured himself some water from a plain clay pitcher. As soon as the water touched his lips, he heard a noise. Placing the cup on the counter, he went into the living room and found the front door wide open. A cool breeze flooded the room. The smell of wet grass and mud wafted in from the outdoors. The trees outside weren't blowing hard enough to force the door open, making him wonder what had caused it.

As Davohn closed the door, he felt a twinge of panic. A slim shadow shifted on his right from inside the room. Before he could react, shooting pain tore through the back of his right leg, forcing him to the ground. There was a second strike to his head, knocking him prone. As he fought for consciousness, he was unsure of what exactly happened. Warm blood ran down the side of his face and pooled around him. Davohn cringed as his hair was jerked up and the weight of a grown man sat on his back. Cold, razor- sharp steel pressed against his neck.

"Where is the mage?" the figure said with a raspy voice.

Davohn could hardly understand him. "What mage?"

The blade was abruptly taken away from his throat, and the pommel was pounded into the side of his head a second time. Then the blade came to rest under his chin again. "Answer me, woodcutter. I know he lives here."

Davohn screamed inside. Another blow would knock him out. He must not die, not like this. He felt he blade move from under his chin. It was now or never. Before the blow could land, Davohn turned his weight and hunched forward. He felt the man flail as he toppled over his right shoulder. Davohn struggled to his feet as his weak legs shuddered under him. He stumbled to his chair and reached for the axe but, to his horror, it was gone. Davohn dropped to the floor and frantically searched the darkness while the intruder laughed. "You didn't think I would just leave that crude weapon there so you could try to stick it in my chest, did you?"

Without pause, Davohn turned and ran for the window. He lowered his head and outstretched his arms. He heard the sound of breaking glass and the rush of night air as he toppled head over feet, landing in the soft mud on his back. He slid a few feet before scrambling up and running into the dark forest. Sticky blood dripped into his eyes. As he tore away a sleeve and tightly wrapped his forehead, he could feel pieces of glass and wood protruding from his arms and shoulders. After a quick inspection for serious injuries, Davohn's mind raced. Who was that man, and why was he here? What mage was he looking for and who in their right mind would hunt one?

What if Lance came home? That murderer would kill and torture the poor boy when he arrived. With new resolve, Davohn headed back to the house. As he neared, he could see a thin haze of smoke as it filled the forest. Davohn ran through the trees as fast as his old legs would carry him. His house was completely engulfed in flames, lighting the area like a noon sun. Davohn raised a hand against his face to shield it from the intense heat pouring off the blaze. Then he screamed in pain as the flat head of his axe rammed into his right leg. His shin shattered, sending him face first into the mud. Davohn turned over and stared at the man's face. The assassin raised the axe over his head and plunged it deep into Davohn's chest. The dying woodcutter gasped, trying to claim a breath that would not come.

"Your boy should not have crossed Grascon the Nimble." The assassin stood over him with his scarred face twitching violently.

As Davohn's vision began to fail, he stared at the face of his killer, at the single-toothed smile and the ugly scar that went from his nose to the corner of his eye. Then he stared at nothing.

Lance shifted uncomfortably in his saddle as the autumn sun beat down on his pale brow, making him sweat profusely. His back and legs ached and his head hurt from the long, arduous ride. He was hungry, and worst of all, he didn't like the smell of his horse. The damned filthy animal reeked. This trip was turning out to be more than he bargained for. Lance turned his weary head around and looked at Jude. The swordsman was on his horse with a wry smile, heavy hips rolling with the sway of the animal in a strange melodic dance. He showed no sign of discomfort. In fact, he seemed to be enjoying himself. He wore a new suit of chain armor that glistened in the light, and his large sword hung across his back, the leather strap holding it crossing his chest from left shoulder to right hip. Jude's long brown hair dangled about his shoulders as he plodded down the trail.

Lance wondered how his large friend was so accustomed to riding, but resigned to the fact that any proficiency on a horse took time. Just as he studied long and hard to be a skilled mage, Jude must have studied equally hard at learning to ride.

He wiped his brow with his sleeve as the unusually hot sun baked him in the dark sable robe. The trees alongside the trail loomed over them, but seldom blocked the sunlight. The trail was overgrown with grass, save for two parallel marks worn by wagon wheels.

Jude picked his teeth with a twig. "So... uh...where are we going?"

"I thought you were a hired sword." Lance knew how Jude hated being the last to know about anything; much less something he was involved in.

"Well I am, but if I'm to use that sword you hired, I might need to know who to use it against," Jude said, now smirking more than Lance.

"You're to use it against anyone who might harm us," Lance said sarcastically. "It's a good thing I'm doing the thinking on this journey."

Jude looked forward and frowned. It was bad enough his friend trapped him in this trip, let alone treated him like any other sell sword. But for two gold pieces a week, he would endure just about anything. "When an enemy attacks, be sure to remind me which hand to swing my sword with. I wouldn't want to be accused of thinking."

"If these armored men coming down the road attack us, start with your right hand. I'll advise later if you need to switch." Lance's smile faded.

Jude glanced ahead, straining his eyes to see through the haze. A hundred yards up the trail, he could see three men riding toward them, clad in brass-colored scale armor with bright red silk capes hanging behind them, lifted by a light breeze over the horses' rumps. The war horses had thick barreled chests and wore brass-colored barding over their heads. Two men rode side by side in the rear while the center man rode a few feet ahead. He had a wooden standard affixed to the left side of his saddle that rose a few feet above his head. The red and white flag depicted a tilted crown with a sword through the center of it. The flag was red on the left side of the crown, and white on the right.

"Beyklan high guards," Jude said. "They shouldn't

be this far south unless they're up to something." Lance recalled his childhood terror, now transformed into anger. "The uniforms these men wear are the same as those who murdered my parents."

"Don't get any bright ideas, Lance. Not even ten gold coins a week would be enough to become an outlaw to the crown of Beykla."

Lance spoke in a deep, quiet voice. "My soul screams for vengeance."

Jude swallowed hard and moved his horse closer to Lance. "These men would have been but babes when your parents were killed. Don't hold them accountable for crimes of the throne."

The soldiers' finely trained animals stood still with their ears back as they halted in front of Lance and Jude.

"Good afternoon, citizens," the leader said with a loud voice. "I am Sergeant Oswald Thorrin."

Lance and Jude remained quiet, and the sergeant shifted uneasily in his saddle, looking them over. He decided to explain his intentions better. "We are looking for a vagabond. He is wanted for committing many crimes in Central City, among them murder and extortion. The man is about ten hands high with dark hair. He is missing all but one front tooth, and he has a scar from the corner of his nose to his–"

"What did he steal?" Lance asked.

The sergeant scowled at Lance's rude interruption. "What he stole is unimportant!"

Lance urged his horse forward, ignoring the sergeant and pushing his way between the soldiers' horses. Jude followed, and the horses stumbled to get out of the way of his war horse.

The sergeant jerked his horse's head around roughly. "You dare ignore a sergeant of the Royal Beyklan Army?"

Lance continued to ride, not turning his head back as he shouted over his shoulder. "If you are unsure if I dare, sergeant, wait until I and my swordsman round this bend and are out of sight, then ask yourself the question a second time. If you are too daft to come to a conclusion at that point, I am sure one of your lackeys will enlighten you."

Jude chuckled under his breath. "I don't think this is a good idea, at all."

The sergeant's square-jawed face flushed red, and he trotted ahead of them. Then he turned his horse to face them. "You dare insult the king?!"

Lance and Jude continued their horses' slow walk. The dry leather of Lance's saddle creaked as he looked around the sergeant in a haughty fashion. "I don't see any king, only a corpse if he continues to pester a wizard and his swordsman. But if I did see the king, and he asked such preposterous questions, I needn't insult him, for if he spoke as you do, his own stupidity would do it for me."

The sergeant drew his sword and leveled it at arm's length at Lance. The finely crafted blade shined in the afternoon sun. "You will watch your tongue, boy, or I will cut it out!"

Jude thumbed his huge sword and looked at Lance nervously, waiting for the command to cleave the men.

"You will bow down to me and beg forgiveness from the crown!" Spittle sprayed from the sergeant's clenched teeth as he growled.

The other soldiers slowly drew their long swords and trotted up from behind. It was obvious they were intimidated more by Lance and Jude than the sergeant.

Lance calmly cleared his throat. "Sergeant, you cannot make demands when you are asleep on your horse." He channeled the magical energies that swirled around all things, weaving a thin green net over the man's head.

The sergeant tried to resist, but soon his arm lowered. Then he dropped his long sword and slumped forward. His horse sidestepped under the shifted weight. The other soldiers looked at each other and urged their horses backward. It was clear they were afraid.

"Your sergeant is fortunate that he only sleeps." Lance said. "When he wakes, tell him he is alive only because I didn't wish to kill him today. If he returns and I see him before the moon cycles again, I will strike him dead with a word. Do you understand?"

The soldiers nodded, grabbed the reins of the sergeant's horse, and pulled the dun along the trail as his body slouched over the saddle.

As the guards faded into the distance, Jude turned to Lance. "One of these days, you'll tell me all the tricks you can do, so I don't swing my sword prematurely."

Lance smiled at him. He'd never seen his friend so disturbed. Lance knew it had something to do with the encounter, because Jude didn't like the use of magic, but Lance hadn't believed that anything could spook him.

"Did I alarm you, Jude?"

"Once he finds that thief he's looking for, he will surely come to us with some kind of a charge. That, and I just don't like things you can't see or feel."

Lance shrugged. "Well, I'm sure the sergeant felt it."

Jude didn't respond immediately. Instead, he faced the road with his thick jaw muscles flexing while he ground his teeth. "You hired me for my sword, yet you make me feel as if I was hired for company rather than protection."

Lance shifted in his saddle and chuckled, dismissing his friend's concern. "Jude, believe me, when we encounter someone worthy of your blade, I shall be the first to scream your name in my defense. I just felt those guards were undeserving to die at the hands of someone such as yourself."

Jude leveled a stern gaze at him. He decided to concede the point, though, even if Lance thought he'd played into his hand. Jude despised battles of wit and simply wanted to be an equal. "Look, I'm sorry. I'm just not taking well to being your hired help. How about I return your gold and we spend the rest of the journey, regardless of where it leads us, as the friends we've always been." Jude offered half a smile. He thought it came out better than it sounded in his head.

Lance grinned wide, exposing his perfect teeth. "As you wish, but we do need someone to watch the money. And since I have a flair for the extravagant and you're known to be quite frugal at times, you can manage our adventure fund."

"Well, I could but–" "Good, then it's settled."

Jude shook his head. "You could talk a dragon right out of his scales."

Lance reached over and jovially slapped his hand on the back of Jude's armored shoulder. "I hope you're right. That might be useful someday."

They traveled on through the vast countryside. Lance gazed in wide-eyed wonder at the expansiveness of the Beyklan land. It was a beautiful kingdom with forests as vast as oceans. As far as the young mage could see, there were rolling hills and large trees, speckled with an autumn coat of deep reds, yellows and browns. Lance knew from speaking with wandering adventurers in Bureland that Beykla was having difficulty with the dwarves of the Pyberian Mountains in the Northwest, near the kingdom of Adoria. Adoria had begun a civil war with Andoria, and most of the dwarves' income came from trading with the feuding nations. Beykla angered them by outlawing trade with Andoria. The dwarven high council met with the Beyklan king, Thortan Theobold, and he refused to hear their pleas for an end to the sanctions, thanks to a dispute regarding the dwarves' taxation on their mined goods. After his refusal, the dwarves returned to the mountains and hadn't paid taxes since. That was almost two years ago.

The civil war lasted nearly eight months before Andoria was conquered. Lance knew little of warfare, but was aware that eight months was a short war. There were rumors that the Ka-Harkians, a kind of mountain people, had aided Adoria to gain land from what was left of Andoria. Lance had never met a Ka-Harkian, but he knew them to be expert swordsmen. Even the women were skilled with a blade. Ka- Harkia had never been conquered, or even attacked, because all the plants growing on the mountains were highly toxic from minerals eroded by rainwater and the melting glaciers slowly roaming deep in their country. So, in turn, all the animals were toxic to outsiders. The Ka-Harkians, however, were immune to most poisons by simply living off of the land.

Lance wasn't sure what lay beyond Adoria. He knew there was a great swamp, but other than that, it was a mystery. Though he had seen little of the kingdom he lived in, Lance felt as if the world was at his feet. He was finally on his own, to do as he wanted.

Lance placed his hands on the rear of his hips and stretched his back. The sun had nearly set. As the bugs began to chirp and the air turned cool, Lance wondered if Davohn was angry with him for leaving without saying goodbye in person. Lance hoped the letter he left was good enough for the difficult but loving man. He sighed and turned to Jude. "So when are we going to camp? I'm more than ready."

"Whenever you wish, but I was hoping to ride at least until dark."

"Till dark? That's at least an hour away." Lance's feet were tingling, his inner legs were sore and felt a few inches longer, and his back felt like he'd chopped enough wood for Davohn to burn for a lifetime.

Jude seemed to enjoy his torment. As Lance grimaced, his grin grew. "Well, if I knew where we were heading, I would have a better time gauging how long to ride or how early we could camp."

Lance groaned in defeat. "Okay, Jude, we're heading to Central City, then to Dawson if necessary." Jude's expression turned from curious to excited. "Dawson! Why would we go there?" He was beginning to get worried. Dawson was a great city. In fact, it was the greatest city in several kingdoms.

And Central City was bigger than most in any direction. Jude had only been there once as a child, and even then, it was a frightful place. The buildings were all made of stone and towered over the streets. Some were so high, only the noon sunlight could shine on the street. He knew of a great coliseum there, plus many celebrated swordsmen and great thieves. In fact, Jude guessed just about everybody who lived in the city was someone great. Jude was comfortable in his proficiency around Bureland because he was one of the most skilled fighters there, both feared and respected. But he knew that no one in Central City would have heard of him and worse, he may have to prove his skills, which could bring trouble from the magistrate.

"Do you read Nalirian?" Lance asked from nowhere, acting as if the mere question alone would solve all of Jude's fears.

"What does Central City have to do with Nalir?" Jude had heard of Nalir. It was an evil kingdom to the far south on the west coast of the continent. He feared the answer Lance might give would be as dubious as the answer to where they were going.

"Well, I don't speak or read Nalirian; therefore I'm forced to seek counsel at Central City's library." Jude fingered his thick leather saddle horn. "Well if we must go there, then we must, but I've been there before. It's a dangerous place."

"Jude, you've grown large and strong by eating the food you cook yourself, and I can think of nothing more dangerous than placing those toxic substances into your mouth. If you can survive that three times a day, I assume the realms hold no terror you could not surpass."

Jude let out a chuckle, but his face remained tense. Lance was frustrated at his friend's strange superstitions. He'd seen him wield a sword in such a way as to make the skilled look less than novices, yet he was terrified of this place. Lance decided he needed to find a way to ease Jude's fears.

"Do the gods really exist? My mother often spoke to me about the goddess of mercy. She had been a loving goddess who forgave all. She understood why some men were driven to great evil by being victims of it themselves. She had explained to me that evil only begat more evil, that it was a long chain which sometimes never ended. She explained that when someone wronged us, it was better to find out why they wronged us. What had they suffered to cause them to act so?

"My father loved my mother, but he argued that it mattered little. Their wickedness was a chosen action, and by their own decision, they brought the hammer of justice down on their own heads. I used to listen to them argue for hours about it. My mother always seemed to win, much to my father's dismay, but he loved her for it. He used to brag he had never met a man with her wisdom, let alone another woman. I miss my mother. I will do as she says and pity the men who took her from me, but as my father taught, I will pity them to the dark recesses of the Abyss!"

- Lancalion Levendis Lampara

3

The Will of the Stonehearts

"I have had it! We are leaving!" Fezbahn pounded his fist on the table. He'd been his clan's ambassador for thirty-five years – a short time for a dwarf. "The bloody Beyklans are trying to suck our coffers dry and extort Clan Stoneheart!"

His assistant nodded and added, "Ye have tried yer best, sir. The stinkin' Beyklans will have it no other way."

"That's not true!" Henry chirped. "Our country is poor and weak from the orc wars. It only seems like Clan Stoneheart is being unfairly taxed. But honestly, it's a matter of percentages."

Fezbahn regarded the young human diplomat. He had worked with him for several years. Henry tried hard, but never offered anything tangible for his government, only lies and deceit smothered in the honey glaze of honesty. "Bah!" Fezbahn countered. "We have maintained this embassy for nearly one hundred years, time enough for three kings. Never have we been so mistreated. How dare king Theobold try to tell Clan Stoneheart who we can and cannot trade with? We are not a clan of warriors. Your silly king has nothing to fear from us. You'll go and sign Apollisian's petition, or we'll pull out our embassy and return home."

Henry lowered his head. "I cannot back Apollisian's petition. He's not a representative of Beykla.

He's not even a representative of Central City."

"Then, there is nothing more here for us!" Fezbahn started tossing mugs and other things into a sack.

Henry stepped forward, but the dwarf's glare gave him pause. "Fezbahn, you mustn't leave. You must maintain diplomatic relations! What can be gained by closing this embassy?"

Fezbahn cinched up the sack and stuffed it into his backpack. He hoisted it on his shoulder and motioned for his assistant to follow him out the door. "What can be gained, Henry? My clan will gain the respect it deserves, and the people of Beykla will no longer grow fat from the sweat and toil of my people." He slammed the door of the stone structure that had served as the Stoneheart embassy for over a hundred years.

Fezbahn tossed his backpack into a small wagon. Two brown ponies flicked their ears and stomped the ground impatiently. Henry stepped out of the embassy and shook his head as they rode out of the city limits. He knew the king would be furious. He walked toward city hall, wondering how far the silly dwarves would go to keep from paying their taxes.

Tharxton Stoneheart stood in the deep underground tunnel. His long braided red beard had two large golden rings woven into the bottom tip. He wore metal plate armor affixed by leather straps to his chain mail tunic. Ancient dwarven runes danced up and down the thick plates covering his arms. His hand rested atop the hilt of his hammer that hung upside down on his side. It was made of a dark black ore that had been heated, then shaped countless times until it was forged. The head was over fifty pounds and bore intricate runes of his clan lineage. At the center of the head was a ruby that glittered in the passage's flickering torchlight. The hammer had belonged to his father, and his father's father, and so on. Over twenty generations of Stoneheart dwarves had wielded the fantastic weapon.

He surveyed his clan as they shaped and cleared the passage they'd been excavating ever since the Beyklans began taxing them to recover economically from the orc wars. The bearded folk relentlessly tunneled through the rock under the forest that was east of the Pyberian

Mountains.

Tharxton ran his calloused finger over the expert craftsmanship used to sculpt the gigantic passage. Huge oaken timbers, saturated with oil and tar, were fastened together by iron plates. Rail tracks brought huge carts from the darkness, spilling ore and debris. Occasionally, the dwarves found a vein of precious metal or gems that they'd quickly mine, but for the most part, they worked diligently at lengthening and widening the passage.

Tharxton eagerly rubbed his hands along his beard. How he longed for the day he could lead his armies down the passage and smite the Beyklans for their treachery. He was pleased that the dwarven elders had approved his request for war. He knew the diplomat Fezbahn would be unable to remain in Central City long, and he could strike a blow against the greedy Beyklans. When trade was outlawed with the Andorians during the war, Tharxton's family, as well as most dwarven families, lost everything they'd saved. Without trade, the dwarves lacked many of the foodstuffs and medicines needed to survive. Unlike most clans, the Stonehearts dwelled in the Pyberian Mountains, rich with precious metals, gems, and ores, but few natural caves containing nourishment. Clan Stoneheart relied on trade from Andoria and Beykla to supply the goods they could not find naturally. But since the demise of Andoria and the sanctions from Beykla, they were relying more on a barter system for commodities.

The Beyklans maintained that they were trying to ensure no one interfered in the civil war between the Adorias, but the dwarves believed they were trying to cripple them, to keep the clan submissive by charging outrageous taxes. Though Tharxton was king, he also had to obey the clan's elders, so his attack against the Torrent Manor – the keep that the Beyklans erected twenty years ago to monitor their taxation – was delayed, which proved to be a blessing in disguise. The dwarves had a passage under the mountain over thirty miles long that had taken decades to build. Tharxton had ordered his army to resume digging directly under the Torrent Manor, located between the Beyklan capitol of Dawson and Central City on the west road.

The king smiled wide with anticipation as he imagined destroying the keep along with the western Beyklan Army. Tharxton was young for a dwarf, and he seldom wore silk or fine garments like a king. He kept his long beard braided and was rarely seen without his weapons or armor. Tharxton was also an expert smith. He forged his own armor, complete with ancient family runes, and the reddish tint to the metal gleamed like a warm ember when he was in the sun. He wore a great helm with a red plume that hung behind him to his rump. He'd forged weapons for most of his life, trying to make them superior in weight, shape and style. In time, he learned to wield the weapons with mastery, enabling him to rise through the ranks of the army until he was made general. The former dwarven king, Dalton Thornfist, had no son and named Tharxton king before he died. Tharxton was afraid at first and begged the king not to force him to accept the crown. Tharxton complained that he knew nothing of being a king, that he was still unskilled at being a general, but his pleas fell on deaf ears. Clan Stoneheart didn't mourn the loss of their old king long. They embraced Tharxton with open arms and made him proud to lead them. And lead them I will, he thought. His men had nearly completed the tunnel, and it would soon be time to set the hammer in motion.

It was nearly noon on the sixth day of travel when Lance and Jude arrived at the first farmhouses near Central City. Lance gazed wide-eyed at the rolling fields surrounding the dirt path. The wind blew the browning wheat, causing a ripple like a rolling wave on the open sea. The people tilling the fields seldom raised a hand to him, though he frequently raised his.

Jude rode quietly, unimpressed.

"Jude, do you not gaze on such farms with

wonderment? Surely they're the greatest you've ever seen!"

Jude chewed on his bottom lip as he thought for a moment before answering. "Central City is full of many wondrous things, but it's important that we don't become enthralled by them. That's when the cutpurses hit us!"

Lance frowned. "In the daylight? Surely they wouldn't be so callous as to try something in the middle of the day!"

Jude chuckled and shook his head slowly. "The thieves here are very skilled and could easily steal from you during the day."

"What about the local magistrate? Don't they arrest these thieves?"

Jude was becoming frustrated with his friend's ignorance. "Trust me, Lance, they wouldn't do it if they couldn't get away with it."

Lance didn't come all this way to get robbed by some second-rate thief. He'd study spells to foil those foolish enough to stick their fingers into his pockets. "Let's find a farmer to put us up for the night." Jude slowed his horse. "Dusk is seven or eight hours away. Why would we want to stop now?"

Lance ignored his friend's stare. "Well, we could both use a good night's sleep, and I would like to learn as much about this town as possible."

Jude hurried his dun alongside Lance. "What makes you think a farmer would put us up for the night?"

Lance shrugged. "If they're anything like the farmers back in Bureland, they'll welcome some silver." Jude nodded. In truth, he could use a nice sleep, even if in a barn, and the thought of soft hay to lie in made him yawn. He decided Lance had a good idea, though he doubted his assumption that a few silver coins would sway the farmers.

They turned and rode slowly down a dirt trail. Tall brown grass grew along the sides, and the autumn branches of large trees loomed overhead, enclosing the path with a cave of vegetation. A cool breeze drifted by, lightly blowing the leaves. As they approached the trail's end, it revealed a two-story house made of wood and stone with bright green shutters and a porch extending from the front to the side. Two wooden columns, with carvings of flowers and vines winding around each other, supported the porch. Behind the house were three larger buildings along with a smaller, one-story structure similar to the house, but lacking a porch.

There was a silo on the south part of the farm made of smooth sandstone-type bricks, and stood twenty-five feet tall. The conical top was made of thin wooden slates, layered much like the roofs in Bureland. Cows and other livestock gathered around the base in a fenced area. Men were working all over the farm, and few paid more than a glance to Lance and Jude.

"Maybe we should leave," Jude said. "This is one of the largest farms I've ever seen. I'm sure the owner won't enjoy visitors." Using his experience as a warrior, Jude noticed several tactical advantages that normal farms lacked. Jude's biggest worry was the narrow slits in the silo's roof. He knew expert marksmen often lurked behind such transoms to rain down arrows on unsuspecting enemies.

"Nonsense!" Lance grinned wide. "I wish to speak to the owner and congratulate him on his beautiful home!"

Jude began to disagree when a middle-aged man approached. He was dressed in a plain leather tunic and breeches. His long brown hair bounced on his shoulders as he walked. He bowed courtly. "Greetings to you from Master Hentridge."

Lance smiled. "Greetings to you. My name is Lance, and this is my friend, Jude." He motioned to the swordsman. "We have traveled many days and are seeking refuge from the elements."

The man gestured back toward the farm. "We are simple farmers, good sirs. I'm afraid that we have not the accommodations you might be accustomed to, but if you please, I shall take you to see Master Hentridge."

Lance nodded. "It would please us greatly, sir, for we surely seek shelter, but good company would please us even more."

They dismounted and were led to the house as Jude nervously glanced around the farm. Many people toiled about but, against Jude's suspicions, he saw no visible weapons on them. He carefully watched the farmhands caring for the livestock, tending to a large garden behind the house, and loading grain from a wagon to begin planting in one of the many fields.

The man took them to the rear of the house, near the garden where an uncovered wagon was parked. It appeared as if it would take several horses to move the huge farm cart. It listed to the right front side, where they witnessed a pair of legs jutting from underneath.

"Master Hentridge, travelers here to see you, sir," the worker said.

"Eh, what was that?" an average-sized man mumbled as he crawled out from under the wagon. He had thick, short brown hair that made his ears stick out. He had grease and tar on his face and hands, and was covered from head to toe with wood shavings.

Lance and Jude handed their horses' reins to the servant and waited for an introduction. Master Hentridge wiped his hands on his pants and shirt as he labored to his feet. He smiled as he extended a hand in greeting. Lance looked at the greasy hand hesitantly. Jude took it in a friendly embrace while shooting Lance a frustrated look.

"It's a pleasure to meet someone of your standing, good sir. I am Jude and this is my traveling companion, Lance." He gestured to Lance, who was still repulsed at the offer of a filthy hand.

Lance frowned. "Yes, it is a pleasure to meet you, good sir. We have been traveling for most of the week. We'd like to stay the night at your grand establishment and partake of any stories or advice you may feel in your heart to give us."

"So Ima guess'in you want to pay for a night's rest?" Master Hentridge turned to Lance with hands on his hips. "I be needin' a silver piece from the likes of you two to stay at my farm. All meals are served at the ringing of the bell. You have but a few minutes to get served and eat before my men start back to their chores, so I suggest you don't lollygag. You will stay in the servant's quarters." He gestured to the small building built under the silo. "I have a few empty beds there you can have. Any questions?"

Jude and Lance looked at each other and then shook their heads.

"Good, and don't get in my men's way. Also, everything on this here farm, including a dead rat if you find it, is mine, got it? So no getting your grubby mitts on my stuff or I'll have them whacked off." The greasy man called for a stable hand to tend to their horses, then picked up his sack of tools from under the wagon and walked away.

"This way, please," said the middle-aged man who had led them there. He took them along the garden to the south part of the farm. They passed a large fenced area that was home to over a score of cows and oxen. The fence had a stone base with wooden rails on top. It was over six feet in height, connected to a large barn which housed the animals. The silo was connected to an auger system that fed the livestock. The auger was made of iron, set in a stone trough that was sixty feet long. A wooden side panel covered the blades to keep the livestock from getting their noses too close. It appeared to be cranked by a wheel capstan, powered by several workers.

A few farmhands regarded Lance and Jude as they were led to the servant's quarters. Jude looked up at the silo's roof to the murder holes, half expecting arrows to fly down from them. Lance seemed more interested in the workers, often looking them up and down while testing his theories as he watched them carry out their duties. Satisfied at his estimation of leaders and workers, Lance focused on where he was being led.

The servant's quarters were about forty yards from the silo's base. Jude tried to estimate whether it was in bow range, while Lance was busy admiring its simple architecture.

Inside were twenty bunk racks crammed into narrow

rows to strategically allow equal space. Every bunk had a folded sheet and blanket on a canvas mattress. Jude and Lance found a rack at the far end of the room and placed their gear on it.

Lance climbed onto the bottom rack and laid down, placing his hands behind his head as he sighed. "Just think, Jude. You thought this was a bad idea. We have a good bed and a dry place to sleep tonight with little worries of the beasts in the forest."

Jude grunted as he climbed onto the top rack. "I'd rather face the beasts of the wild. At least you can see their fangs as they lust for your blood. I bet the likes of these hounds would be more inclined to stab at our backs instead of our bellies." His bunk sagged and groaned under his massive weight. Lance gasped, jumped from his rack and ran to the wall.

Jude gave him a puzzled look. "What's the matter with you? Find a mite in your bunk?"

"I bet oxen would be better supported by the top bunk than you! Perhaps I should rethink our sleeping arrangement."

Jude shrugged and hopped down to the floor. He grabbed his dirty leather pack, tossed it on the bottom rack, and placed the coin purse on his belt. Then he neatly slid his sword under the mattress, and practiced drawing it until he did so with a swift movement. Satisfied, he placed his hands behind his head and drifted to sleep.

Lance placed his pack next to Jude's before climbing onto the top bunk. He gently removed the Necromidus and began to read. The book's cover was made of animal hide. Lance was unsure of its exact origin, but he thought it to be elven.

The pages were made from papyrus, yet the letters were all made into strange symbols and scratches. Lance rubbed his sleek chin as he tried to imagine how anyone made sense of the arcane writing. He knew of mages casting encryption spells on their books, but he wasn't sure if this was encrypted or not. If they were enchanted, Lance could relax his vision, and if the item he was looking at had any magical dweamors about it, he could slowly begin to see the weave. But as he stared at the Necromidus, he saw nothing save for the twisted symbols.

Lance thumbed through the pages, looking for pictures that might shed light on how to begin the incantations. Toward the end of the first book, he saw sketches of hand movements but didn't dare try them without the correct invocations. He'd heard many stories of wizards trying to cast spells without having all the components, and they always ended in disaster. Lance strained his eyes on the ancient script, and the deep symbols and sketches began to swirl in a myriad of directions, forming small codes and meanings. Lance blinked in astonishment, and the script returned to its previous state. He rubbed his eyes and refocused on the page. It began to swirl again before him. Just as he was about to make something out, he would blink and it would be lost to the original nondescript signs. Lance slammed the book closed in frustration, then reminded himself to be patient. His mother had told him to beware the fury of a patient man, for his vengeance would be untimely, ever-burning, and inescapable.

Lying back on the lumpy mattress, Lance opened the pouch he had received from the rogue in Bureland. As he had done many times throughout his journey, he tried to decipher some of the text. Again, he only became more frustrated. He shoved the hard-covered manuals and text back into his pack and jumped down from his bunk. He looked back at Jude, who was sound asleep. It was in the middle of the afternoon, so Lance decided to take a walk around the farm. The room was dark and congested, anyway, and he desired more of a sociable setting.

The door to the servant's quarters groaned as he pushed it open. The sun shined from behind white billowing clouds. Lance saw few workers moving about. He walked through the farm on a northern dirt trail, which wound up the eastern hill and passed by a hut. He peered in and saw a portly man wearing a leather apron. He was covered in soot and wore heavy gloves that were stained and burned in places. In one hand was a pair of metal tongs that held a red-hot horseshoe, and the other hand grasped a scarred hammer. The man placed the horseshoe on an anvil that was about three feet all, so large that Lance wondered how it was ever moved from where it was created. He doubted even Jude could budge it, let alone lift it.

The man ignored Lance, hammering the shoe over and over again, shaping the shoe. The ringing was intense as Lance approached the burly smith, who was middle-aged and showing signs of balding. As Lance neared, the man stopped hammering, looked at the horseshoe, and tossed it into a wooden pail of water next to the anvil. The shoe sizzled for a moment, and then became silent in the bottom.

The man wiped sweat and grime from his brow with a yellow-toothed grin. "Eh, what'cha want from me? Make it quick, I have work to do."

Lance stroked his chin as he gestured around the farm. "Where did everybody go?"

The smith used the tongs to reach into the water for the cooled horseshoe, studying it as he spoke. "They went to work. The field hands are in the fields and the others in Master Hentridge's house preparing supper." He snatched another shoe from the coals of the fire and rudely pounded whenever Lance started to speak, making it clear he had no desire to continue the conversation.

Lance walked out of the tent toward the barn at the northern part of the farm. It was the biggest he had ever seen. Its wood was aged and somewhat warped. There was a door about ten feet off the ground, revealing an expansive hayloft that was almost empty, save for a few rogue bails tossed about. Lance saw a stable of horses through the two huge foyer doors that gaped wide. Inside was a young boy, maybe thirteen years old, tending to the animals. The boy smiled when his eyes met Lance, and he hastily closed the stall in which he was working and trotted over. Lance wasn't a large man by any standards, but he towered over the boy.

Lance smiled and extended his hand. "My name is Lance, good sir."

The boy's face reddened at being called 'sir.' He shyly shifted on the dirt floor and reluctantly shook Lance's hand. "Hi, my name is Keldon, I'm the stable master."

"Good afternoon, Keldon. How are you today?"

Keldon was unresponsive. His eyes scanned the farm, uneasy.

"I hear you're doing a fine job as stable master." Lance hoped his compliment would smooth things over.

Keldon gestured to the stables with pride. "Over thirty head of horses. Well, thirty-two counting your pair, and I am in charge of them all."

Lance smiled at the stable boy's newfound bravery. He guessed if he did indeed run the stables at his age, then by the looks of things, he was doing a fair job. The stables encompassed the entire ground floor. It looked as if they could house another ten horses without difficulty. The stalls were made of solid wood bulwark with bars at the top to allow feeding. The feed and hay were neatly stocked in bins near the far end of the barn, and the tack and saddles were oiled and in good order.

"So what is it I can help you with?" Keldon asked.

Lance fished a gold coin from his pocket and turned it over and over in his nimble fingers. "Well, Master Keldon. My friend and I had two horses brought in here. I was hoping to exchange them for some better ones."

The boy followed the coin wherever Lance moved it.

"This coin could be yours, master Keldon..." He left the rest to the boy's imagination. Lance could see the dreams of wealth gleaming from his face as he hungered for the coin. But as he was reeling him in, the boy stopped, turned, and walked toward the feed bins, stealing an occasional glance to the stalls. This was a grand farm, yet the need for so many horses weighed on Lance's mind. He'd counted maybe two score of oxen, more than adequate to run the place. He was no businessman, yet he guessed the cost of feeding and housing so many horses would be high, very high.

Lance stepped around the stable boy to one of the stalls. The wood was too thick. The animal inside was surely no normal plow horse. Lance could see its corded muscles rippling under a thin hide. The horse was large, even for a war horse, though Lance was unsure how to tell one from the other. This horse had patches of hair missing near its mouth and the side of its nose, and he recognized the scars as unaccustomed to plow horses: they were reined from the side of the head, pulling away from the muzzle, not across it. Lance noted this fact with scrutiny and was even proud of himself for making such a distinction.

The walls of the stall were wider than normal, an additional oddity.

The stable boy saw Lance's scowl as he examined the stalls, and decided his new visitor had seen more than enough. "It's time to go, sir. Your horse is not in that stall."

Lance gave him a glare, but said nothing. He was angrier at himself for allowing his own suspicions to be noticed. The last thing he wanted was to uncover some thieves' guild or a hidden outlaw sect. All he wanted to do was get to the library and have the Nalirian text translated. He didn't have time for petty distractions.

The boy shrugged and led Lance down the aisle, deeper into the stable. "Your horse is down here, sir, I didn't mean no disrespect. I was just worried you might try to hurt the master's war horse."

Lance beamed; he'd been right. The animal was no plow horse. Lance wanted to get Jude and share these revelations with him. He still suspected this was no ordinary farm. He stopped. "Never mind, good sir, if Master Hentridge has a mighty war horse, then I am well assured my beasts are in the finest care." He turned to walk away.

The stable boy followed closely on Lance's heels. "Good sir, you said I might be able to earn that gold coin." He rubbed his hands together, staring at the pocket where Lance had placed it.

Lance slowed and tossed the boy a silver coin. "If you do not spend this coin and my horses are in good order when I return to claim them, I shall give you that gold penny." He patted his pocket.

"Yes sir, I will sir." The boy picked up a pitchfork and resumed his daily duties. "I'll hold you to our deal. I'll be sure to tend your horses right nice and I'll be expecting my coin when you return."

Lance smiled and waved as he hurried toward the barracks to tell Jude what he'd discovered, and to see what the swordsman had to offer on this subject. He inhaled the deep rich smell of the autumn forest surrounding him, smiling at the excitement of being on his first real journey as a man.

"You pestering my brother, outlander?" came a soft but deadly voice from behind him.

He turned to see a young woman with long straight red hair. She was wearing a dark blue outfit that hugged her hips and breasts, showing her elegant body. She had a sable cloak that hung over her shoulders and flowed in the slight evening breeze. It was bunched at the top by a ruby pendant, and the hood dangled over her back. Her beautiful green eyes seemed to penetrate all that was hidden.

Lance smiled awkwardly as he fidgeted with his hands, then placed them behind his back and clasped his fingers together. "Oh heavens no, I was just asking him to show me the stables."

The woman's tone softened after seeing Lance offered no threat. She eyed him up and down, measuring his every feature, from his thick jaw to his manicured hands. She looked for rings but found none. She searched for any sign of a weapon protruding from under the folds of his fancy black and silver traveling cloak, but without result. He stood flat-footed to her, and his finely groomed hair told who he was. "A filthy noble or mage," she whispered under her breath, too soft for Lance to hear.

Lance felt her scrutinizing eyes falling over him, though he was too taken aback by her beauty to notice her comment. He held his gaze, transfixed on her visage as if entrapped in the bowels of a spell.

The woman noticed his blatant staring and after a few

moments, she realized that he was maybe a full four years younger than she. It was unlikely that he was a mage. She'd come across a few in her day, and any talent were older, yet this boy had all the markings of one, even down to his stance which would spell certain doom for someone trying to wield a blade. Perplexed, she offered her name. "I am Tamra. Who might you be?" She relaxed somewhat, but kept her muscles tight, ready to spring if needed.

Lance extended his hand eagerly. "I am Lance from Bureland, traveler to Central City. I'm pleased to meet you." He kept his deep green eyes fixed on hers.

Tamra was mystified. Rarely had she met a man that was disciplined enough to keep his eyes where they belonged. Though in truth, she enjoyed his handsome visage. A pity, she thought. At his age, the dogs of Central City would mark him for easy prey. "What takes you to Central City, boy?"

The insult bounced away unnoticed as did the fact she didn't take his hand in greeting, but the mention of his trip ripped him back from infatuation. He wanted to impress her in some way, yet he was not at the farm to impress a pretty face. He was on a desperate mission to learn about his past. He doubted Tamra would harm him, though he considered himself above her talents. However, Lance knew he may have been followed, either by the betrayed thief, or by the magistrate itself. He didn't want this beauty to have any knowledge that might bring her harm. "Well, my lady, my motives are my own, though I admit they are purely honorable."

"So be it, Lance from Bureland." She flashed a wry smile. "But take heed, the dogs of that cursed city will give you many fleas if you dally in your departure."

Dumbfounded, Lance stood in front of her awkwardly, trying to think of something witty to say. But after a few moments of silence, she gave him a farewell wave and headed toward the main house.

As soon as she was down the trail, Lance ran to Jude smiling the entire way.

"I remember my chance meeting with beautiful Tamra. Though I never spoke with her again after we left the farm, her image stayed with me. She was a radiant beauty, whose inner light shined more brightly than most. Surely, she underestimated the power dwelling deep within me. But how could she have known? Even mighty Jude could not fathom the inner strength I possessed. Perhaps that is what my giant friend feared. Not my power, but the measure of it. Poor Jude, smart as he may have seemed, he was merely a swordsman. He lacked the intelligence and wisdom needed to truly understand the secrets of magic. But just as a swordsman studies the pommel of an enemy's sword and gazes upon the nicks and scratches that told the tale of countless battles, just as he sees the confident way a sword hangs from the wielder's hip and the measure of stride that he uses with the constant shuffle of weight for the flow of balance to enter combat at a single moment...

"...a mage displays similar attributes, as does a thief or person of any skilled trade. A true master will learn to appreciate these subtle, but powerful tools. I did. Though in truth, had it not been for my friends through my journeys as a young mage, death would have long ago claimed my soul. But now, even Death himself fears my name."

- Lancalion Levendis Lampara

4 Dwarven Blood

The setting sun cast rays of red and orange through the autumn trees, giving the farm a celestial glow.

Insects flew about, eaten by songbirds taking breaks from their evening ballads.

Lance rushed to the bunkhouse and burst into the room. He could only see a few silhouettes of workers as he scanned the area. Some were lying on their racks while others played a game of stones in the dimming light of the far window. As Lance closed the door, many of the workers grumbled at the disturbance. He paid them no mind as he went to Jude, who had now awakened from the commotion.

Jude ran his fingers through his hair and shook his head. All eyes were on Lance. His friend was skilled at many things, but the amount of wisdom he possessed was lacking. And for that reason alone, Jude was glad to be with him on the journey.

Lance whispered, "We need to chat. I've discovered a few things that you should know about."

Jude leaned closer. "Is it dangerous? We attract too much attention whispering like two youngsters in church." He wanted to go back to sleep, confident that they were safe for the time being. A few of the men had even spoken to him and offered a sip from a flask. Though the company was less than pleasant, Jude was more comfortable there than on the trail.

Lance nodded slowly. "Perhaps you're right. In the morning, then." He crawled onto his rack to run the thoughts of the day over in his mind. He was no closer to figuring out the text, but the adventure was exciting!

"My king, my king, we've nearly broken through!" a dwarf proclaimed as he hurried down the wide underground chamber.

"Steady, good miner, pipe down," Tharxton said with a soft voice as he clasped his shoulder. "How much farther do we need to tunnel, first miner?"

The dwarf blushed under a thick layer of sweat and soot. The title 'first miner' was one of great admiration and respect. "Me guess is just a few dozen yards of soft clay, then we break through the dungeon wall and into the pigs' soft underbelly!" He rubbed his hands together excitedly.

Tharxton smiled and stroked his braided red beard while recalling the reports that Fezbahn had abandoned the embassy and returned home.

The miner wiped the damp soot from his eyes and smeared it on his trousers. He looked down the passage and then back to his king, who was deep in thought. He bowed low at Tharxton's feet. "My lord...." he swallowed hard in anticipation. "...shall I fetch the watch and give word to assemble the clan?" Tharxton nodded. "Aye... fetch the watch. For on the morrow's night, we shall avenge the wrongs our people have suffered under the greedy hand of Beyklan tyranny. They shall feel the power of our wrath, and loathe the day they decided to grow fat and rich from the toil of clan Stoneheart!" He said a silent prayer for his people as he watched the back of the dwarf running eagerly down the corridor. Tharxton felt a deep sadness for them, knowing many of his kin would die in battle. He feared the attack on Torrent Manor would only be the beginning. The Beyklan people were a proud nation and would not easily accept defeat.

He moved back toward the tunnel's entrance, gazing at the giant wooden beams that supported the ceiling and the arches spanning the large rooms at the front of the mine. He marveled at his people's artwork, carved into every inch of the polished stone. Tharxton lowered his head. They were peaceful by nature, artisans and craftsmen. The king knew they would lose more than their lives in this excursion, though they had little choice. A sigh escaped his lips as he left the tunnel and stepped into the west valley.

He raised his hand to shade his eyes from the sun.

General Amerix Stormhammer approached. He was a scruffy dwarf who was over four hundred years old, one of the oldest in the clan. The king doubted there was a single soul who could best him in combat. He was cruel, ruthless, and cunning, the perfect warrior. At almost five feet tall, he was exceptionally tall for a dwarf, and had seen more battles than Tharxton had seen days. His dull plate mail armor bore a thousand nicks and scratches, and his shield a thousand more. His silver-streaked black beard hung to his knees and shook as he walked. Other dwarves jumped out of his way as he strode confidently toward Tharxton.

"A rumor has reached me ears that we a'be fightin' them human dogs soon," Amerix said with an evil grin.

Tharxton stared into his steel blue eyes. How many horrors danced in his mind? How many battles did it take to turn a good dwarf into a cold killer like Amerix?

"Aye, it's true," Tharxton replied solemnly. "We will march at the morrow's dusk. It will be a bloody affair and many a dwarf will die."

"Aye, but many more humans will bleed the ground red with their stinking blood!" Amerix pounded his chest.

Tharxton's face reddened. "Are you so eager for war, General? If you need to have another nightmare, I can send you alone against the humans!"

Amerix matched his tone. "Aye, you could do that, me king. And 'twould be a grand pleasure to be alone, spilling our enemies blood, than to be standing next to one of me own kin that was more suited for kitchen duty of the womenfolk than glories in battle!" Amerix noticed Tharxton grasping the pommel of his war hammer. He'd longed for a battle with the young king.

Tharxton caught the general eyeing his hand and

relaxed as a small crowd formed around them. He knew that many of his people looked up to the old dwarf, himself included, and a confrontation would help neither of them. "You may have seen many a battle, but I am king. If I deem kitchen duty is to be had by a simpleton or a general, it will come to pass."

Amerix leaned forward so no one could hear. "'Tis true, you are king and I am general. But anytime you wish it, you may draw your hammer and we'll see who remains in what authority."

There was an eerie silence as they stood with their eyes locked in a deadly gaze, neither blinking for several minutes. Finally, Tharxton said, "General, your men await. Are you going to continue this childish game or prepare for the war you lust so much for?"

Amerix remained silent for a moment. He desperately wanted to put the boy king in his place, but there was much to do before setting out with his men. "Aye, you win this round, but beware. General Amerix Stormhammer is your ally only in war. In politics, he is your bitter enemy." He turned and walked toward the crowd, barking orders.

Tharxton sighed and hung his head, but a wry smile crept on his face when he thought of the men of

Torrent Manor facing the general. If there was ever a dwarf who could march into Torrent Manor and single-handedly defeat every soldier within, it was Amerix Stormhammer.

Intense anger rippled through Amerix's old muscles. As he shouted commands to prepare for the upcoming battle, the dwarves raised their arms and cheered about going to war.

A young dwarf stood next to Amerix and said, "Why does our king hang his head? We are about to have our greatest victory! Maybe he's a coward like the others are saying."

Amerix turned to the dwarf and poked him in the chest. "A crown is a heavy mantle indeed. If ye wore it, me doubts you would hold your head as high for any period of time."

The dwarf didn't miss the opportunity to hurry off and aid in battle preparations. A disapproving look from Amerix was more than required to send any dwarf running, let alone a painful poke in the chest.

Amerix glanced around. Soldiers were everywhere, nearly six thousand in all, readying their weapons. Sounds of song and praise to Leska, the earth mother goddess, echoed throughout the valley. The morrow would be a great day, indeed. The songs were too soft and happy, however, to be of his liking. Durion, the mountain god, would never allow such songs to be sung before a feast, let alone a battle! The Stonehearts were such a pathetic clan.

Tharxton marched them down the shaft, and they camped a few miles from the Torrent Manor entry site. They were nervous about the following night, but Amerix relished it. It had been over fifty years since his last major battle, and the grizzled old general feared he might die withered in a bed, rather than the battlefield. Now, he had a chance to die like a true warrior.

Amerix laid out his sleeping roll and began the rituals of his god. He came into clan Stoneheart after his own people were decimated by an army of dark elves and a white dragon. He was forced to take an oath by Leska, though he secretly retained worship to Durion, the clan Stormhammer's god, because he was warlike.

The general cleaned and oiled his ancient plate armor and sharpened his axe. Its double-bladed fury had silenced many foes. When he finished caring for his equipment, Amerix laid back and closed his weary eyes. He dreamed of screams from the humans as they fled the cut of his blade.

He was awakened by his aid from outside the tent. Amerix only trusted his aid and a few hundred other dwarves with his life. Though he served under the young king, Amerix longed for the day to take the crown, either by force or political ascension – force was preferred.

He rose slowly and glanced at his muscular arms. There were scars on top of scars, yet somehow he'd managed to survive each one. He rubbed his calloused hands over them. His muscles were once strong and harder than steel. Now, they hung weakly from his bones. He was still stronger than most of the clan, but two hundred years ago, there wasn't a dwarf around that could best him in any feat of strength. He was the largest dwarf in clan history, a legend among his people. The dwarves followed Tharxton's orders because he was king. They followed Amerix's orders because he was their hero.

Amerix rubbed the sleep from his eyes and said to his aid, "Watch." "Yes, General," a gruff voice answered.

"Ye will stay behind with King Tharxton. He won't be marching with us. Meself and most of our brethren will set out and attack the manor at dusk. The king, in his distaste for battle, will remain behind and arrive after we have secured victory." He began to remove his sleeping robe.

The watch was stunned. "Our king won't be joining us in battle?"

"Aye, 'tis true. But I value ye as a faithful aid, or I would not have told ye our king's true motives. 'Tis better this way, watch. Our king is wise to leave the fighting to the true warriors. He doesn't have the stomach for it."

The watch fumbled with his hammer. "General, I've seen King Tharxton fight. He's second to none, save for you."

"Aye, I agree the king's battle prowess rivals even me own honed blade, but he hasn't just ordered us to defeat Torrent Manor. He has ordered us to slaughter all the inhabitants."

The watch gasped and grabbed at his chest in horror as he slumped back. "Even the human womenfolk?"

"Aye, even them. The king wants to strike fear into the hearts of the Beyklan dogs. He wants the survivors to return to their beloved Torrent Manor and see their men killed, their women raped, and their children slaughtered. Only then will our enemies fear clan Stoneheart! Tell the men that the king said any who lack the courage to do what's necessary to preserve our own families' safety, can stay behind with the womenfolk! Let the glory be for the brave on this fateful night! Now go, watch. Wake our brothers and spread the word. I'll be marching from the end of the tunnel in thirty minutes. Have them and the miners ready."

The watch stood staring in disbelief.

"Now!" The general shouted.

As the watch scurried into the camp to carry out his orders, Amerix reached for his armor as he had done thousands of times. He ran his stubby fingers over the nicks and scratches. Would this be his last battle? He doubted it. He was beginning to think Durion himself protected him. He'd been in countless situations where he should have perished but survived. He was a sight to inspire fear as his thick arms fastened the chest plate with its leather supports. After sliding his mammoth axe into place over his back, he gave a silent blessing from Durion for all the mountain ranges in the world, and placed his great helm over his head. The armor had dwarven runes from top to bottom and the helm bore hundreds of small dents. It had a row of small iron spikes from the nose guard and over the top, and two weathered ram horns spiraled on each side.

As Amerix stepped from his tent, the cool stagnant air of the mine washed over him. He longed for the fresh scent of blood, instead. The soldiers were awestruck of the ancient general. His large shield swayed as he walked to the gathering at the end of the tunnel.

Amerix drew his giant axe and raised it high into the air. "Let us show them Beyklan dogs how a true army fights a war!"

The men jabbed armored fists toward the cavern ceiling.

Amerix led his army to the end of the shaft, where the miners were hard at work burrowing deeper toward the dungeons of the Torrent Manor, creating a passage thirty-five feet long and six feet high. The ceiling was rough with a few timbers, rigged to collapse as they withdrew to either bury opponents or seal off any way to follow them.

Amerix looked behind him at the wave of soldiers

marching with him. There were a little over five thousand soldiers following. He imagined king Tharxton awakening to find he only had eight or nine hundred soldiers left. A wicked grin stretched across the general's weathered face. When they neared the end of the tunnel, Amerix gave the order to begin the drums of war. The dwarves eagerly began to pound their swords, hammers, axes, any weapon they had, against their shields, causing a thunderous booming that rattled debris. Amerix felt his heart beat with their pounding.

"What was that?" A ragged prisoner asked his guard as he sat up.

The sentry, clad in red-stained leather armor, rose from his rickety wooden chair. "You mean that vibrating from the floor?"

The prisoner listened for a bit, then shrugged as he slumped back against the stone wall. His cell was plain, except for his wooden dish for food and water – mixed together in a soupy concoction. He glanced around at the other cells, set in twenty-foot squares. The stone ceiling was over ten feet high and wooden rafters loomed in the darkness. There were a hundred prisoners, underfed and starving, and all were male except a woman – he guessed she was a thief – who was brought last night. The guards had shackled her to a large ring mounted to an iron plate on the floor. He wondered how she'd reach her food bowl. The guards had been rough with her, but he didn't think she'd been raped or beaten. He'd waved at her but she ignored him, which he was used to.

The sentry walked to the far wall and pressed his ear to the floor.

"What do you hear?" asked a prisoner with his dirty face pressed between two iron bars.

The guard raised to his knees, reached for a food dish, and dumped out the contents, much to the prisoner's complaints. He placed the empty dish on the floor and poured water into it. The guard and a few prisoners watched as the water rippled from the steady vibrations.

"What is that all about?" called one prisoner.

Ignoring him, the guard hurried down the hundred-foot corridor to the stone stairs at the far end of the dungeon. He fumbled with his keys in urgency at the iron door, hands trembling as he turned the key. He strained to open the heavy door and scooted to the other side, closing it behind him.

The prisoners talked amongst themselves nervously. The vibrations were more audible now, as if someone, or something, was pounding and scraping the wall from the other side. A tiny hole formed four feet from the floor. Rock and dust made a tiny pile underneath. The prisoners were too transfixed on it to notice the lone female pull a piece of metal from her mouth. She placed her long brown hair behind her ear as she diligently worked the lock. Within moments, the lock clicked and fell to the floor with a loud clang. The other prisoners looked back, but they saw only darkness and the rusted chain that once held her in place. One prisoner began to protest but four guards burst into the room before he could speak.

They wore red and gold leather armor, followed by a man in polished brass, banded mail. His red silk cape trailed behind him as he strode down the hall. His heavy boots thudded past the cells, oblivious to the woman's empty confines. Every prisoner hurried to the opposite ends of their quarters; many had been stabbed or beaten for getting too close to the duke's son when he patrolled the dungeon.

"It was here, my lord." The first guard pointed to the wall at the end of the hall. "I heard it plain as day, some kind of thumping."

The duke's son stuck his finger into the pile of rock dust. He trailed up the wall and found the small hole. He turned to the guards and wiped the dust from his hands. "It seems something has been burrowing behind this wall, probably for some time now. It shows how well you observe your surroundings."

The guard stepped back. "But, my lord, I could feel it from this side."

The duke's son removed his helm and held it in his left hand. He wiped his long blonde hair from his face and placed his ear just above the hole. "I don't hear anythi–"

A hollow thud from the other side interrupted him. He stopped speaking, though his mouth remained open. His lower jaw and lip began to quiver. His eyes were wide in shock and a gasp escaped his mouth. To the other sentries' horror, a trickle of blood flowed from under his chin and dripped onto the stone floor. There was a barrage of dwarven voices from the other side. The wall trembled, shook, and collapsed!

Amerix stepped to the wall and peered through the hole they'd made. He could see a hundred-foot stone corridor. It was a bit narrow, but large enough for the dwarves to march three abreast. They needed to charge through quickly, in case the humans tried to barricade them in the dungeons. It would be a bloody affair fighting their way out.

Amerix studied the cells walled off with iron bars. They held dirty, underfed men. A horrid odor wafted from the hole, making the general scrunch his large nose in disgust. He ran his fingers across the thin remaining wall. His miners had done an excellent job at fragmenting it.

His troops' drumming of weapons on their shields had caused enough vibration that the scraping was difficult to hear.

Movement on the other side caught Amerix's eye. He watched four men hurry down the hall in confident strides, followed by a man in a Beyklan royal guard uniform – complete with helm and flowing silk cape.

They approached the hole but did nothing else. He could hear them speaking, but the human tongue was foreign to him. He watched the armored figure, assuming him to be a leader, bend down and look at something at the base of the wall, then remove his helm and place his ear against the partition. Amerix debated on fetching an interpreter, but decided to speak his own language. It was universal with all races: the language of war. He studied the height of the man and motioned for a miner to give him a pickaxe. Amerix rubbed some dirt into his hands for grip and steadied the tool in his massive hands. With a mighty swing, he drove the pickaxe through the wall. He felt it pierce the stone and lodge into the soldier's head. Amerix peered through the hole as the armored man quivered in the troughs of death. Smiling sadistically, Amerix ordered his men to charge, and they rammed through with their shields outstretched. The stone collapsed under the force. Dust and debris fell for a moment, clouding the air of the dungeon, and Amerix burst through to find the four guards standing wide-eyed in disbelief. He hurled the pickaxe with enough force to strike the first man and impale him on the wooden shaft behind him, lifting him from his feet. Before the others could react, Amerix drew his axe and plunged it into the second man, who cried out as he tried to hold his entrails together.

The remaining guards turned to flee, and Amerix swung at the closest one. His axe tore a deep gouge into the back of his leg, and the force of the blow nearly tore it off. He toppled to the floor, grabbed at his wound and screamed. His pleas for mercy were silenced by the wave of soldiers that followed. As the last guard reached the heavy door, he fumbled with the latch and pulled on the iron ring. The door creaked and the hinges squeaked as it opened wide.

Amerix took a measured step and hurled his axe down the corridor. It whistled through the air as it tumbled end over end before slamming into the soldier's back. It hit his spine just above his rump. He crumpled to the floor and started dragging himself up the stairs.

Amerix ran to him and ripped his axe away. As the grizzled general started up the stone stairs, the sound of the soldier's skull being crushed brought another smile to his demented face.

When they reached the top, the army burst from the dungeon into the small room beyond. Its walls were made of wood with a few inexpensive tapestries hanging from them. Amerix kicked over a wooden table, spilling drinks and a leg of mutton from it, and barred the door before facing his soldiers who continued to fill the room.

"Okay, me men, now the fightin' begins!" Amerix bellowed. "First group will head for the portcullis. I want its controls smashed and make sure it goes down. Second group pours into battlements and take down their arches. The remaining troops will focus on survivors in the south quarter. They'll be cowering like dogs in the main building structures. Cut every living human down. I want the horror of today's battle to forever ring in the hearts of these scumbags. Let the vultures feast today, me men, for this is the day of Stoneheart, the day of our liberation!"

The evening sun had set an hour ago. Dark silhouettes patrolled the edges of the battlements. Small pyres were mounted on poles to light up the keep's walkways. The local farmers and merchants had closed shop for the night and had either left or returned to their residences among the towers and buildings littering the interior. Many families of soldiers resided in the keep, as did peasants or drunkards who spent more time in the dungeons than roaming the fairways. Atop battlement one, overlooking the west road into the Torrent Manor, were the watch commander and several sentries. Security had been increased after talks with the dwarves had broken down and their embassies in Dawson and Central City were pulled. Though it was unlikely that they had the resources to create siege engines or feed and equip an army to march against the sturdy walls, the king had ordered a second detachment of soldiers to remain inside, and he sent a hundred tons of grain along with several score of cattle.

A young sentry rushed up the stairs of the west

battlement, excited and out of breath, and reported to the watch commander. "Sir, the watch reports that he heard some kind of commotion from the magistrate's office."

The large man looked across the vast forest with his hands grasped behind his back as he enjoyed the cool night breeze. "Never mind the sounds, watch. You know as well as I how the Duke's son enjoys interrogating the criminals. I'm sure he's having a time with that farm girl who claimed he raped her." He smirked. "No one of his stature would ever be with a farm girl, let alone rape one. She probably threw herself at him and he rejected her, so she tried to get even. Besides, the whooping and hollering were probably the prisoners showing her what rape really is."

The watch glanced back toward the magistrate house, then back, afraid to tell the watch commander there had been reports of dwarven voices inside. He realized how absurd it would be; there was no way dwarves could have broken in unnoticed. He knew they were poor thieves or assassins, known best for carving, mining, and making weapons and armor. He thought about mining for a moment and gained courage. "Sir, there were reports of dwarven voices coming from the magistrate's offi–"

The watch commander cut him off. "Dwarven voices? Come now! Your concern is duly noted. But how do you suppose they got inside of our keep? Hmm? By tunneling, perhaps? I tell you this: no dwarves are going to tunnel some three hundred miles underground to attack a keep. They would never be so bold, and if they were, we'd cut them down like the bearded pigs they are."

An alarm was sounded from within the keep. The night officer and the sentries turned to see dwarves pour out of the magistrate's office into the courtyard, toward his battlement and portcullis.

"Sir, a scout force has snuck into the keep!" one sentry shouted.

"Drop the portcullis before they manage to hold it open!"

The horns of alarm echoed into the night sky. The

soldiers used heavy wooden sledgehammers to pound the large hooks that held the brake. The portcullis lurched and fell with a thunderous boom, imbedding itself deep into the ground.

The watch commander ordered half the archers to watch west for the main force, and the other half to cut down the dozens of stocky shadows flooding the courtyard. He watched in disbelief as hundreds more continued to emerge from the magistrate's office and storm the inner portcullis housing area, but he was unconcerned. The weight of the gate made it impossible to be mechanically hoisted. In order to raise the gate, they'd spend hours digging it out of the ground.

He stared in confusion as they hammered the gears and cogs of the gate, destroying them, even while archers rained arrows on their heads.

He chuckled to himself. The fool dwarves had sealed themselves in the keep. But as he watched the courtyard fill with more than five hundred dwarves, and more still storming from the tiny office, he realized this wasn't a force to link up with an outside army. This was the army. The dwarves did the unthinkable, tunneling through three hundred miles of earth and stone. The watch commander staggered back against the stone rail of his perch, watching agape as nearly a thousand dwarves battled his soldiers. His heart sank, for he knew the Torrent would soon be lost.

"Arrogance. It is known by men to be a foolish state of mind, yet many fall prey to it. Champions are defeated, thrones are stolen, and kingdoms are crushed, all by that simple yet profound little word. King Theobold was arrogant in his belief that he had the dwarves cowed. The commander of the Torrent was arrogant in his belief that his keep was unshakable, and even Tharxton Stoneheart was arrogant to believe he unequivocally ruled his clan. And because of this, all three suffered.

"Some say Amerix was arrogant, but I say nay: he was confident. He did not have a steadfast belief in his men, or his ability to lead them. He merely knew what was needed to achieve victory and he exploited this knowledge. Arrogance and confidence: these two words with profoundly different meanings can easily become lost into one."

- Lancalion Levendis Lampara

5 Champion of the Torrent

"Cut down the dogs!" Amerix shouted as he charged into the grassy courtyard. The dwarves' silhouettes in the torchlight betrayed them, and Amerix held his scarred shield high as arrows rained down.

"Extinguish every torch yer eyes see!" The old general led thirty of his kin to the battlement stairs, rushing past the bodies of the portcullis guards who'd stood against them. He hacked off a corpse's foot as he passed, as did the others, chopping the dead into unrecognizable masses of flesh.

Amerix reached the oaken door of a stairwell leading to the upper levels. He kept his shield raised as more arrows zipped past, and he shouted a roar to Durion. His men peered around at the other wave, now entering the northern battlement. While Amerix furiously chopped down the door, dwarven screams and curses came from the north wall as they retreated. Covered in a steaming black substance, they clutched their faces and ripped their armor away. Some rolled on the ground, kicking and screaming, while arrows rained down into their unprotected neck and chest. Soon, the smoldering wave was dead.

"General, they'll pour scalding oil on us!" a dwarf shouted.

"Aye, it'll sting a bit, but me blade hungers for blood!" Amerix kicked in the remaining pieces of the door and plunged into the darkness.

The dwarves hesitated before following him.

Amerix ran up the spiraling stone steps, and as he rounded the top, he witnessed six Beyklan soldiers standing near an iron pot of bubbling oil. They pulled down on the iron rods and dumped five hundred gallons toward the general and his brethren. Amerix put his shield up and charged through, ignoring the searing pain ripping through his legs and neck. He could hear the screams of his kin behind him as they tried to follow their crazed leader. Sticky oil dripped from his helm and armor. Steam formed a swirling wall of mist, and the Beyklan men panicked when they saw him rise out of it with a sinister grin. They hastily picked up crossbows from a table and let the bolts fly. One bolt pierced the general's shield and entered his left forearm. Another ripped through his right leg plating and struck a few inches above his knee, yet he continued on and swung his axe down. His finely crafted blade easily killed a Beyklan soldier with one blow. The other men drew swords and attacked the dwarven demon. Amerix ducked a slice from the right while his shield deflected one on the left. He swung his axe at the next man's head, severing the top half of his skull. In the same fluid motion, the renegade general knocked one man to the ground and hacked through another's chest.

A severely burned dwarf crawled to the top and stared in wonder while his general fought with a ferocity he'd never seen. The two human soldiers who were still on their feet backed away.

"This is for me homeland!" Amerix drove his axe down, shattering the blade of the soldier beneath him and slicing into his shoulder and neck. The dying man gurgled in response.

"This is for me wife that died because of your taxes!" He blocked a half-hearted strike with his shield and chopped the next soldier's legs out from under him. The last man backed against the wall and dropped his sword. It clanged on the stone floor as Amerix's rhythmic breathing echoed throughout the room. The soldier dropped to his knees and pleaded for mercy. Amerix cleaved the man's head from his shoulders and walked toward the battlement door.

A burned dwarf entered the room. "General, what did the human say as he went to his knees?"

Amerix adjusted his oil-covered helm and spoke through clenched teeth. "I know not the words from dogs! But it looked as if he begged to be killed mercifully." He pounded his axe into the next door, tearing chunks of splintered wood away and kicking the rest in. Pieces still clung to bent hinges as he stepped through to the battlements. The autumn night air felt crisp on his skin. He glanced around with weapon ready, but the narrow area was empty. He cautiously stepped onto the railing. The entire north side was dark with only a few torches still lit. Amerix calmed and lowered his shield. Everywhere he looked, there were hundreds of dead Beyklans.

He smiled and rubbed his singed beard. "Summon my sergeants. We'll regroup and lay waste to the southern buildings."

The closest dwarves to him obeyed while Amerix addressed the others. "You all go round up some mead. I won't entertain me sergeants without some drink." They all set off immediately.

Amerix stepped off the rail and leaned against it. Everything was going as planned.

The watch commander tried to formulate a plan to either stall the onslaught or flee to the southern part of the keep and prepare a counterstrike.

He moved from the battlement to the walkways leading to the southern area and watched his archers shoot down many dwarves, but at least two thousand had come from the hole in the earth, and more poured out every second. If the roving watch who had warned him survived the battle, the commander would be arrested and probably hung.

As he walked, he spied the roving watch and pointed at him. "You!" The watch turned to face him. "Me, sir?"

"Yes, you." He approached him. "I want you to gather five men and make a stand at the first level of the battlement when the dwarves..." he paused to speak more optimistically. "If the dwarves make it up the stairs, dump the hot oil on them before they reach you. None of the bastards will survive. Then, secure the door and retreat to the southern buildings."

"Yes sir!" The watch and five other men began rigging the cauldron to pour down the stairwell instead of over the wall. The watch commander took the remaining men with him. As he left the battlement, he secured the door from the outside by laying a metal rod across the handles.

A soldier gave him a puzzled look. "Sir, won't they be trapped inside?" The watch commander shrugged. "Yes, but so will the dwarves."

The soldier gave a final glance back at the doomed men before running off. All over the Torrent

Manor, flags and commands were given to retreat to the southern quarter. Men, women, and children alike fled as fast as their legs would carry them.

Amerix and his sergeants perched atop the tallest battlement in the Torrent Manor. Their bloodied plate mail armor gleamed in the moonlit sky. They sat on wooden barrels and feasted on fine wine, bread, and cheese. Amerix stood, raised a wooden mug and proclaimed a toast to victory. The other dwarves raised theirs in cheer. The old general watched as the final few hundred came from the tunnel. They were each carrying kegs topped with a black, saturated cork. He turned back to his sergeants and began his speech. "Greetings, me kin! As we sit under the night sky of Leska, our enemies scurry like rats to hide from ye blades and hammers. Let us enjoy this moment and know that Leska has blessed this battle. She came to me in a dream last night."

The sergeants gasped and leaned forward.

"She came to me and said, 'Great general, I come to ye to bid yer blade to be swift on the morrow's night, for yer enemy will try to crush ye after victory.'"

The dwarves smiled at the mention of the triumph.

Amerix sipped from his mug, savoring the frothy drink before continuing. "After the battle, ye must march on to Central City and crush it!"

The crowd was shocked. Destroying an unsuspecting keep of a thousand or so men was one thing, but attacking a human city was another.

He ignored their disbelieving looks. "She said 'I will bless the great Amerix Stormhammer, for ye will lose not more than two hundred brethren, and in yer final siege, ye will lose barely double that amount. Yer axe will be sharper than a demon's dagger, and no enemy will be able to kill ye.'" He pointed at the oil clinging to his armor and the crossbow bolt that still jutted from his right knee. "These are testaments to Leska's power! I have suffered many wounds but I don't feel pain. The oil should have cooked me in me armor, but I pressed on, just as Leska ordained! Even as we speak, we're pouring thousands of gallons of oil around the southern buildings. We'll burn the nasty humans in the fire of our vengeance!"

Another dwarf, badly burned and covered in bandages, spoke up. "'Tis true, me brothers! I stormed the stairs behind Amerix. He went face first into the burning oil! He ran through it unhurt. The humans cried out in terror at the sight of him! The bastards that rained down the oil were killed in an instant when fearless Amerix reached the top! His axe even cut through their swords as if possessed by the gods themselves! "

Amerix's old face creased as he smiled. "Aye, me brethren, let us march to Central City. Leska has promised me that all who kill at least a score of humans in that battle will be given the gift of immortality!"

The sergeants were enthralled by the story and personal accounts, and after glancing at each other for support, were soon eager to march. Amerix finished the meeting and left to oversee the battle's final stage: the burning.

He slowly walked down the oil-covered spiraling stairs. His burns were blistering and his punctured knee was beginning to ache as the surge of battle drifted from his mind, a small price to pay to fulfill the lies he'd told his brethren. He disliked deceiving them, but soldiers needed to believe in something if they didn't believe in themselves.

The coppery smell of death crept over him in the courtyard. He took a deep breath and exhaled in pleasure. It had been too long since he last knew battle. The smell of blood, the sting of a fresh wound, and the sound of steel ringing on steel... which echoed in the distance. Amerix turned abruptly and faced south. He squinted, grabbed a sergeant by the beard, pulled him close, and yelled, "What's going on?!" Spittle flew from his mouth.

The sergeant looked confused. "There's a human champion guarding the ones holed up in the buildings. But no worries, General. He has only slain about forty dwarves. We'll soon reach two hundred casualties. Then the human dog will be powerless, even to our weakest soldier. Leska has ordained it."

Amerix shook his head. "Isn't anything easy?" He placed his battered helm back on his head. He'd have to slay this human champion before he lost two hundred men.

He walked with a confident stride across the courtyard and saw a Beyklan sitting atop a giant white horse. Amerix hadn't seen a horse so large in all his years. It was almost twenty hands tall with metal plates strapped to its head, shoulders and flanks. Amerix remembered mention of such horses. He thought it was called barding, though he had difficulty remembering. What he did recall was that humans who adorned their mounts in such armor were considered important. Amerix pushed his way through the dwarven crowd who held the human at bay, noting that a few of the arrow shafts protruding from his dead brethren were different from the ones used by Beyklans. These were embedded three quarters up the shaft, as opposed to the humans' arrows which rarely penetrated dwarven armor, and the fletching was from some kind of green bird.

Amerix strengthened his resolve and pressed farther.

As he reached the front of the crowd, he witnessed the human warrior, adorned in full plate armor from head to foot. He wore a long violet cape instead of the red ones the Beyklans wore. His armor bore runes like Amerix's but they appeared to have been carved by an elven hand, and his long sword was equally as ornate, fantastically crafted and shining despite the dark night. Amerix studied the man closely. His right gauntlet was leather on the inside with plating on the outside, while his other was completely housed in metal, indicating he favored his right hand. His helm was full with only a thin visor for the eyes. Amerix shook his head; even the human champions were stupid in their choice of protection. They were so afraid of being wounded, they gave themselves sight disadvantages in combat. Getting hurt was part of the glory of war. How was a hero to tell his tale with nothing to show?

Amerix looked around for the archer. The champion bore no signs of a bow or crossbow, and his helm was unsuited for firing with any accuracy. Soon, he saw a slender woman on the roof of a small building behind the human. Amerix pounded his bloody axe against his shield in challenge. The entire dwarven army hoisted their weapons high and let out a mighty cheer.

Apollisian surveyed the damage from atop his horse, and his heart sank when he saw the dwarven and human bodies. The paladin was sent by his church to try talking the local nobles into backing the petition, but they ignored his wisdom. All they cared about was rebuilding the kingdom's economy after the orc wars. True, the dwarves were not being taxed a greater percentage than the Beyklan peasants, but since the dwarves mined so much more, the amount paid was higher. When Apollisian was notified that the dwarves had closed down the embassy, he knew it was only a matter of time before the Stoneheart clan moved to war, but had no idea they would act so fast or so viciously.

He'd ridden several weeks to arrive from his church of justice in Westvon Keep. His squire, Victor DeVulge, and his elven friend, Alexis Overmoon, had arrived over a week ago to investigate the accusations that the manor was in place to unjustly tax the dwarves of the Pyberian Mountains. Apollisian was restricted from most areas of the keep and locals were instructed not to talk to him, so he made little headway. The duke and his son were less than accommodating, forcing them to camp outside.

It was Apollisian's final day at the manor when the dwarves attacked. Though his suspicions were then solidified, he faced a greater dilemma. The dwarves had disregarded his attempts to surrender and marked him as an enemy. Apollisian was unaware the Pyberian dwarves were so evil. He knew their king, Tharxton Stoneheart, and didn't see him anywhere. The dwarves spoke of Amerix as their leader.

Apollisian was forced to kill two score of the little folk, and Alexis shot a few who tried to flank him.

Now, the dwarves surrounded him and stood a safe distance away. The champion of Stephanis waited for the dwarven leader to show himself. His sword, Songsinger, sounded a shrill hum when he fought evil enemies. What disturbed Apollisian was that his sword had yet to sing.

"He will come," a soft voice from the sword echoed in Apollisian's head, and he nodded. Sometimes, it was more of a feeling than a voice.

Apollisian watched helplessly as the dwarves soaked the buildings with oil and placed wooden debris by them. Alexis shot down any who approached with a flame, but the paladin knew there was no escaping or defeating them. Instead, he hoped Tharxton or Amerix would show up and listen to reason.

A gruff old dwarf approached, towering over the others at more than five feet tall. His black beard was mottled with gray and swayed in the breeze. As he neared, Apollisian saw grievous burns on his face and neck, and oil dripped from his armor. He had a broken crossbow bolt protruding from his shield and another from his right knee. His shield bore a different standard than the others, a strange design of half circles and lightning bolts, not the banner of Stoneheart: a hammer encircled by a red sun.

Apollisian smiled as his sword began to vibrate and hum, and he called out in the dwarven language, "King Amerix, I presume?"

In Amerix's four hundred and eighty years of life, he'd known only a few humans who could speak his tongue. "General Amerix to ye, dog! Me king wouldn't soil his blade with the likes of yer human blood."

Apollisian's horse shifted and its ears flickered eagerly, sensing the tension and preparing for the rapid commands that precluded battle.

Amerix asked, "How does a dung heap like yerself learn me tongue?"

Apollisian remained silent, gauging the other dwarves' actions to see if they were loyal to the general out of fear or admiration. He sensed both.

Amerix gripped his axe tighter, sure that he'd bear many a scar from this encounter. The human champion was but a whelp, but it was obvious he had seen more than his share of skirmishes. No matter. Amerix had dispatched foes many times greater.

"I am Apollisian Bargoe of Westvon Keep. I came here to stop the unfair persecution of your people, but war is not the way. Depart, General, spare the innocent women and children of this keep, and I shall continue to lobby on you and your king's behalf to put an end to this injustice."

Amerix narrowed his eyes. "You'll what, human?"

Apollisian's spirit soared. Perhaps he was wise enough to listen. "I will lobby for your clan, great general!"

Amerix snorted. "Tell me how yer weak tongue is gonna bring back me boy? How is it gonna bring back me lover?"

"General, I cannot bring back the dead. But what I can do is help. I can help convince the Beyklans to stop or modify the taxation."

Amerix pointed his axe at the paladin and yelled, "What do ye think I be doing here? This keep will persecute us no longer! Now, step aside so I may burn the bastards in the fire of me vengeance!"

Apollisian readied himself. "I can't allow you to harm the innocent women and children of this keep!"

Amerix smiled and spit on the ground. "Ye do too much talkin' and not enough bleedin'!" He swung his axe and cut Apollisian's horse from under him, slicing through its left front leg and severing the cannon bone. The horse toppled forward, sending Apollisian to the ground head first. Amerix raised his shield as two arrows with green fletching slammed into it. The force staggered the old general and he fell to the ground.

The horse kicked and thrashed while hundreds of dwarves let out a battle cry and charged the buildings with torches raised. Apollisian rolled from the fall and came up to his feet with Songsinger held in a defensive posture. The blade's wail of warning echoed into the night.

Amerix stood slowly and looked at the human champion. They circled one another, each weighing the other's strengths and weaknesses. Amerix wore a grim visage adorned with determination. Apollisian flexed his fingers around Songsinger while listening to the dying moans of his faithful war horse. Anger tore through his body, begging him to cut down the murderous dwarf. But there was more at stake than vengeance for his horse or the already slain men. He had to think about the innocents who were still alive, huddled in the southern buildings that were now beginning to burn. He had to offer the general one last recourse, knowing that his life would probably end in the battle. Even if he defeated the dwarven nightmare before him, he'd be unable to stop the army.

"General, you've crushed this keep. It is no more. Its armies are vanquished. All that remains are the innocent. Show these men your true strength and have mercy on the meek." Apollisian added a silent prayer.

Amerix spoke through gritted teeth. "Mercy? What mercy did these scums show me wife? How about me boy? Where were you then, great diplomat? Aye, I'll show mercy to the human whelps; I'll show 'em all the mercy that they showed me loved ones!"

Tharxton was awakened by a voice calling into his tent. "My king, scouts report the sun has set. We're ready to move."

He spoke softly as he rose to his feet. "Aye, fetch the miners; we'll set out in fifteen minutes." He rubbed the sleep from his eyes. "I want to be at the end of the passage by midnight."

The dwarf stepped into Tharxton's tent, letting the heavy flap fall closed, and looked at the ground uneasily. "Uh... my king, why do we need the miners, if you don't mind my asking, sire?"

Tharxton gathered his chain mail to put on. "We need the miners to break into the dungeons of Torrent!"

"But sire, Amerix departed just before sunset. He probably burst through over three hours ago. He said you were leading the second wave to finish off any stragglers that might flee and return later."

"What?!" Tharxton screamed. He suited up quickly and grabbed his weapons. He burst from his tent into the thick air of the mine and looked at his army. Maybe a thousand of his brethren remained and they were just waking. He shouted commands and they scrambled to ready themselves.

"My king, why do we make haste?" A dwarf asked as he placed a metal chest plate over his head and slid his thick arms through. "Surely Amerix hasn't finished the battle yet."

Ignoring the comments and questions of his men, Tharxton bellowed, "Attention, my kin! You have been tricked by General Amerix! I believe he will slaughter all of Torrent Manor, not just the soldiers." The men exchanged uneasy looks, and one shouted above the others, "But my king, you ordered that earlier."

"Never have you heard those words from my mouth! Surely such a cowardly act would bring the Beyklans to make war against us!"

The dwarf scratched his head. "Isn't that what we want?"

Instead of answering, Tharxton marched down the chamber toward the Torrent Manor. The others finished dressing and followed.

Apollisian circled the dwarf with his sword outstretched, "Your life is now forfeit, Amerix, but surrender now and I'll spare the life of your kin."

Amerix smiled wickedly. "Me life is forfeit?" He chuckled. "I'll tell ye what, boy. I won't bury yer corpse after I kill ye, so the buzzards can eat yer eyes and their droppings will pile on yer chin." He screamed as he charged.

Apollisian brought up his shield as the dwarf's axe bit into it. Sparks and metallic chips cascaded around them. The paladin swung his sword low at the general's head, who ducked and rolled, deflecting with the top of his shield. As he rolled, Amerix laid a thin slice across Apollisian's leg. The paladin glanced down and saw a trickle of blood ooze from under his armor.

The champions squared off and charged again. Amerix dove in with his axe whirling, his face bent with fury. Apollisian caught most of the blade with his shield, but felt it bite into his arm. He jabbed forward, over Amerix's shield and into his shoulder. Amerix winced in pain and disbelief – the sleek blade sliced his enchanted armor as if he wore none at all.

They clashed again and again, their weapons meeting and nicking the other. Though each bore many wounds, none were crippling or fatal. Both were mottled in blood and the pain in Amerix's shoulder was unbearable. The wound was deep, but the dwarf drove on, placing Apollisian on the defensive. He wielded his axe with such precision that with each slash, he came closer to striking his opponent down.

Apollisian grunted with each parry, coming closer to meeting his god, but battled back with mad determination. When Amerix swung low, he'd sidestep and strike into the dwarf's weak side. The axe was powerful but not designed to block strikes as keenly as his blade.

The general recognized this, aware that he was as close to defeat as he'd ever been. He whispered a silent curse to Father Time. In his youth, his strength alone would have cut down this human dog, a mere whelp in dwarven years. Yet the paladin fought with uncanny skill and resolve.

Amerix began to feel every pound of his axe. His wounds screamed for him to lie down and die. But as he started to succumb to it, he caught himself, just as he'd done a thousand times in the past. If he died, it'd be after his enemy exhaled his last breath, not before. Even as Apollisian slammed his streaking blade into his axe and shield, he smiled. Apollisian charged with his sword low, forcing Amerix to stumble to his left.

The paladin slammed his shield into the general's face. The bone-crunching blow knocked Amerix to his backside, but he rolled with the jolt and was back to his feet with a hellish fire in his eyes. With axe and shield in an offensive posture, Amerix launched a barrage of dizzying attacks.

Apollisian was amazed at the display. Amerix was bleeding from head to toe, bearing many deep, disabling cuts, yet he twirled his axe in a myriad of strikes and feints, all with a wicked grin. Apollisian had never faced such an unyielding foe.

They circled and clashed again. The wound in Apollisian's leg was burning and he was dizzy from the loss of blood, but he was unable to flee. He stole a glance over his shoulder and saw the southern buildings in a blaze. The roar of the fire was smothering the sound of ringing steel and smoke hung heavy in the air.

Amerix noticed his concern. "Ye need not worry 'bout yer elf friend. Me brethren have captured her alive, but she'll beg to be killed after we have our way with her."

Apollisian half-turned, frantically scanning the rooftops to steal a glimpse of Alexis. All he could see were the flames lighting the night sky and the smoke rising into the darkness.

That was all the distraction Amerix needed. He drove his axe forward at the paladin's exposed shoulder. Apollisian tried to block the attack, but the axe struck his sword hand and the metal plates of his gauntlet surrendered to its keen edge. Pain ripped through his arm, forcing him to drop his sword.

He bent over, clutching his hand as warm blood created a puddle between his legs. He struggled to remain conscious while Amerix struck harder, driving the human back toward the fire. Apollisian deflected each cruel strike with his shield while trying to flex feeling back into his hand.

Amerix pressed him to the double doors in front of a building, ignoring the searing heat while he faked a low attack at Apollisian's wounded leg. As the paladin moved his shield down, Amerix swung his axe high. It tore through Apollisian's armor and into his shoulder, knocking him through the crumbling doors to the inferno.

Amerix moved back from the fire to join his men and watch with satisfaction as the women and children of the Torrent Manor screamed in terror and agony, burning alive.

He looked around at the hundreds of slain humans piled in awkward and humiliating positions. He glimpsed down at his wounds, turning the ground red under him as they bled. He felt light-headed and wanted to lie down. His body ached for rest, yet Amerix forced himself to take step after step, trudging forward to his men. After a small but difficult march across the courtyard, he addressed his sergeants weakly. "We have won the day, but I've learned that Central City has already formed a militia and sent the murderous dogs out against our homeland." He tried to regain composure, but his ancient body was taxed beyond limits. The dwarves didn't notice, listening eagerly to his every word. "We must set out at once for Central City. Gather yer brethren and have them grab whatever provisions they can find. Meet at the south wall in thirty minutes."

The dwarves rushed to spread the word while grabbing provisions.

"Therrig!" the general called out as he leaned on his axe for support.

A short squat dwarf, Therrig Alistair Delastan, stepped from the masses. He bore a few minor cuts from the skirmishes and if they bothered him, he showed no signs of it. His orange hair was slicked back over his wide head, and his braided beard hung loosely from his solid chin. He had a purple scar on his neck from battling the dark dwarves who'd invaded his original clan when he was young. Therrig was faithful to Amerix for being as ruthless as he was cunning. Amerix had no friends, only enemies and allies who followed out of necessity, a kind of rationale that appealed to Therrig.

Amerix took a moment to gather his waning strength. "Therrig, I want you to take the miners and drop our attack tunnels."

The lawless dwarf smiled wide at the notion, exposing yellow teeth. "Before Tharxton enters them?"

Amerix nodded angrily while Therrig slumped his shoulders. He began to protest but Amerix cut him off. "I may not agree with me king, but he is me king and the leader of the Stonehearts..." He pointed to Therrig, then his own chest. "...and the Stormhammers. We don't remove our kings in such dishonorable ways."

Therrig growled in agreement and hurried to the mine, forcing a path between the mass of curious soldiers gathering around them.

Amerix stood straight and pressed his large hands into the small of his back. He felt a few pops and relief swept over him. He walked a little quicker, and more upright, toward the portcullis to watch his dwarves work. They'd already enacted a work line, organizing foodstuffs into various piles. He called to a sergeant, who rushed over to him. "Yes, me general?"

"Wouldn't it be grand if our enemies came to this destroyed keep to see their loved ones all slain, only to fall into a horrid pit trap as they approached the portcullis?" Evil glimmered in his old blue eyes.

The sergeant nodded eagerly as Amerix continued. "And wouldn't it be even grander if the ones who survived the pit trap, navigated to the other side of the portcullis and hit yet another trap designed exactly the same?"

"Aye, it would be grand, sir."

"Then grab some men and do it! You have twenty-five minutes! Don't fail me." Amerix surveyed his army, the greatest he'd ever commanded. He rubbed his straggly beard and tucked it into his belt. He drew out a blood-soaked cloth and wiped oil and gore from his armor. As he ran his stubby fingers over the intricate runes along the plates, he remembered a time when clan Stormhammer was thriving, long before the dark dwarves came from the bowels of the earth to annihilate them. They would have had a chance if not for a great white dragon. Amerix strained hard to recall its name, though the memory of pale scales and cold breath was clear. He remembered the screams of terror from his brothers as they tried to vanquish the mighty foe, but its name escaped him. He shrugged and dismissed it, but every man, woman, and child of Beykla would surely know the name of Amerix Alistair Stormhammer. And there would never be a day that their grandchildren's grandchildren would struggle to recall it.

Apollisian lay motionless on his back inside the burning building. He could see fiery rafters above him dripping burning embers. He coughed on the smoke that grew thicker at every passing moment. Closing his eyes in defeat, the paladin prepared for death. He couldn't move either arm, and he was dizzy from the loss of blood. It was a scream that roused him.

He cursed under his breath and forced himself to roll to his side. People were trapped inside the fiery tomb, and he was still alive to save them. The young paladin screamed as he forced his mutilated arm to his shoulder, struggling to inch his hand to the mortal wound. He tried to chant, to channel the healing power of his god, but his lungs had filled with blood. The only sounds to pass his lips were sickening gurgles. Apollisian scooted across the floor through soot and ash, leaving a blood trail. He wedged his body against the stinging-hot stone wall, his hair smoking from embers landing on him. He let out another gurgled scream as he forced his tortured body to sit upright. The blood in his lungs was clearing, so he tried to chant again. As he spoke, magical energy coursed through his hand and into the shoulder wound. Soft blue light reached deep into his chest to heal the gash. Apollisian slowed his breathing, closed his eyes, and waited. Soon the wound was closed, but he still bore a deep scar that could easily be torn open if he exerted himself too much.

The paladin applied a tight bandage to his mangled sword hand and crawled under the smoke down the long marbled corridor, filled with red-hot oaken beams. Two boys were huddled in a corner, clinging to each other and choking while tears streamed down their faces. Apollisian rubbed his eyes and looked at them again. They looked exactly identical! He'd heard of such births, but they were usually feared by people and kept hidden from others. Often the youngest was slain.

Apollisian called out to them between coughs. "Come over here boys, but stay low, under the smoke." They obeyed.

The boys appeared to be six years old, dressed in scorched peasant rags. Their greasy brown hair hung to their shoulders, mottled with ash.

Apollisian led them out of the small room. He could hear the support timbers collapsing and searched for cover. When he reached the far end of the corridor, he witnessed a giant marble pillar that had fallen over, landing on another that lay flat. After crawling under it, he pulled the boys close. He tore clothing from their shirts and doused it with his water skin. He then wrapped the wet cloth around each boy's nose and mouth while saying a prayer to Stephanis, and they waited for the fire to subside or burn itself out.

"My lord, my lord!" a robed figure shouted as he entered the dining room of King Hector De Scoran. The two attendants near the king jumped as the man passed by. "We've done it! We deciphered the text's true meaning!"

After a sip from his golden flagon, Hector took a bite from his mutton, ignoring him, and casually leaned on the giant oak table while he chewed.

The man slowed his pace and spoke slower and softer. "My lord, we deciphered more of the text's meaning. When it pleases you, I'll show you what we found. I'm sure it would please my lord very much." He wiped sweat from his brow on his sleeve.

Hector rotated the mutton leg and looked at the pinkish meat. He swallowed his bite and took another long draw from his flagon, swallowing several times before dropping the leg and wiping his mouth with a white silk cloth. As he walked behind the robed man through the dining room, he wiped his hands and tossed the cloth to the floor next to a dining attendant, who didn't move until they'd left.

Hector followed him down the hall to one of his private studies. The man pulled a brass chain of keys from his corded belt and opened the door. The study was circular, adorned with tapestries depicting lush forests and magical runes. He led Hector to a bulky podium littered with wax mounds that were once candles, then opened the text to read the prophecy:

"A day shall come to pass when the mother of mercy shall bear child. This child will be like no other, for gods and men alike will seek to vanquish him. The hate from the hells dwells within his mind, as compassion for the meek guides his heart. If allowed to live, this child will bear the false testimony of the gods as he ascends the throne of righteousness, while working the magic of evil.

The evils of the realms will oppose him, but they will be crushed asunder as the scorpion under an anvil of fire, for he shall command evil and good alike unto his ascension." He pointed to the first section and read again. "A day shall come to pass when a mother of mercy shall bear child." He thumbed through his notes. "The mother of mercy has already bore her child, my lord."

Hector shrugged, figuring as much. He'd sent patrols out every time someone fit the description of a mother of mercy, and had her and her family slain. Yet, it didn't surprise him that this mother of mercy had eluded him thus far. "Who is she? I'll dispatch a raid and she will be no more."

"We believe she's already dead, my lord. She was killed by one of your raiding parties almost eighteen years ago."

Hector smiled and crossed his arms. "Then we have nothing to fear."

The robed man cleared his throat. "Well, not exactly, my lord. See, the mother of mercy was slain, but not before she bore a male child."

Hector was growing more impatient. "Then fetch some clerics. Find the woman's spirit in the afterlife and order it to divulge the identity of her son, so that we may slay him."

The robed man was getting nervous. The king often had the bearer of bad news slain, and he knew of no worse news than what he was about to give. "We did that, my lord, but it seems the woman has no spirit."

"Nonsense." Hector waved his hand in disbelief.

"It's true, my lord. We know why she was called the mother of mercy."

Hector's ever-growing scowl began to frighten him. "Why was she called the mother of mercy?"

The robed man moved to the opposite side of the podium as Hector and began his speech: "My lord, we learned recently that there was a fallen goddess named Panoleen.

"She was the goddess of mercy, forced from the heavens

by the council of gods for some kind of transgression. We're unsure of what, exactly. She was called what is known as a Breedikai, or original god, created by Dicermadon to preside over mercy. Once banished, she dwelled here on Terrigan. Since she was created as a goddess, she had no soul. When she died, she ceased to exist. On Terrigan, she met a paladin named Trinidy, who she married and bore a child for, eighteen years ago."

Hector rubbed his jaw. "Why is this child a threat? Surely no boy could overthrow my empire."

The robed man shook his head slowly, fearing Hector would strike him dead at any minute. Sweat beaded on his flushed forehead and trickled down his face. He wiped it with his sleeve and continued. "My lord, Panoleen's child would be gifted with her innate power as a god. He could easily rise more powerful than any man who ever existed, thus making him a threat to both mortal men and the very gods themselves, just as the prophecy states."

Hector pondered this new twist of information. This boy could prove to be dangerous, but he was just a boy. The king smiled. "What is your name, young sage?"

"Spencer," he stuttered, unnerved by Hector's depiction of him. Though a low-ranking sage, he was nearing his fiftieth birthday.

Hector went deep into thought. Who was this boy? And how would he be a threat? Might he carry some plague to his nation? Or might the wrath of the gods descend on them for some act or failure to act? He had to know more. "Spencer, you said this son of Panoleen would be more powerful than any mortal. But why don't I recall there ever being a goddess of mercy?"

Spencer shrugged. "Her name started appearing in the old texts as if it had always been there. We think the gods themselves have some sort of play in this, as if they also want him to be found." "Started appearing, or had been overlooked?"

Spencer's mind raced. Had he said that? Was Hector trying to trick him into something? He swallowed hard. "Her name just started appearing."

"Good, then no matter how powerful he is, he can be killed. You said it yourself, he's mortal and the gods themselves want me to do it. You've done well, Spencer, but now the true question. I hope you came with more knowledge than the other sages gave you." Spencer trembled as Hector went on, murder dancing in his eyes, "What is the name of this boy?"

"I don't know, my lord. Soran is going to see the dragon, Darrion-Quieness, soon. We hope his ancient knowledge might aid us."

Hector's mind wandered. Darrion-Quieness was the most powerful of all the white dragons on the continent of Terrigan. The name "Quieness" was of nobility among his kind. He dwelled deep in a mountain lair in northern Nalir, and any meeting with him was expensive, costing at least one life plus thousands of gold and platinum pieces, or the dragon's favorite, diamonds. Hector pondered who or what Soran might pay to gain information on the fallen goddess.

Hector knew he was going to kill Spencer. In fact, he was looking forward to it. He disliked bad news, and he always adjusted better with the pleasant screams of death, but he was too intrigued with the interpretation of the text and the addition of Darrion-Quieness. He'd used the dragon in the past to wipe out a small clan of do-gooding dwarves in the Pyberian Mountains of northwestern Beykla. By eliminating the clan Stormhammer, the dragon earned countless gold and jewels. A few of the clan survived, but that was many years ago and they hadn't surfaced yet.

"Go away from me, Spencer. I should kill you for being unable to answer all of my questions, but today I shall not."

Spencer grabbed the folds of his robes in his delicate hands and ran. Hector smiled as he watched him flee awkwardly out of the chamber.

"Evil Amerix Stormhammer. That's what history called him. But if a slave rebelled against his persecuting master, is he then evil? If a man sought justice for the murder of his wife and child, is he then evil? Some say that justice and revenge are two different entities. I say nay, they are one in the same. Goodly men, hidden behind the mask of their own view of morality, often cross this delicate line and forever become lost in the swirling quagmire of justice and revenge. They unintentionally twist revenge into justice when they try to give back some of the pain they do not have the strength to bear. They often hide this need of revenge behind a guise of justice. I say justice is not an action that "evens" the score, so to speak. But more an ideal that goodly men possess. Justice can never be as equal as the event demanding it.

"There is no justice anyone could exact on a demon, short of suffering it the same endless torment it has given since creation. If that was justice, Amerix would be "just" in his brutal killing of the men at the Torrent Manor. Surely the lives lost, including his wife and child, were a direct result of the greed from the Beyklans. Though, when Amerix mercilessly slaughtered the men and women of the Torrent Manor, he crossed that narrow line between justice and revenge. But why was that line crossed? Because Amerix could have killed every man, woman, and child in all of Beykla, and his wife and son would still be dead. Would this sedate his ignorant need for revenge? No. The only justice that could come would be the renewed strength in clan Stoneheart, by forcing the Beyklans to relinquish their taxes. An action Tharxton would have succeeded in doing, thus making the dwarven way of life better than it had ever been. That would have been justice.

"Every goodly man knows the difference between justice and revenge. But when the soul is clouded with emotion and the searing white hot pain of those loved and lost, justice and revenge become pervaded into one emotion that we unintentionally create. What a sad irony, for there is no justice for a man wronged. I do not fault, or even hate, Amerix Stormhammer. I recall a time not so long ago that I became mired in that swirling abyss of emotions between justice and revenge."

- Lancalion Levendis Lampara

6 A Time of War

Lance awoke from his slumber to find a slender hand gently shaking him. He strained his eyes through the darkness to see Tamra's beautiful face. Her red hair hung across her shoulders and her green eyes were alight with youth and vigor, though her whispered voice spoke with urgency. "Lance, get Jude up. You need to leave."

Lance rose up on his elbows and rubbed his eyes. "What do you mean? What's going on?"

Tamra climbed over the top bunk's rail to lean closer. He could smell the sweet scent of her hair. He'd never been so close to a woman, feeling her hot breath against his cheek as she spoke. "My father's..." She paused. "My father's friends from the northern farms say the dwarves of Pyberia attacked the Torrent Manor last night. Central City will soon be closed to outsiders. It has a large militia, but reports say the dwarves number over five thousand. If they were to attack..." She struggled to keep her voice steady. "Many would die."

Lance pulled away to look into her eyes. "Why are you telling me? Shouldn't you be getting your workers ready to run?" He could tell she was struggling to find the words so he'd understand without betraying her father. He wondered what truth she was dancing around. Both looked down at Jude as he tossed and turned in his bunk.

"Lance, you must flee. Go back the way you came. Go away from this place and Central City, away from the dwarves and the danger."

Lance frowned at her. He was confused why she only wanted him and Jude to flee. He knew little about dwarves, except that they weren't surface farmers. Even if they burned Central City to the ground, he doubted they planned to inhabit the area. He chuckled at the idea of a hundred bearded folk manning plows and sweating in the sun, but Tamra seemed truly worried about him. No one other than Jude or Davohn had worried about him, yet Lance was distrustful by nature, figuring she must have a hidden agenda. No matter, it must be close to sunrise. He and Jude would get a head start to Central City. If the dwarves were coming, he needed to reach the library before they burned it down.

"Okay, we'll leave, but I still don't understand why you're telling me." He guessed that Jude's original notions about the farm may have been right.

Tamra smiled. As the daughter of Master Hentridge, she'd seen a hundred men as handsome as Lance, and much more important or wealthy. But she sensed something about him, something she couldn't put a finger on. "We'll be fine." She climbed down and walked toward the door.

Lance noted that she moved with stealth and grace, another surprising revelation of beautiful Tamra. He'd have to visit the farm again when he returned from the library. He climbed down and reached to wake up Jude, but found him already getting his equipment together.

Jude placed his chain armor over his head. "Lance, why do I get the idea that you tricked the woman, the same way you've tricked me over the years?"

Lance smiled back. "I didn't trick her. I simply told her I'd leave the farm, and so we shall, but we'll head directly to Central City." He paused. "How much of the conversation did you hear?"

Jude pulled the leather straps of his chain armor tight. "Enough." He chuckled as he slipped on his backpack. "You ready?"

Lance put on his much smaller backpack. "Let's be off, my friend."

They stepped outside and were greeted by the cool morning air. They closed the door and Lance wondered if any of the men inside were awake as they departed, faking sleep but listening as Jude had. They went to the stables and found their horses were saddled and ready to go, tied to the wooden rail outside the building. Jude checked over the tack to ensure everything was in good order while Lance scanned the silo for a sign to settle his growing suspicions of the farm, but saw nothing unusual.

They rode swiftly away, curious of any truth to Tamra's tale. He doubted the dwarves of Pyberia would ever come against Beykla. Neither race, nor country had ever succeeded in conquering the fierce nation, let alone a small clan of dwarves. Yet Lance failed to think of a plausible explanation for Tamra telling them to leave. So he took the warning as misguided concern.

Along the trail toward the road, birds began to chirp at the eastern sky, and the forest became alive with sounds for the approaching dawn. Lance reached into his pack and removed a small lead chest. It was smooth on all sides, shaped more like a book with two silver hinges on one side and a gold locking mechanism on the right. He ran his fingers across the engraved runes on top, curious of their meaning. He lifted the first of the four books. Its cover was black and it had silver runes about it. Lance had decided they were symbols for death or some likeness of it. Yet, he continued to open the ancient tome without worry. He was nearly finished studying its first spell and was eager to try it.

Jude glanced over at Lance, and he almost gave a word of caution but didn't feel like wasting his breath. He knew Lance would say, "Is a sword wielded by an assassin any more evil than one wielded by a paladin?" Jude couldn't refute the logic, yet he still feared for Lance.

They rode for most of the morning. Lance studied his book in depth, uttering only a few words of recognition as he frowned and rubbed his chin. Jude continually scanned the horizon for an army of dwarves that he was reasonably certain he'd never see.

The forest around them gave way to open fields and small farms. The farmers paid them little heed, and Jude noted that some were packing things on their animals like grain, clothing and food stuffs, as if to survive away from home for a while. If they were packing for the marketplace, they'd be using their oxen and wagons to carry bulkier loads of one or two products.

Jude pointed to them. "What do you make of that?"

Lance was startled by his sudden question. "What? Are we there?"

Jude lowered his voice. "It's a good thing I watch the road. A dragon could sweep down and swallow you whole, and the only way you'd notice is it'd be harder to read that blasted book in the monster's gullet!"

Lance snickered. "That's why I hired you, to watch the road for me."

Jude pointed at the farmers again. "Doesn't that strike you as odd?"

Lance glanced at the horses and then turned his attention back to the book. "Nope." He retraced the page with his finger to find the most recent line read. Jude sighed and shook his head. If there wasn't an army of dwarves coming, it was an army of something.

Tharxton and his men emerged from the far end of the tunnel and he surveyed the dungeon. It had taken his dwarves almost nine hours to burrow through the wall of collapsed rock that Amerix had dropped for them. The stench of death hung in the air like a fog. Everywhere Tharxton looked, he saw torn, decapitated bodies of half-starved men. He looked at how their bodies laid. The human prisoners had clawed at their cell walls, or tried to force themselves between bars as they were cut down. As Tharxton marched on slowly, he drummed his thick fingers across the pommel of his hammer, shaking his head as he walked up the stairs. From there, he smelled smoke and heard the crackles of fire.

"Do you think Amerix is still here with our brothers?" one dwarf asked.

"No," Tharxton answered. "If he was, he would have posted guards at our only path of approach."

The dwarf pondered a moment. "Maybe Amerix

feared his guards would see their king and betray him."

Tharxton turned to face the dwarf, who stepped back a bit. "Do you think the general is surrounded by dwarves he cannot trust? Or even more disturbing, do you think the general is so foolish that he would post a guard with questionable loyalties?" He pointed angrily at the dwarf as he spoke. "You'd better re- think your enemy! He's more cunning than you can imagine, and more deadly than any you have ever faced. He could cut you down with a thought. So until you understand the depth of our danger, don't open your fool mouth!"

The dwarf stood silent, embarrassed. Tharxton stormed up the stairs while the rest followed cautiously. They'd never heard the king raise his voice.

Tharxton stepped out into the courtyard, and everywhere his stern eyes fell were the mutilated bodies of women and children. Tharxton fought back rage and despair, realizing that if he didn't find Amerix soon, his forces would be unable to stop the human retaliation. He would then be staring at a similar sight, but with slain dwarven women and children. Tharxton looked south, at what was left of the once-proud keep. Its buildings were made of marble and the highest quality wood. The Torrent Manor must have been beautiful indeed, made so by the sweat and tears of Stoneheart blood.

Tharxton slowly walked around the courtyard, taking in every gruesome scene. He'd ordered his men to look for survivors and as they milled about, he closed his heavy eyes. No, he thought. This is not the way. Tharxton now understood his people's reluctance of military action. The Beyklans were too proud to back down, and the dwarves couldn't hope to win a war against them. Yes, they'd dealt a decisive blow, perhaps enough to give the dwarves some bargaining power, but he knew the Beyklans would demand justice, and the head of Amerix.

Tharxton was jarred from his thoughts by the call of a dwarf running toward him. "We found a survivor!"

"One?"

The dwarf smiled. "Two, actually, though only one is

human." "Well, what is the other one?"

"An elf."

Tharxton growled under his breath. He never liked elves much. They were a goodly race, but too fancy for his taste. He liked races that drank stout drinks, worked hard, and fought. Elves were nothing like that.

He walked toward the rubble where the pair was found. They'd been moved to a grassy area in the courtyard. The young, brown-haired human in burnt leather armor was conscious. His face was blistered and his hands scorched black. Tharxton's soldiers had chained him to the wall and warned that he was an aggressive one.

The elf was a female with long blond hair braided in the back, though it was now singed. She clutched a white ash bow that suffered little scorching. She was bleeding from a piece of wood protruding from her right shoulder. Both of her legs had been buried under a heap of burning stone and wood, and her right was broken. When Tharxton approached her, the human lunged at him. The chains on his wrists and neck jolted taut, jerking him backward to the ground. The human spat words that were gibberish to the dwarves, and they had a hearty laugh.

Tharxton turned angrily at them. They quieted, looking elsewhere for tasks to do, and he stooped low to the elf. As he felt her cheek, the human leapt at him, and again the chains jerked him back.

Victor shouted through clenched teeth, "Step away from her, you murderous bastard, or so Stephanis help me, I'll spend the rest of my days hunting you down, pig!"

Tharxton kept his eyes on the elf as he responded. "You think the rest of your life will be that long?" Victor gasped at hearing the dwarf speak the common tongue. Tharxton called for one of his clerics in his native language, then knelt just out of the human's reach. "If I wanted you dead, you'd be dead. I'm searching for a rogue dwarf named Amerix that took a small portion of my army." Amerix had taken nearly all of his army, but Tharxton hoped that when he released the man, he might tell the dwarven numbers to be much higher, buying negotiating leverage.

Victor tried to calm himself. "He fled south, toward Central City, but he'll soon be dead. The city's militia is the size of his army, and the western Beyklan army is also stationed there."

Tharxton had learned long ago that Amerix didn't die easily. Tharxton motioned at the dead soldiers around them. "Does Central City have soldiers like these? How many did you say? Let me tell you something, boy. Though I hold no love for General Amerix, and I hope he's slain in battle, his meager army lost only a hundred or so against the Torrent Manor. Do you think he'll lose many more against Central City?"

Victor winced at the thought. The dwarven onslaught had been unstoppable.

Tharxton smiled at the human's humbled pride, and began again, softer. "That's why I must catch up to Amerix before more innocents are murdered by his evil hands."

Victor sat confused when Tharxton's clerics removed the stake from the elven maiden and healed her. He cleared his throat. "I am Victor DeVulge, Squire of Apollisian Bargoe of Westvon." He pointed at the elven maiden. "She is Overmoon, Apollisian's scout and friend." Victor stood and wiped off as much soot and dirt from his pants as he could, then extended a hand to the dwarf king.

The king gently accepted as the clerics approached to heal the human. "I am King Tharxton Stoneheart, fourteenth King of the Pyberian Mountains. Well met, Victor DeVulge, well met."

He'd been following the Ecnal for over a week, with only that cursed Jude preventing him from exacting revenge. The rogue had witnessed him cut down many men in Bureland, so he knew to keep from his reach. The stealthy rogue watched and waited to make the boy pay for his treachery. The swordsman had to leave Lance's side, eventually.

The rogue took a deep breath and sighed. It appeared

they were traveling into Central City. The rogue had a long history with the guild there and he was no longer welcome, and they would especially disapprove if he slayed someone in their streets. He'd have to wait until Lance returned to the trail. The rogue's mouth twitched in anticipation. He ran a finger along the scar extending from his nose to his ear. His lack of patience had helped in earning that wound.

The rogue had been operating comfortably in Bureland until Lance double-crossed him, forcing him to flee. That wound would also be avenged. He turned and melted into the shadows, leaving no trace that he was ever there.

Lance and Jude arrived in Central City late in the afternoon and gazed at the magnificent city. It was made up of small houses much like Bureland. There were many lower class people about, carrying groceries from market tents that littered the streets. Several citizens led mule-drawn carts in and out of the city, some carrying goods to sell and some buying goods for the farms. The mood seemed tense, but when Lance smiled at people, most grinned back. As they rode into the heart of the city, the buildings were jammed together, creating a myriad of dark twisting alleyways. The people traveled in fancy leather- encased carts splashed with colors and driven by armed men. The people walking around wore fine silks and gave a wide berth to Lance and Jude. But while the streets seemed safe, the alleys held dangerous figures lurking in the shadows, as if hiding from the very sun. Most buildings were at least two stories, and as many as thirty people lived in a single structure. Lance gawked at the spectacle, yet as he rode on, he saw buildings ahead that dwarfed the others.

Jude noticed more than one building with windows boarded up, and many citizens openly carrying weapons as they hurried about. Most took little or no notice to the pair, and Lance seemed oblivious to it, plodding on with a calm smile. Jude, however, marked everyone's actions on a long list of reasons why he should have stayed in Bureland.

The cobblestone road was wide enough for three wagons to travel abreast, and every hundred feet, they passed a wooden pole with lanterns affixed to the top. Lance paused at an intersection, looked west, then east, and then turned to Jude.

The swordsman shrugged. "Could be any direction. Perhaps we should enlist the aid of a villager."

Lance glanced around. The west road led toward a building that was at least five stories tall. Across the street from it was an oval-shaped structure made of marble and was at least twice as tall, yet it had no windows. The road between the buildings curved to a northerly route. Lance looked east and saw another marbled building with pillars resting on a wide staircase. The windows were oversized and with stained glass. He saw no holy symbols, though he thought it to be a church of some kind. On the other side of the street, he saw a three-story building that he immediately recognized as an inn. Lance motioned for Jude to follow as they made their way toward it. They passed many men dressed in the Beyklan high guard uniform of brass-colored mail with red flowing capes and plumes. Lance waved to them, but as expected, they made no attempt to acknowledge his presence. Jude stared hard at them, noting a look in their eyes that he recognized well, for he'd worn it many times as a young soldier preparing to battle orcs.

Jude moved his dun horse closer to Lance's steed. "I believe Tamra's warning, my friend. This city is on edge, preparing for some kind of defense. Even the guards march with nervous steps. I believe the dwarves are indeed coming."

Lance looked at his big friend. "Then we must hurry before they arrive. Let's find someone at the inn who can direct us to the library." He urged his horse into a quicker step. They headed east to a building next to the inn with wooden double doors, opened wide. Several horses were inside and tack was strung along the walls in a disorderly fashion.

A ten-year-old boy approached them. He had one front tooth and smelled as if he'd never bathed in his life. "Ye be stayin' a day, or a week?"

Lance dismounted and handed the boy the reins. "We'll be here only for a short while."

The boy frowned and held out his dirty hand. "Gonna cost ye a silver as if ye stayed a day."

Jude also dismounted. "Then silver, I guess, we will pay." He reached into the pouch while the boy stared greedily until he was given one.

"A silver piece fer each horse." The boy pocketed the first silver and held his hand out for the second.

Jude began to argue, but Lance was entering the inn. He mumbled a few curses and paid the boy, then hurried to his friend's side. Lance glanced up at the sign as he entered: Welcome to the Blue Dragon Inn. It had a long blue dragon coiled around the words. The common room was the largest Lance had ever seen. It could easily house over three hundred patrons and had a polished stage at the far end. The bar was to the right of the entrance and it curved around the west side. There were hundreds of wines and whiskeys on shelves behind it, as well as wooden kegs of ale and honey mead, dealt by four bartenders while twelve serving wenches worked the tables. The ceiling was almost fifteen feet high and housed giant rafters of polished wood, which supported a score of candle chandeliers at the far end of the room, just above a bleached white skull the size of a man. A bright brass plaque hung under it with the name "Gorsaat" on it.

There were over fifty patrons ranging from royal guards to peasant farmers. Lance and Jude sat at the bar and a small but robust young man with thick, uncombed red hair came to them. "Welcome to the Blue Dragon Inn. My name is Fifvel. What would you be drinking, my good sirs?"

Lance balked at the way he spoke, feeling somewhat out of place. This was nothing like the Inn of Aldon in

Bureland. It bulged with class and prosperity. Lance guessed that for the cost of the chandeliers alone, they could buy Bureland's inn outright.

"I'm looking for the library," Lance said in his best attempt of a nobleman's voice. "I have need of a scholar there."

Fifvel eyed his strange black cloak with symbols at the hems. "You one of them spell casters?" His rough accent was nothing like the rehearsed greeting he spoke before. "'Cause if you are, we don't take any spell casting in here. If you do try it..." He pointed to a big man sitting at the far end of the bar. "Glaszric will rip off your arms."

Lance looked at the man and then back to Fifvel and smiled. "It's hard to cast spells with no arms." "'Tis true," Fifvel said.

Jude looked at Glaszric, who was almost six inches taller with long black hair kept in a ponytail. His skin had a green tint, and he had a sloped forehead. He had a great sword, almost six feet long, that scraped the floor as he sat on the barstool. Jude watched him take a sip from a wooden flagon and noticed two small yellow tusks protruding from his lower lip.

"Damn half-orc," Jude muttered under his breath. Half-orcs were usually not ones to be trifled with, fighting with the ferocity of an orc but capable of human intelligence. Jude had tangled with one in his day and barely survived. Since the orc wars were recent history, Glaszric's skill with a sword must be quite accomplished to be living in Beykla.

Fifvel pointed out the window. "Well, if you're looking for the library, it's right across the street." Lance leaned on the bar to peer out the window. He saw the marble building with the magnificent pillars, and a smaller one with a statue of a totem pole. "What's the other building?" "Are you going to buy some ale or torture me with questions?"

Jude tossed three silver pieces on the bar. "The first coin is for telling us where the library is. The other two are for whatever Fifvel deems them for."

Fifvel slid the coins into his pocket while Lance and Jude left.

Amerix stood motionless in the black of night. The rain pounded his helmet and stung his face. Water streamed from his elbows. Though the storm brought no wind, the rain made the ground slippery. Each flash of lightning created a still image of the dwarven army. It never rained in the under-mountain, so the dwarves loathed the autumn storm.

A young sergeant approached and yelled with water flowing down his face. "General, yer scout reports the city has been warned of our approach, and even as we speak, the human dogs ready their defenses." He removed his horned helm to wipe his face, then replaced it on his head. "Shall we advance? It is only an hour's tromp. Though, Leska curse this rain, it will probably take two." He spat as water flowed over his lips once again.

Amerix remained emotionless. He ignored the stinging rain. He ignored his old aching bones and fresh wounds. He ignored everything save for his vision of a burning, destroyed Central City. Even the humming sword he'd stolen from the human champion was little more than a minor distraction, despite giving him a headache several days prior.

The sergeant began to turn about when Amerix spoke. "The storm, sergeant, is because of me fury." The sergeant looked confused and shifted. "What do ye mean?"

"It's spawned from me fury."

The sergeant didn't respond, staring blankly at the general. Amerix gave him such a murderous gaze that he stepped back in fear. "Me axe will strike as quick as a lightning flash." He pounded his fist against his breast plate. The gauntlet made a dull ringing sound as it thudded against his chest.

"Me cry of vengeance shall echo like thunder across a barren valley," he said in a louder tone, bringing his fist to his chest again, causing a more acute ringing sound of metal upon metal. Other dwarves looked over to see what was causing the noise.

"The blood of the human dogs will bleed the ground red, choking the life from every plant miles from here!" Amerix screamed as he pounded his breast plate once more, making a thunderous sound. The others began to fall into rhythm with him. They pounded their chests while chanting songs of war and death to their enemies, then stopped abruptly when Amerix thrust his fist into the air. All was silent save for the constant sound of the driving rain. Water trickled down his arm and into his matted beard.

"This rain is a sign from Leska!" Amerix shouted. "She now washes away the evils that ye will soon be forced to commit! Let us bow our heads and thank Leska for her cleansing rain!"

In unison, the dwarves put a knee to the muddy earth and their mail creaked in the night. As abruptly as they kneeled, the dwarven army rose.

"There is a small cavern about an hour from here." Amerix pointed southwest. "It leads back to our homes in the Pyberian Mountains." He paused and grinned wickedly, exposing yellow teeth. "It also leads within a mile of Central City's sewers. Come, my brethren. Let us march onward to victory!"

"It's not Nalirian," the old man said after examining the ancient parchments.

Lance fumed. "They have to be!" He feared that he'd been duped by the thief in Bureland. Doubt flooded his head about his parents. What if they weren't really killed? Lance calmed himself. In his dreams, he could feel their souls crying for justice from beyond the grave.

Jude placed his heavy hand on Lance's shoulder. "Well, sir, you say they're not Nalirian. So be it. But it's obviously some kind of writing. Do you know what it might be?"

The sage smiled and shrugged. "I'm familiar with every text, rune and national writings throughout the land of Terrigan, and I assure you this writing was not done by any man such as you or me."

"Then, what kind of a man?"

The sage pointed at the small pile of gold coins on his oak desk. Lance and Jude were a minor success playing this game with him, and at the cost to their purse. Jude sighed and tossed another coin down.

The sage crossed his arms. "An elven man wrote these words."

Lance stared at the old man for a moment, then furiously grabbed the parchments and placed them back in his leather case. He stomped toward the door with Jude close on his heels.

"Don't you want to know more?" the sage called to their backs as they started out the door.

Lance turned around. "Sure, I would like to know the day of your death, so I might come to your funeral and sneer at your lifeless body!"

The sage said nothing, but with a wry smile, he pointed down to the pile of coins. Lance bit his lip and slammed the door. He considered opening the door again so Jude could slam it hard enough to cave in the frame.

"Well at least we know it's elven now," Jude said.

Lance remained silent. They'd spent a small fortune with the sage, and the task was becoming more impossible with the knowledge that the writing was elven. How much, and how long would it take to find an elf who would translate it? Lance had never met an elf, but he'd heard how elusive and indifferent they were to humans. And even if he did find an elf willing to read it for him, he surmised it would turn out to be a cooking recipe or some other elven thing.

"What now?" Jude looked around the deserted streets of the city. It was almost dark and he watched as a linkboy went about lighting the lanterns on the wooden poles.

Lance rubbed his chin, deep in thought.

Jude motioned across the street. "Perhaps we could return to the Blue Dragon Inn. We paid for a night on our horses. We'd might as well get a room."

Lance stared eastward at the stone columns of the river battlements. Central City was sitting next to the Dawson River, which flowed from the Sea of Balfour, north of Beykla, to the bottom of Terrigan, crossing many nations. Central City was one of the few areas to cross the mighty river, having constructed a magnificent stone bridge. It served as a byway and also a defensive battlement from invaders from the East. Though no other human kingdoms dwelled in that direction, there were several elven nations. Yet even then, the elves were not known for making war.

Jude was anxious to leave the city as soon as possible. He was intimidated by the sheer volume of people, but more afraid of the rumored dwarven army. Jude had never seen an army of dwarves, but he'd heard tales of dwarven warriors slaying giants in single combat. The thought of being caught in the path of an army of them terrified him. Thunder sounded with an occasional flash of lightning from an approaching storm, so Lance and Jude knew they would need shelter.

Jude grasped his friend's shoulder. "Let's stay one night, then be off from this cursed city in the morning."

Lance only nodded as he slowly crossed the street to the inn.

"Determination. It can allow men to achieve the unachievable. It can give the strength to overcome trials and tribulations they would not normally overcome. I once stood at the foot of despair and stared long and deep into its great chasm. Yet, my determination allowed me to soar above it on the wisps of the wind, when I should have been unable to do so.

"This is why Amerix has not died. There is no magic keeping him so, other than his own resolve to refuse surrender. It is his own wicked tenacity not to fail that keeps his old stocky legs moving. I often wish I possessed his determination in all the times of my life, rather than during small periods of brief emotional turmoil. Just imagine the great things I would have accomplished had I not been led by emotion rather than blind obduracy."

- Lancalion Levendis Lampara

7 A King's Anger

Apollisian awoke huddled under the damp, singed blanket with the twin boys. They were still unconscious and their scorched hair was covered in soot. He rose and meticulously burrowed out from under what was once the great hall. When he poked his head above the rubble, his heart sank. Dwarves were all around the burned-out buildings of the Torrent's south quarter. He was relieved to see that Amerix was absent, especially being without his sword. He'd need the enchanted blade if he was to face that demon again. The twins stirred, and he whispered for them to keep quiet before taking a deep breath, savoring the fresh draw of air like it was his first. The paladin had been buried for hours, and his lungs burned with the gases he'd inhaled. His first duty was to get the boys to safety, then find out if Overmoon and Victor were alive. He suspected the elf could slip away somehow, but Victor would have been an easy kill.

While Apollisian searched for an exit along the collapsed south wall, he noticed two large forms among the dwarves. It was surely his companions.

Tharxton sat on partially burned timbers that served as a makeshift bench under one of many tents he and his men had constructed while searching for survivors. An autumn storm had soaked the remnants, extinguishing most of the fires, and white smoke still erupted from the debris. Most of the bodies had been gathered and a mass funeral was soon to be held. Despite the extent of the human casualties, Tharxton found his mind wandering to the identity of the elf. He was certain he'd heard of the Overmoons, but was unsure if there was a historical hero or perhaps some political relations. Tharxton cursed himself for not listening better to his childhood lessons. The only rule he could recall was not to call elves by their first names. For a non-elf to do so was punishable by death. He chuckled at the idea of the elf trying such a thing with his brethren around, but he'd seen stranger things and creating yet another enemy was a bad idea. He tried to discern from her actions if she was royalty, but those damnable elves were so prissy as a culture, it was too difficult to tell peasantry from royalty. He shrugged and decided that regardless of her station as an elf, the farther away she was from him and his men, the better. The approaching dawn would bring troves of humans to investigate the smoke that was undoubtedly visible for miles.

Word was, three more survivors were found under rubble in the south sector: a young warrior named Apollisian and two small children. Tharxton remembered Apollisian, having spoken to him ten years ago during the initial negotiations with the Beyklans. Hopefully, the young knight would take the elf away and out of his hair.

The king was roused from thoughts as Apollisian entered his tent. Tharxton swallowed hard at the sight of him. He remembered a boy in chain armor the last time he spoke with Apollisian, but standing before him was a full grown man. The king knew that humans aged much faster than dwarves, but it still amazed him. Apollisian stood much more confident now. His long blonde hair no longer carried the stain of blood and soot, and his armor had been cleaned.

"Any word on the location of Amerix?" Apollisian asked.

Tharxton had explained the story of General Amerix Stormhammer, and Apollisian dreaded facing the deadly dwarf again, but knew in his heart that if he didn't, many more would die by the renegade's axe.

"He fled into some caves south of here. No doubt back

en route to the Pyberian Mountains to rouse his supporters for a coup against me. So I'll take the remainder of my army back through the tunnels to deal with him there. After he's caught, I'll try him for treason." "And try him for murdering the innocent people of Beykla."

Tharxton nodded nonchalantly. He could tell Apollisian was afraid of Amerix, and commended him for surviving a fight with the general. Not many dwarves could have survived, let alone a Beyklan.

Apollisian left the tent deeply troubled. Could he trust the king with the capture of Amerix, or should he seek the general's head himself? The edict taken when he became a warrior of his church dictated that he was to hunt the scoundrel until either he or the dwarf was dead. But Apollisian had the young Overmoon in his charge, not to mention he had to get the orphaned boys to Central City, first and foremost. Overmoon's father, King Minok, desired for his daughter to learn the ways of justice, not die in the pursuit of it. But how could she learn of justice if he ran? He'd explained to King Minok the dangers his daughter might face, but he was sure the elven king hadn't imagined they'd be hunting the wickedest and most powerful foe Apollisian had ever faced.

It was a long journey for the paladin and his crew. They only had two horses, those that belonged to Alexis and Victor. Apollisian walked alongside Victor's horse, and the men would occasionally switch places to conserve energy. The animal was about the same size as Apollisian's, but neither beast was accustomed to carrying armored riders. Apollisian would stroke the tired equine's neck as he walked, missing his own faithful steed. Alexis rode her horse most of the journey, while the twins, Cerebron and Corwin, rode double on Victor's horse, since it was larger than Alexis' and less spirited. Cerebron was in the front with Corwin on the back.

They stopped frequently to let the animals rest and

allow Overmoon to hunt. Had she not been so proficient at the task, it would have been a much hungrier trip. Victor performed his duties as squire during the three-day trip. Overmoon, who had a childish nature, seemed cheerful and often played with the boys. Corwin warmed up to her during the day but cried for his lost parents at night. Cerebron, however, sat in his own silent solace, eating and drinking only enough to sustain himself. Any attempt at conversation was met with cold resistance or a blank stare. Apollisian worried for him, seeing an unquenchable inner fire in his heart. Hopefully, the church of justice in Central City would help show them the light of goodness.

"I'm worried about the boys," Apollisian told the elf as they walked.

Overmoon stretched her elegant arms wide, exposing the tattoos along the inside of her forearms.

"Are we to just drop them off at some church and abandon them?"

Apollisian turned to her and gazed into her compassionate brown eyes. He took in her beauty not only as an elf, but as a woman. In that moment, he was lost. There was nothing but him and her. No Amerix, no war, nothing but the ignorant bliss of a man staring into the void of what he could never have. Aside from the vow of chastity made to Stephanis, the god of justice, he could never marry an elf. Elves lived ten times as long as a human, and as he grew old and weak, she would retain her youth. A curse, he thought.

"What is a curse?" Overmoon asked. "What are you talking about?" "What?" Apollisian was somewhat embarrassed.

Overmoon fumed. "I ask you a legitimate question, and you look at me as if I'm an idiot and say, 'A curse.' I know I don't know all the human customs yet, but what are you talking about? And don't patronize me; I'm three times as old as you and twice as smart."

Apollisian could feel blood rushing to his face. "Save that tone for the children, elf. Perhaps you need reminded who is in whose charge. If you dare to speak to me like that again, I'll send you back to your father. You can explain to him how your childish tongue ended your journey!"

Overmoon turned and sneered as Corwin snickered. She whipped back and was cut off by more of the paladin's condemnations.

"Furthermore, I care not for your age, and if I were you, I wouldn't mention it again, for your lack of wisdom is an embarrassment not only to me and my god, but to the entire Overmoon family." Apollisian paused and softened his tone. "Now, to answer your question, the curse I'm referring to, is the curse to do what is right. I'd much rather chase Amerix to Hell and back, but instead I'm traveling with three children and my squire."

Overmoon glared at him with such anger that he thought he might need to draw his sword, then she walked closer to Victor, who was wise enough to remain silent. Apollisian rubbed his scarred hand over his empty scabbard. As soon as he dropped off the children, he'd find Amerix and reclaim his blade. Then he'd claim justice for the slain innocents.

Overmoon was quiet for the rest of the day, and at night, she sulked by the campfire. Victor tried to warm up to her, but whenever he spoke, she only stared at him. The squire dared not comfort her, though he was as taken by her beauty as Apollisian. Unfortunately for young Victor, he lacked the resolve or the wisdom of the paladin, and he was unable to recognize that his infatuation was fruitless.

Apollisian watched as Victor struggled with her rejection and decided that a walk might do him some good. "Do a walk around the camp, Vic. We'll be going to sleep soon, and we ride into town, tomorrow."

"Yes, my lord." Victor nodded and stepped into the darkness.

Apollisian unfolded his bedroll for the boys. Corwin smiled and crawled inside while Cerebron sat at the foot of it, hugging his knees into his chest. Apollisian leaned against a tree and sighed. His body ached from the fight. He'd been healing himself each day but was still a few days from a full recovery. His emotional healing, however, was much slower. He often awoke at night to the screams of those burned alive, or tortured himself over the battle with Amerix, thinking that he should have done this or said that.

"Cerebron won't make it," a soft feminine voice said.

Apollisian turned to see Overmoon standing next to him. He marveled at the fire's light as it danced across her almond skin. Her braided blonde hair was coiled around her head in a tight circle. He looked back at the boys. "I agree that he's troubled, but it's early to make such morbid predictions."

Overmoon stared at the pair. Corwin was fast asleep, but Cerebron sat staring blankly. "Once, when I was a child..." She looked Apollisian in the eye. "...long before your father's birth, my village was attacked by orcs. I lived a privileged life, but I remember a young maiden who lost her true love on the battlefield. She sat in the same chair that young Cerebron sits in now. She neither cared if she lived nor died. It was soon after that, she took her own life. And do you know why?"

Apollisian cleared his throat. "Because she felt that with the love of her life gone, she could no longer bear to live?"

"No. She realized that the tragedy she'd endured had robbed her of her sense of right. She no longer cared for right or wrong; the two became blurred into something she could not comprehend. She was so dead inside that she held no regard for her life or anyone else's. She knew that only in death, her soul might be freed from the shackles leavened upon it." She pointed at Cerebron. "That child has no sense to even realize what he's lost. Evil will overcome him and he'll most likely live a life of crime, committing many times over the acts he suffers for now."

Apollisian shook his head. "That's why I'll take him to the church of Stephanis, so he can learn about justice through worship."

Overmoon placed a hand on his shoulder. He could feel the warmth of her touch through his tunic.

She leaned close and whispered into his ear. "Do you think Stephanis is known by humans only?" He watched her walk away and then lowered his head. It was going to be another long night.

He awoke from his deep slumber and his pale lids fluttered, slowly revealing vivid green eyes. Darrion-Quieness, the great white dragon, licked the outside of his toothed-filled maw and yawned. The ancient beast stretched his limbs and rolled over on his giant pile of gold and jewels. His pointed nostrils sniffed the frigid air and detected intruders in his cave. They were at the entrance of his lair, so he had time to wake up before devouring them. The whites were among the weaker dragon races, but he'd survived a millennium and grown to mammoth proportions: three hundred feet from head to tail. His scales had changed from gleaming white at birth to a murky opaque. His black claws were long and hooked, protruding several feet from his toes. His oversized head was well-armored, and a spine extended out with a sail crest angling back toward his body. His long leathery wings permitted flight, but he lacked agility.

Darrion-Quieness glanced around his lair. Many frost giants littered his cave in solid ice. They were his favorite food, and abundant in the tallest peaks of the mountains. With the ability to control weather, he made it a perpetual winter around his mountain home. It attracted colder climate creatures that he was more than happy to feed on. Most intelligent beings stayed far away, but the occasional foolish hero, usually a human, would try to rid the world of the horrible evil named Darrion-Quieness, and the dragon would toy with the thoughtless morsel before eating him.

But something was different about today's group. The dragon smelled many humans, but he didn't detect weapon oil or armor. This troubled the great white. If they had no swords or armor, they were probably spell casters, and they posed the largest threat. He hated fighting them because it was difficult to discern their abilities. So instead of provoking the mages, he would barter with them.

The intruders sheepishly rounded the corner to the main cavern. He counted seven in all, wearing black robes with the mark of Nalir. Darrion-Quieness smiled a pearl-toothed grin. He was going to get many diamonds as payment, which he loved more than anything else. He scanned the humans, trying to see the pouch where the diamonds were kept, but he could not see it. The humans were crafty for hiding them because he was known to take the diamonds and eat the people rather than speak to them. The dragon thought he might test their might and get both dinner and diamonds.

One of them stepped forward. Darrion-Quieness could smell magical enchantments about him. He was small for a human and kind of old.

"Darrion-Quieness, it is I, Soran, that calls your name today. We have sought you out so that you might aid us. We've brought the usual payment. It will be delivered upon receiving answers to the questions we seek." His voice quivered from the mere sight of the beast. Soran had cast spells to protect him and the other mages from the dragon's aura of fear. Yet, he could still feel the powerful magic prying at his mind's defenses.

Darrion-Quieness ignored whatever the human was saying and thought about the wonderful diamonds he'd receive from the day's transaction. Soran took the dragon's silence as permission to continue: "Before, we came to you and asked about the prophecy. You told us that a man was born who would crush the kingdom of Nalir. You said he was an orphan with the surname Ecnal. We have slain every Ecnal in the land of Beykla, where the orphans have such a surname. What–"

The dragon interrupted, "How many beautiful shining diamonds did you bring?" He picked his teeth with his black talon.

Soran stammered. "Y-you will be p-paid when our question has been answered and we are safe from your lair."

The dragon frowned, and his glare made the mages gulp nervously. He inhaled deeply and his throat swelled as he lowered his head. A giant cone of blue air rushed from his mouth and covered the wizards. The dragon swept his head from side to side as he exhaled, then he paused to raise a claw to smite any survivors. To his pleasure, only Soran remained alive, pinned in a coffin of ice with his head and an arm free. Soran tried to speak but was unable. He fought for consciousness, staring helplessly at the terrible beast before him.

"Hector!" The dragon called out. "I know you can hear me. I can sense your weak scrying. How dare you send your goons to disturb my sleep and have the gall not to send any diamonds? I know of your talents, King. I demand payment now!"

A blue light formed and an image of Hector De Scoran appeared, adorned in black and silver plate armor with intricate designs of scorpions on the shoulders; their tails stretched down the king's arms.

"Fitting that you show a weak image instead of appearing in person," the dragon taunted. "Afraid you will suffer the same fate as your lackeys?"

"Do not tempt me beast. I've allowed you to make a home on my land. I'll come to your lair only to claim your hide as my trophy."

Darrion-Quieness spread his wings and roared. The cave shook and debris fell.

The king continued, "But for now, you're useful to me. I've brought your diamonds, and I offer these men as tender morsels to placate your perpetual hunger."

Soran gasped. He didn't understand why his master would do this to him. Kalen, he, and his colleagues had done as the king had asked. They'd deciphered the prophecy; they had... deciphered the prophecy. It made perfect sense to the doomed wizard. His group was no longer useful and their knowledge of the prophecy made them a liability to the wicked king. The trapped mage struggled but could not move.

The image of Hector produced a large bag of diamonds

that dropped to the cavern floor. The dragon reached out and tore open the bag with a single claw. He purred in delight at the hundreds of diamonds spilling out.

"Ask your questions, Hector, and then be gone."

Hector De Scoran smiled and paced the floor. "Did we succeed in slaying all of the Ecnals in Beykla?"

The dragon laid down, slowly counting his wonderful diamonds. "No." "How many did we miss?"

"One."

"Where is he?"

The dragon stopped counting. "You waste your time, Hector. The more you seek to invalidate this prophecy, the more you'll enforce it."

"So it can be changed?" Hector asked eagerly.

Darrion-Quieness exhaled and resumed counting. "All prophecies can be changed, but they seem to have a strange way of fulfilling themselves."

Hector pondered the dragon's words. "Where is this Ecnal?"

"He's in Beykla, in Central City, and he owns a Necromidus which should prove interesting." "What is he doing there?"

"One hundred thirty-seven." Hector frowned. "What?"

"One hundred thirty-seven. That's how many diamonds you gave me." "What does that have to do with anything? That's more than enough!"

"Goodbye, Hector. Don't disturb me again for one hundred thirty-seven days, or I'll fly to your castle and test your boasts of power." The dragon waved his hand and the king's image was gone. The beast looked down at the terrified wizard.

"What is your name?"

"S-S-Soran."

The dragon shook his head. "No, your name is Lunch." His massive jaws snapped on Soran's half- frozen body. The dragon crunched and chewed as he climbed back onto his mound of gold and jewels. After his nap, he would take a trip near Beykla to see what was so special about the son of a fallen goddess.

"Damn that lizard!" Hector screamed as he tried to re-establish his link to the dragon's lair. He focused his mind and channeled powerful weaves into the spell. After several unsuccessful attempts, he turned his attention to what he'd learned: the Ecnal was in Central City.

"Guard, send for a sage or one of the wizards," Hector commanded. The guard nodded and left the king's chambers. Hector thought about his many agents in Beykla. His favorite was the wererat guild, run by Pav-co.

A few minutes later, a sage rushed into the room. "Yes, my lord. You sent for me?" The man stammered, falling to the imposing king's feet.

Hector looked down with an arched eyebrow. "Spencer, is it?" "Y-yes, my lord," the sage whispered.

"I recall you've always served me well," Hector said with an evil grin.

Actually, Spencer had failed to answer a question recently, and the king had threatened to kill him on a later day for it.

Hector seemed to have forgotten this, and Spencer had no intention of reminding him.

"I always serve with my all, my lord." A trickle of sweat ran down the side of his face.

"Well, Spencer, I have a minor task for you."

"Yes, my lord?" He scooted on the floor closer to Hector's feet.

"If you perform it expeditiously, I'll forget I planned to kill you."

"Yes, my lord. Name it and it will be done." His voice cracked with fear.

"Go to the library and tell my first wizard, Kalen, that I need to get a message to Pav-co." Hector stroked the blade of a silver curved dagger. "I want Pav-co to find the Ecnal and kill him. He is to return the Necromidus to me as proof of the deed."

"Yes, my lord," Spencer said and scurried from the room.

They worked feverishly night and day, burrowing through stone. Amerix had sent close to three hundred of the dwarves down the passage to Mountain Heart, the underground village of his people, and instructed them to leave as many clues as they could so Tharxton might think they'd all marched in that direction. Of course, he'd told his men that it was to throw off any Beyklans who might follow them into the cavern. One sergeant showed concern for tricking them into traveling straight to their vulnerable families, but Amerix assured him that any human army lacked the ability to march the hundreds of miles underground to Mountain Heart. The amount of oil needed to keep torches lit, as well as food and drink to keep the men from weakening, would be more than they could carry.

With that plan in place, Amerix led the rest south, following an old limestone deposit that ran parallel with the Dawson River. When the passage ended, they began digging their way, rigging the new tunnel to collapse, covering their tracks. Since the cave was relatively close to the surface, they faced few of the dangers normally associated with traveling underground. They were well into their second night before encountering their first dilemma.

Therrig roused the sleeping general. "My lord."

Amerix rubbed the sleep from his eyes, yawned, and looked around.

Therrig cleared his throat. "Are you ready for the report, my lord?"

Amerix's black beard shook as he nodded. "Aye, but me hopes it is better than the grim expression ye bring this day." He rose from his satchel and began the tedious task of donning his armor.

"Well, my lord, we've found a large cavern full of

mushrooms and precious water. The lake is large and we suspect that there are many beovi swimming in its depths."

Amerix smiled. Beovi were underground fish that fed on plants. They grew to be quite large and were a delicacy to dwarven kind. Unfortunately, lakes of beovi usually attracted other humanoid races. "So who are our new neighbors?" He tugged on his leather boots.

"A group of kalistirsts. Maybe a hundred, no more." Therrig had a lust for battle in his eyes.

Kalistirsts were an underground race resembling a cross between a mole and a dwarf, with no eyes and covered in thin fur. Their three fingers and three toes sported six-inch claws that could burrow through the earth in moments. The claws prevented the race from using tools or weapons, but they could double for both. They were friendly, but would join whichever side offered the best price. Amerix entertained the idea of massacring them. After all, kalistirsts contributed to the downfall of clan Stormhammer.

Amerix sighed. It wasn't this group. "I'll go down with two others and make contact with the kalistirsts. I'll tell them we're going to fish and gather supplies, then be on our way." He stared at his great helm. The ram horns were moldy and the iron spikes were showing rust. He placed it on his thick head as he did a thousand times before.

"And if they refuse?" Therrig drummed his fingers on his hammer.

"Then we kill them."

Therrig smiled. He was tired of digging and gathering food. Rubbing the scar on his neck, Therrig wandered off, entertaining visions of kalistirsts running in terror.

The cavern ceiling was fairly low, and there were sedimentary rifts along the walls that acted as ledges, but their limestone composition made them fragile. Water seeped through the walls and trickled into the pool, the sound echoing through the large cavern.

Amerix navigated his descent from the dwarves' rocky perch to the cavern's base. He recognized the limestone for what it was and didn't spend any more time on it than was necessary. With a small grunt, he plopped down from the final ridge onto the hard floor of black clay. The old general glanced around as he approached the pool. Though he couldn't see any kalistirsts, he knew they must be burrowed nearby. Their first reaction to any intrusion was to hide.

Amerix walked slowly to a level base near the pool. It was murky from all the minerals, but it seemed deep. Amerix removed his battered helm and called out in his native tongue. "Show yerselves, mole people. I know ye be hiding."

He waited but no one appeared. After a few minutes, he shrugged, replaced his helm, and trudged back to his men.

The army spent the next day fishing and resting. The cavern was large enough to hold them comfortably for a few days, and Amerix watched as his men caught hundreds of beovi. They cut the giant, white fish into strips and cooked them on calours, a flat sedimentary rock that was heated by fire. They then salted the strips and smoked them using burnt cartilage and bones. The process took little time and effort, plus it bolstered their morale. Amerix had many sentries posted in case the kalistirsts decided to take the lake back, but they never showed.

The general had his miners collapse the tunnel they'd burrowed to keep Tharxton from following them, though he explained to the miners that he feared humans might have been following them. The miners new that Amerix didn't fear that event coming to pass, but could not guess the real motive behind Amerix's wishes. But in truth, they were not overly concerned with it. He gave the orders, they followed them. A few of the dwarves were grumbling about not hearing from Tharxton, but that was as far as it went. Though, Amerix knew his army was fickle at best, and he needed to strike Central City within the week or risk many of his men that were loyal to Tharxton to become suspicious.

By the eve of the second day, the dwarven army was

getting cramped in the cavern, so Amerix decided to push on to the southern corridor. It was much smaller than the one they'd dug, but it was made of weak clay and Amerix feared it wouldn't hold any shafts they might carve into it. So they marched, single file in some cases, toward Central City. Toward what the old general felt would be another decisive victory.

"What is the reason for war? Could not ideas and influences be spread without the threat of death or dismemberment? How does one define a war? Could someone fight a war without killing anyone? No one has to die to win a military campaign. If a castle is under siege and the attacking army does not let any food or water get into the castle, the defenders would have no choice but to surrender. How could they not, unless they allowed themselves to starve to death. But if they did choose death over surrendering, then I ask why?

"Why do men and women choose to die rather than give up? Could a war not be settled by fighting dogs or by a sport of some kind? Could not a war be fated on a single battle, where each side places their trust in a champion?

"The answer is simple, it could. The problem is men, as a society, lack honor. If all men had honor, or followed a set of humane rules, there would be no need to fight to the death. There would be no fear of losing that would be great enough to warrant giving one's life. Given that truth, why can't men create these rules? Men can come together to build towers that reach the sky. They can build ships that can sail to the far reaches of the world. They can even wield and control forces that are unseen and contain enough power to shape the very earth they live in. Yet despite all of these abilities they possess, humans lack the basic fundamentals to achieve the simplest of all, peace. Peace is not a structure to create or a spell to bring someone back from the dead. It is merely the omission of violence. Are humans so cruel and wicked that they cannot keep themselves from committing acts of violence? Strange on how the simplest of tasks is so far beyond those that can achieve almost anything."

- Lancalion Levendis Lampara

8

The Foe Beneath

Hard rain pounded against the shutters of Lance and Jude's window. They'd rented a quaint room on the second floor. Thinking the bargain price was a steal compared to the other rooms, Lance soon learned why it was so inexpensive. Spurts of water flowed through the splintered shutters and soaked his wool blanket. He wanted to move the bed away, but it was secured to the floor with metal plates. Jude slept against the door while Lance sat at the other end of the room, studying the Necromidus. He strained his eyes in the candlelight as the wind raced through, nearly extinguishing the flame again and again. The rain played out its song until Lance grew weary and drifted off to sleep.

The storm had been a fierce one, and when sunlight finally peeked through the shutters, dotting the bare floor and walls, Lance awoke, gathered his pack and roused his friend. "Get up, we leave the city today."

Jude slowly opened his eyes and stretched his thick arms. With a mighty yawn, he rolled over and pulled the blanket tighter around him.

"Come on, Jude, I thought you'd be thrilled to leave. All you've done is complain since we arrived."

Jude finally sat up after a few more prods. He rubbed his eyes, smacked his lips, and rummaged through his pack for his water skin. He took a long draw, letting water spill from the corners of his mouth, then tossed the water skin on top of his pack. He belched and wiped his mouth before plopping back down and pulling the blankets around him. Lance groaned and forced the door open, pushing hard against Jude's legs. If the big man noticed at all, he didn't show it until the door slammed shut. Then he cracked a smile.

Lance descended the stairs to the common room, and was greeted by the overwhelming smell of venison and eggs. He was surprised to find the room rather empty, save for a few tables of militia guardsmen and farmers. Lance strolled to a table against the north wall and waited for the serving wench. After getting her attention, he ordered a plate for him and Jude. He savored the fresh meat while contemplating where else he could have the text deciphered. The old sage had told him the writing was elven, but there were many types of elven races, and each had unique languages.

Jude rose and dressed, happy to be leaving the city, even if it was early in the morning. Though their stay was a little over a day, it was too long for the swordsman. He donned his chain armor shirt and strapped his sword over his back. Hoisting his leather pack over one shoulder, he opened the door and trotted downstairs. He spied Lance sitting at the table, staring intently at nothing. He dropped his pack on the floor and took a seat across from the mage. The aroma of the meat and eggs wafted up into his face.

Jude shoveled a heaping spoon-full of egg in his mouth, took a bite of bread, and spoke while chewing. "Hey, Lance, what's up?"

Lance shifted his gaze from the wall to the floor, but said nothing. Jude swallowed and said, "We'll find an elf to help us." "We're not elves. They won't help us willingly."

Jude guessed he was right. Elves rarely spoke to humans except for kings or heroes, and they were anything but that. "Perhaps you could trick one, like you've tricked me." He smiled, but Lance only shook his head.

Jude sighed. "Well, I could put my ear to the street and see if anyone can help us." Lance cracked a grin. "We might be forced to stay a few more nights."

Glad to see his friend's spirits lifted, Jude folded his arms behind his head and propped his feet on the table. "Well, if I'm to suffer a few more nights in this city, I'll need better housing."

Lance finished the small amount of wine at the bottom of his flagon. "Let's go rent us a fine room, then."

"We shouldn't dally too long, though. I don't want to be here if the dwarves attack. I think every day that we linger, we're pushing our luck."

Amerix stepped through the small opening from the tunnel his men had carved. His leather boots splashed into a two-foot-deep stream of putrid water. Methane and ammonia hung in the air of Central City's sewers. The shafts were about nine feet high and twenty across, and the gray stone walls were covered in a slimy green moss. There was a three-foot-wide ledge lining each side of the water, and the passages were dimly lit from a sewer grate a hundred feet above. The sunlight reflected off the moss, giving the area a green hue.

Floating debris swirled in the water as Amerix waded to the ledge on the east side of the passage. A few of his commanders exited the tunnel and gagged on the odor. Amerix chuckled. "Ye gots the stomach for war, but ye can't deal with a little stench."

One commander doubled over and vomited. Amerix clapped him on the back and laughed again. "Let us be a movin' to a more favorable place so we can stage a command and map the area."

The commanders nodded and covered their noses and mouths, fighting to keep the remaining contents of their stomachs down. As the soldiers moved into the passage, the reaction was the same. Human waste clung to their legs as they waded, carrying their weapons high to keep the blades from being soiled. Their dwarven eyes scanned the corridors. Like many underground races, their vision was much better in the dark than surface creatures. But though they could see over a hundred feet in complete darkness, they were oblivious to the other eyes that watched back.

Hand signals in the shadows above asked, "What are they?" Ryshander impatiently signed back to Kaisha, "Dwarves."

Kaisha frowned. She'd called the sewers her home for over a decade and had never seen a dwarf there, let alone a parade of them. She strained to look past Ryshander toward the corridors. She could hear them splashing down the grinder, and her keen sense of smell detected heavily oiled weapons and armor. Kaisha dared not move. She'd learned from Ryshander long ago about hiding in the shadows. Often, even the slightest movement could spell disaster.

Ryshander studied the dwarves. His well-honed muscles clung to the thin crevices of the wall without complaint. He noticed that the dwarves were unfamiliar with the grinder and moving in the sewers. They splashed around and spoke loudly. He tried to gauge their ages, but he'd heard tales that they lived for hundreds of years. Ryshander was almost thirty-five, and Kaisha was twenty-seven, though they looked to be in their teens. Being wererats kept them from aging and prevented them from being injured from nonmagical or silver weapons, but they still knew the value of caution.

They remained motionless, save for the occasional hand gesture. When the dwarves were out of sight, they both sighed. Ryshander lowered himself from the small alcove near the base of the ceiling, and then offered his hand to aid Kaisha. She was equally skilled in climbing, but it was a gesture of respect rather than necessity.

Kaisha signed, "We should alert Pav-co immediately."

Ryshander shook his head. "This may profit us. We should follow them and see who or what they're looking for. Maybe we can aid them and line our own pockets with gold, instead of Pav-co's." He moved quietly down the corridor, his green cloak blending into the moss-covered walls.

Kaisha hurried to him. "My love, what are we to do if we find they're looking for Pav-co? Or worse yet, what if they're looking for others of our kind because Pav-co wronged them? You would stroll into their numbers for the sake of a few coins and leave me alone in this world without you?" She pouted and crossed her arms under her breasts.

Ryshander lowered his shoulders and stroked her smooth cheek with his gloved hands, his dark brown eyes gazing into hers. "Let's poke around ol' Pavie and see if we can learn if he recently wronged any dwarves. Though, I know we're wasting valuable time that could be used to line our pockets with dwarven treasures."

Kaisha smiled thankfully, and they hurried down the grinder toward Lostos, the sewer guild house of Pav-co.

Lance sat in their new room which had high ceilings with intricate designs of swirling colors. The floor was hard-polished oak with a plush rug in the center, and next to each bed was a cedar closet with ivory handles. This room had actual glass windows instead of wooden shutters, and the oaken beds were against the walls adjacent to the window. The mattresses were stuffed with goose down and had fine cotton sheets. The wool blankets were dyed red and gold, the colors of Beykla. Lance ran his hand over them. He didn't appreciate the colors, but realized he was probably one of a small group of people who despised their home country. Lance leaned back on the bed and basked in the warm sunlight that filled the room. He'd been studying the Necromidus for most of the day while Jude was out looking for a renegade sage who worked for a local thieves' guild. Lance had heard of such sages, as well as mages who sold their talents to the highest street bidder. It's a strange environment to study and practice magic, he thought, but no stranger than studying on horseback or in unfamiliar inns.

Lance was close to finishing the first book, yet he was unsure if the spells would work. The magic required the weaving of necromancies on live people to ensure accuracy and effectiveness. He would never try it on innocent people, so he thought he'd experiment during the next conflict.

Lance practiced the incantation several times while waiting for Jude to return. As he weaved his hands in the prearranged motions of the spell, the ends of his fingers tingled as black wispy strands of energy enveloped them. He could almost sense the weaves screaming for release, pulling at his restraint, but Lance resisted. He closed his eyes and struggled to control their order. Beads of sweat formed on his brow, and his body shuddered from the strain. Lance fought the sensation for several minutes before collapsing on the bed. He'd withstood the spell's pull, but it had scared him. Never had any of the dweamors he weaved fought against his cognizant will. Yet this one from the Necromidus seemed to have its own mind of sorts. Lance shook his head as he thought, No, it was not a mind of its own, but more of a will. It was a pagan desire that lusted after the release of its own intense energy. He rolled over, pulled out his pen and ink, and began to scribe in his notes.

His time for revenge was rapidly approaching. After deciding to risk being caught by old enemies, he followed the mage and swordsman around the alleys and streets of Central City, waiting for Lance to be alone. Yet, everywhere the mage went, the damned swordsman followed. Grascon was growing more impatient. The longer he stayed in Central City, the more likely it was that another thief might expose him to the guild.

Grascon rented a room across the hall from Lance and Jude. When they moved, he moved. He didn't bring a lot of gold with him, so the move to the more luxurious room forced him to cut a few purses and necks to afford it. He was excited when Jude went out on his own, but Grascon disliked operating during the day. His victims were at a disadvantage at night, and he'd learned long ago not to underestimate a mage, regardless of how young he appeared. He only hoped Jude didn't return until much later.

Jude was having no luck. He'd wandered through the back alleys for most of the day. He and Lance had only about nine gold coins left, not enough to buy information about the guild. He'd almost gotten into a score of swordfights and was growing tired of walking. It was late afternoon when he decided to enter the sewers to search for guild contacts there.

Jude searched the alleys for a grate away from the observant eye of city guards. When he found one, he grabbed the rusted bars, pulled it up with little strain, and set it on the ground. He peered down into the sewer and saw a ladder extending a hundred feet into the darkness. Jude climbed in and carefully replaced the grate over his head, green slime and water dripping onto his head and shoulders. He covered his nose and mouth as he lowered himself down the chute.

Once Jude reached the dark passage, his feet found one of the ledges and he scanned left and right, his eyes struggling with the dim green glow. He walked down the right ledge, careful not to trip on anything that might send him headlong into the disgusting water. He reached a "T" a few hundred yards down and looked down each passage. He went left, then right, and then left again; making mental notes of each turn. He had almost decided to turn around when he heard strange voices ahead of him.

The two dwarven scouts had been walking for hours. They wore chain shirts and carried large axes. Thick metal helms protected their heads, strapped to their chins under their brown beards. Their armor and legs were stained with excrement as they moved clumsily down the corridor.

"Bah, this stinks!" one of the dwarves called out. "We ain't seen a thing since we came into these Leska-be-damned sewers."

The other dwarf nodded. "There ain't a single human in this rotten hell." He wiped his burning nose on his sleeve.

They turned the corner and stood motionless in surprise. Standing directly in front of them was a large human, probably the largest they'd ever seen. He stood six feet, seven inches tall and was about three dwarves wide. He had a giant sword strapped to his back and wore a chain shirt that hung below his knees. His hands were outstretched with palms showing, and he was speaking some rabble they couldn't understand. After their moment of hesitation, the dwarves did what any other would do when faced by an enemy of sorts: they drew their weapons and attacked.

Jude advanced cautiously toward the voices, thinking perhaps they were some form of thieves' cant. As he navigated the narrow ledge to a right turn, Jude could hear the deep voices growing louder, so he waited as two dwarves rounded the corner and stood in shock. Jude quickly studied the dwarves. He noticed they carried their double-bladed axes in their right hands, and their weapon arms were on the outside of the ledge. Jude was also right-handed, so his weapon arm was on the inside. Therefore, he had a distinct disadvantage if the encounter came to blows. Furthermore, due to the dwarves' small stature, they could launch feints and thrusts without hindering each other's attacks.

Jude outstretched his arms and placed his hands palms out, showing that he bore no weapons. "Friend dwarves, I mean no harm. I'm looking for a renegade sage or some other...." He was cut off by an attack to his left knee. He raised his leg and twisted his body to dodge the blow.

The axe narrowly missed his hamstring and whistled past. The second dwarf launched his axe overhand at Jude's head. Jude, off- balance, managed to avoid the brunt of the blow, but the axe tore a gash through his chain shirt and into his chest. Searing pain burned from the wound and the blow knocked him backward. He lost his footing in the wet moss and with a mighty splash, the cold, debris-filled water washed over Jude as he hit the stone floor under the three-foot-deep rivulet. He drew his sword and his massive form erupted from the water in a defensive stance, holding the sword close to his body with the tip pointing up. The blade glinted in the pale light of the sewer as the fetid water cascaded down. Jude's eyes were inflamed by the filth, and he struggled to see the two dwarves advancing toward him.

With his left hand wiping his face, Jude awkwardly parried another strike from an axe. He backed against the ledge on the far side of the passage. He didn't dare climb onto it, since the moss was too slippery to navigate a battle on. Instead, he grabbed his sword with both hands and took a wide stance.

Ryshander and Kaisha were having difficulty making their way back to Lostos. Every passage they took had dwarven patrols in it. It was as if they'd magically appeared in the sewers. Each patrol was made of two or three wearing light armor and carrying axes or hammers. Ryshander feared a confrontation might harm their chances of making any coin from the dwarves, and the increasing number had Kaisha concerned, so the pair rested under a grate.

"We should flee the sewers," Kaisha signed.

Ryshander's long brown hair bounced as he shook his head. "It's not dark yet, and we'd face more dangers than a few dwarves if we emerged during the day."

Kaisha leaned against the grinder's wall with her arms folded.

Ryshander placed his hand on her shoulder, then signed. "I know what you're thinking, but there are only four alley sewer grates, and we're nowhere near any of them. We can't come out while it's light, so we either keep moving or wait here until dark." Ryshander half-smiled to himself. For once, he was the conservative one. Normally, he was quite ready to take a few chances. But something was different this time. He couldn't put a finger on it, but it was bigger than a few dwarves in a sewer.

"What is it, my love?" Kaisha signed as she studied Ryshander's face.

Ryshander gazed into her beautiful brown eyes, how he loved her. Without her, there was nothing in his world. His sun, moon, stars all began with her name. He shook his head and whispered, "Nothing, Kaisha."

Kaisha's eyes went wide and she began signing furiously. "How dare you speak down here? I understand your passion for all things, but I will not tolerate such recklessness!"

Ryshander could only look down. She was right, but he was so caught in the moment. He wanted to scream at her how he could be at the end of his existence and if he could have but a glimpse of her smiling face, he'd die knowing that his life was complete. Instead, he humbly signed an apology.

She accepted and kissed him on the cheek. She started to sign again when they heard the sound of ringing steel echoing down the corridor.

They silently rushed to the battle. Cautiously navigating down the slick passage, the pair slowed.

They didn't want to wander into a perimeter patrol in case this was a planned attack. Pav-co would severely chastise them if he'd set an ambush and they interrupted.

After checking the ceilings and small alcoves of the grinder, they approached the clamor. As they warily rounded the corner, they watched with deep interest as two dwarves battled a giant of a man.

"Who is the human?" Kaisha signed.

Ryshander shrugged. "Are you sure he's human?

Rarely have I seen a human as big as he. Perhaps he is half ogre."

They returned their eyes eagerly to the fight.

Slime dripped from Jude's arms as he clutched his two-handed sword, holding it toward the advancing dwarves. Blood streamed from the wound in his chest, running down his stomach and legs. He clenched his teeth and emitted a low growl. Jude knew they were not the drunken novices he usually fought in Bureland. He now battled adversaries with more than a hundred years of training and experience. But he was not about to go down without at least drawing their blood.

Once the first dwarf came into range, Jude circled his blade over his head and struck hard from his right. The dwarf brought his axe up to intercept, and the weapons collided with a shrill ring. The force of the blow knocked the dwarf's weapon wide. The dwarf tried to roll with it and return a strike, but Jude had already moved to his right. The man continued to circle the sword. Straining every muscle in his thick arms, he groaned and struggled against the inertia to change the blade's direction, so it came directly down on the second dwarf's head, instead of bringing it into his side. Expecting the latter, the dwarf tried to move his axe to deflect the overhead blow, but he underestimated Jude's speed.

The strike sliced deep into the dwarf's face. There was a dull melon-splitting sound as the blade cleaved the helm and sunk into his skull. The dead dwarf slipped under the putrid waters and disappeared from sight, save for the sword's pommel protruding upward. Jude gripped it and placed his foot on the dwarf's head as he pulled, but his wet, slimy hands were unable to get a firm hold on the hilt. While trying, he took a slice across his left shoulder from the other dwarf. The attacker was preparing a second strike as Jude felt the new wound. His numb arm hung low as warm blood dripped into the water. He began to feel dizzy and fought to keep his balance. There wasn't enough time to free his weapon before the next attack, so he set his feet and waited.

The dwarf came in with a high swing aimed at Jude's neck, and he ducked low, using his wounded left arm to grab the axe at the base of the head. His shoulder sent a painful shock rippling through his body as the bottom tip of the blade stabbed into his forearm. While the dwarf struggled to free his weapon, Jude brought his right arm around and struck him solid in the face. His nasal bone snapped, sending out a fountain of blood.

The dwarf released his axe and staggered back in the water, clutching his face. Jude transferred the axe to his right hand and waded toward him. The dwarf tried to climb onto the ledge and retreat, and Jude followed, quickly closing the gap with his long strides. The dwarf never looked back as his fingers frantically dug at the moss-covered walkway.

Jude brought the axe down into the back of his enemy, lodging it in his spine. As the body disappeared among the sewage, Jude checked his wounds. He could feel the water's sting and knew if he didn't get them clean, he could die from disease. He'd seen many a battle where the victor on the field lost their lives from an infection in a dirty wound.

Jude was worried about how many more dwarves might be lurking about, especially considering the rumors of Torrent Manor, so he wanted to move along fast. He placed the handle of the axe under his left arm and wrenched his two-handed sword free from the other dwarf. After sliding the blood-soaked weapon back in its scabbard across his back, he waded to the other side of the sewer. He was covered in blood that had splattered from the dwarves, and streams of his own blood soaked his chain shirt and arm.

The swordsman slowly stepped onto the ledge and continued down the grinder, toward the ever- dimming green glow ahead. Once the sewer went pitch black in the evening, he would be blind to any more dwarves he encountered, while they could still see quite well. Also, he was wounded to the point that he was unable to defend himself properly. Another battle would have a different outcome. Jude forced the thoughts from his mind and focused on finding a way back to Lance.

"Now what?" Kaisha signed to Ryshander. She was unsure whether they should search the bodies or intercept the large man. Certainly, the battle was heard by nearby dwarves and they were approaching the area.

Ryshander shrugged. "I think we should loot the bodies. We can pocket any coin or jewelry they may be carrying, plus the big man left one of the axes behind. No hurry on alerting Pav-co. He should know of the dwarves' presence by now. We've seen enough of their patrols that they've surely been spotted by other guild members."

Kaisha nodded. "I agree. Plus, I think it'd be foolish to bargain with the dwarves now. They'll be angry at their losses, and their numbers are too large for them to be some kind of adventuring group."

"Not only that, if the dwarves are agents or friends of Pavie's, we can blame the looting on the big man that killed them." The lust for gold shined in Ryshander's eyes.

The pair hurried over to the bodies and searched them, but they found no jewelry, gold, provisions, nothing other than the axe and their armor.

"This doesn't make sense," Kaisha signed and placed her hands on her hips, frustrated.

Ryshander glanced over his shoulder. "Well, we need to move before their friends arrive."

"Let's catch up to the big man and follow him. Maybe he'll lead us to some answers." Kaisha picked up the axe and handed it to Ryshander.

He nodded, took the weapon and hurried down the passage in the direction of the human.

Jude wandered down the corridor, controlling his wits through the pain from his wounds. He was certain he was heading toward a grate. He played the battle over in his mind and was pleased with the outcome. And though he was profoundly wounded, he was certain the injuries would heal. Jude felt more confident. Though he'd easily won many fights in Bureland, it had been many years since he was truly tested by serious combat. His mind wandered to the time he bested a half-orc in the Inn of Aldon. The beast was intoxicated and could barely stand unassisted. That was Jude's main claim to fame in Bureland. The half-orc had everyone so intimidated that even the witnesses to the fight exaggerated the telling of the tale.

Jude reached a corner of the grinder. He paused and listened, unable to hear anything other than his own breathing. He peered around the wall, and his heart danced at the sight of a bluish-green light from a sewer grate to the surface. He moved cautiously toward the ladder. With each step closer, he fought the overwhelming urge to break into a dead run. He didn't look back at the imaginary dwarven horde or other fiendish devils that he felt were stalking him until he reached the rusted iron rungs, and he only saw darkness and vague outlines of the empty corridor. With the aid of adrenaline, he ignored the pain in his shoulder while climbing toward the grate. Finally, he reached the top of the ladder.

Jude hung the dwarven trophy on the top rung and peered at the exit. To his horror, a large wheel was on the iron grate. Jude could see the sky from under the wagon, and he could smell the sweet night air, but all he could do was helplessly touch it with his hand. Jude's heart sunk. How could he have come so close and fail? Did he dare climb back down and stumble around in the darkness, searching for another grate that could be anywhere? How long should he wait? He couldn't tell if the wagon was attached to any horses. Was it stopped for a short time or parked for the night? Jude was wrestling with his options when he heard dwarven voices echoing below.

Jude shoved up against the grate with all his strength, but was unable to budge it. Fear tore through him, but he exhaled softly, concluding that he would have to wait until either the wagon moved or he was slain. He figured if the dwarves tried to come up the ladder, he could kill enough of them to discourage climbing up to attack him directly. The previous pair had no projectile weapons, and he doubted the dwarves could throw their heavy axes a hundred feet up at him. Jude thought if he was lucky, they wouldn't think to look up to the grate. He glanced at the wagon and rethought the luck idea. He had six hundred pounds sitting on the sewer grate proving he wasn't very lucky tonight.

"Luck. What is it? Can it be defined? Is it a tangible force, or some kind of magic that is yet to be tapped into? I know many races that worship Lukerey, the god of luck and mischief. To me, it seems like the religion with the least merit. Any event, good or bad, can be attributed to luck. I cannot deny these unseen forces exist, but is it something that can be harnessed? Is it possible to influence luck? Or are you merely increasing the probability of fate?

"To me, luck is when preparedness meets opportunity. If you are prepared to capitalize on an event, and you have the opportunity to do so, that would be luck. Yet despite my power and ability with the arcane arts, I cannot explain many things that are attributed to luck. They are, for lack of a better explanation, lucky!"

- Lancalion Levendis Lampara

9 The Hearts of Rogues

Ryshander and Kaisha hurried down the corridor, figuring the human would escape the under-city at the first grate he came across, which was only a few hundred yards away. Their soft leather boots slid to a stop when they saw him slowly climbing the ladder. They moved more cautiously, measuring their strides with each other to reduce the echo of footfalls. They could hear the swordsman's labored breathing, and his fresh blood stained the mossy walls and pooled on the ledge.

"What now?" Kaisha signed. The man wasn't opening the grate and she didn't want to risk an axe in the face if they climbed up after him.

"We wait." Ryshander moved to the edge of the passage, positioning himself just out of the human's view. He figured it was too dark for the man to see, but he'd learned that people could be surprisingly resourceful.

Ryshander's keen hearing detected the sound of the axe being hung from an iron rung, then the faint groans as he tried to force open the grate. Ryshander signed back to Kaisha. "I think the grate is locked."

Kaisha frowned. The city never locked them before. Why now? "Perhaps it's barred or blocked."

He shrugged and returned to listening while Kaisha fidgeted nervously. She didn't like the idea of waiting at a barred grate. They were in the middle of a corridor. If they needed to flee an attack from both directions, they were trapped. Avoiding being trapped is one of the first lessons learned in the under-city. Not only that, the thought of the city locking or worse yet, barring the other grates gave her chills.

Ryshander was watching the human from a small

metal mirror he'd removed from his pack. His focus was disturbed by a tug at his sleeve. He looked up at Kaisha's frantic signing. "Dwarves!"

She darted back toward the way they came. Ryshander listened for a moment and heard them talking as their clumsy footfalls echoed down the grinder. He looked up at the human, then back at Kaisha. She was urging him to follow her. Reluctantly, he abandoned the human to his own devices and rushed back toward Lostos, toward safety.

Therrig could hear something shuffling at the top of a chute leading to the city's surface. When Amerix learned the patrol had not returned, he'd sent Therrig and a small band of fighters to discover what had happened. He gripped his two-handed enchanted hammer, itching to spill human blood.

Therrig considered himself Amerix's most trusted friend and his best warrior. He wore thick plate armor with a face shield protruding from his right shoulder up to eye level. His helm was open-faced like most dwarves, and had a bright blue mohawk on the top, held in place by a leather strap under his jaw. If there was a problem, Therrig would deal with it. But much to his disappointment, he found nothing at the chute except blood. Whatever it was, it had escaped. Therrig chewed on his lip and shouted curses at his men for not catching the fiend. Therrig decided to make a wider sweep of the under-city. Perhaps he might find something to placate his ache for battle.

Jude stared into the blackness below him. He couldn't see the stone floor of the corridor, but he could hear the dwarves speaking as they drew closer. His heart began to beat so hard, and he feared the dwarves might hear it. He placed his sweaty forehead against the cool wall of the chute and said a silent prayer to the goddess of mercy that Lance had spoken about. Jude had prayed to nearly every god or goddess he knew of throughout his life, and he'd yet to receive a response. He had never prayed to the goddess of mercy, however, and this seemed like a good time. As he finished his silent plea, he heard the sound of leather creaking and the command for the horses to move. Could it be? Jude looked up to see the wagon rolling away. He didn't waste a second. With renewed strength, he shoved the grate up and onto the cobblestone street with a loud clang. He climbed out, quickly replaced the grate, and sat on the ground for some time to inhale the sweetest air he'd ever breathed. Jude stood up, stretched his tightening muscles, and began the walk back to the Blue Dragon Inn. He was unsure of where he was at, but boy did he have a story for Lance!

Amerix sat in the large sewer room he'd converted into a command center. He had posted detailed maps that his scouts made outlining grates, ambush intersections, and dead ends, in case the battle moved back to the sewers. His men worked feverishly to remove the growth of moss and scrape away the filth and slime that had built up on the walls and floor. The dome-shaped ceiling was twenty-five feet high, and dripped an occasional drop of moisture, so his men constructed a canvas covering for his command tent. The dawn was rapidly approaching and the old general still hadn't received word on the missing patrol. He hoped the humans would remain clear of the sewers. He saw no sign of them in the under-city, and every iron ladder bore an unhindered growth of moss, indicating that the grates hadn't been used in a while. Yet, it was obvious his missing patrol had encountered something or the seasoned pair would have returned. Amerix entertained the idea that they were lost, which angered him since the majority of the under-city had been mapped and he'd made his patrols memorize every detail before going out. He'd sent Therrig with a group of highly-skilled fighters to search for them. Amerix considered Therrig a loose bolt in the wheel of war, but still a proven ally. With each passing minute, he became more impatient for their return. He'd spent enough time in the sewers, so he called for a messenger.

"Yes, my general," the dwarf of barely a hundred years old replied.

Amerix scribed on a damp parchment that he intended to strike in a moment's notice, so the army was to be ready to march at any time. He rolled the scroll up and placed it inside an ivory case. Next he sealed the case with red candle wax and affixed the Stormhammer seal to it.

"Take this scroll to Commander Kestish." Amerix handed it to the messenger without looking at him, then began mulling over which grates he wanted to emerge from. He asked aloud, "Should we split our forces and have a surface unit hit them from the north while we emerge and hit them from behind? Or should we pour out of every western grate, trapping the human scum between us and the Dawson River?" Commander Fehzban frowned. Though he was one of Amerix's most loyal supporters and skilled clerics, he'd been apprehensive about sacking Central City and unsure of the best strategy. Never had a dwarven clan warred with a human city, so there were no battles to study, no experiences to draw from. Fehzban had been equally worried about the Torrent Manor strike and it was a complete success, but he doubted they would be so lucky twice. He knew that Amerix didn't worship Leska, and that his account of visions from her was a drunken stupor at best, but he didn't dare cross his demonic leader.

"Perhaps we could come from the east grates, my general," Fehzban said. He'd served as an ambassador for Clan Stoneheart for nearly thirty-five years and had an intimate working knowledge of the city.

Amerix's face wrinkled in derision. "Why in the name of Durion would we do that? That would leave the human dogs with a clear path of escape!"

Commander Fehzban smiled disarmingly. "Well, my general, we would have much fewer losses–" "So would the human scum!"

Fehzban gave Amerix an incredulous look.

"Go on," Amerix said finally.

"As I was saying, General, the humans would flee, leaving us to pillage and burn the entire city.

Without supplies, our enemies would be desperate and disorganized in the forest, and much easier to defeat or scatter."

Amerix pondered the tactic. "Well, Commander, I like the idea. I'll look at the east grates and see if it's a feasible route of attack." He dismissed the commander and returned to his battle plans. He was certain about one thing: they would attack from somewhere tomorrow night.

Ryshander and Kaisha hurried down the small passage leading to Lostos. The secret door to the hidden guild hall had been a long trip from where they'd encountered the battle between the dwarves and the human. Furthermore, Ryshander had to find a secure spot to hide the dwarven blade. He planned on selling it later and didn't want Pavco to get his hands on it. Kaisha knew they were late and would probably be chastised, but with the news they brought, she imagined their reprimand would be short-lived.

They came upon the small wooden door with intricate carvings depicting a beholder hovering above a small city. This beholder was one of the most fearsome kinds: a floating ball of flesh with a single eye in the center and a large mouth with a thousand dagger-like teeth, gaping in a roar. Its long tongue seemed to reach out of the carving, and it had many small tentacles protruding from the flesh, each with a small eye on the end. The creature was poised to strike dead anything that might oppose it. Neither Ryshander nor Kaisha had seen a real beholder, but from the stories told of the horrible beast, it was unlikely that they'd survive an encounter. They had seen the door a thousand times before, yet they always paused to admire the craftsmanship.

The pair entered after disarming a number of poisonous needle traps attached to the door's handle, then re-arming them once on the other side. They walked down the dry marbled hallway of Lostos while fellow guild members paid them little attention. There were thirty wererats in the guild, more than adequate numbers to control the streets and some politicians.

Pav-co had created the guild fifty years ago, and he'd become severely rich from its operation. The resourceful thief had survived seven coup attempts that Ryshander knew of, and he doubted there'd be more attempts anytime soon.

As they neared Pav-co's room, they noticed anxiety in the air. People were rushing about, ignoring them completely. Pav-co emerged from his room and began walking toward them. Both bowed low to their corpulent leader. Pav-co gently reached down and kissed the back of Kaisha's hand. Ryshander detested his disgusting open invitations to her. Once, Pav-co had flatly propositioned her, and Ryshander was so enraged that he started marching down to duel the loathsome creature, but Kaisha begged him to reconsider. Though Pav-co was much older than Ryshander, she'd seen the plump little man deal out death to the most experienced thieves. Kaisha loved Ryshander too much to let him risk his life over some twisted sense of honor. She knew that if necessary, she could lull Pav-co into her bed and kill him with a long, sharp, silver hairpin saved for such an occasion.

"My beautiful Kaisha." Pav-co's lower lip twitched with lust at the sight of the beautiful woman. She stood at five feet six with long brown hair cascading down her solid shoulders. She wore a black cloak that overlaid a brown and green tunic, sewn with a lighter green stitch. The tunic was low-cut, revealing the deep crevice between her firm breasts, and ended a few inches above her hips, hugging her waist tightly. Her snug breeches were a dark green, velvety material that made little or no noise when brushed together. They extended down to her black leather, knee-high boots. She wielded a short sword strapped to her right leg, and her thin black belt had many pouches that contained her tools of the trade.

Pav-co salivated at the thought of bedding the thief, but he valued Ryshander's talents too much to have to kill him. He knew if he took her by force, the young wererat would certainly seek blood. And no bedroom event was worth endangering his guild's operation.

"What do you have to report?" Pav-co asked. He looked at Ryshander and acknowledged him for the first time.

Ryshander glared at the fat guild leader. "We encountered a giant man that slayed two dwarves."

"We aren't sure what the dwarves are doing in the under-city," Kaisha said. "They had no supplies or tools, other than the weapons the human ran off with. We heard more dwarves as we tried to follow him, so we weren't able to track him on the surface."

Pav-co's face turned red. "You let a human enter the under-city and then escape!"

"We had no choice with the dwarves marching down the grinder," Ryshander pleaded. "If they killed us, how could we warn the guild of their activity?"

Pav-co grabbed at his fat belly and chuckled. "Do you presume you're my only patrols in the under- city? I'm already aware of the dwarves. They've cleared out the old construction room for headquarters. I'm sure they're not looking for us, but I think they're mapping the under-city for some reason. There's about two-hundred down here now, having burrowed into the grinder from an adjacent tunnel, so we know they're not sent by the magistrate. I first thought they were a group of misguided miners, but they're dressed for battle." He stroked his fat chin. "I don't want either of you going against them, for any reason. I've given a guild order to avoid them at all costs. I suspect they're a raiding party that took a wrong left or something, but they've got enchanted weapons and could easily cut our numbers in half. Unless they pose a direct threat to our guild, leave them alone. I think they'll leave in time."

While Ryshander and Kaisha pondered the news, Pav-co asked, "Did you get a good look at the human the two dwarves were fighting?"

They both nodded.

"Good. Follow him and see what he's up to. It might tell us why the dwarves are here, and if he appears to be unaffiliated with them, teach him why humans are not allowed in the under-city." He kissed Kaisha's hand a second time and winked before hurrying back to his room.

"I swear, one day I'll run my sword into his fat belly," Ryshander growled.

Kaisha smiled and avidly kissed him on the mouth, taking time to nibble his lower lip. "There will never be a need for that, my love."

Ryshander's face was flushed as they headed back to the grinder. They only had a few hours to find the giant man who had eluded them.

Spencer rushed into the posh room in the top of the southern tower. He closed the wooden door and tried to slow his breathing. Across the table, a young gray elf laughed and closed an ancient tome hard, the wind from it mussing his long silver hair.

"Spencer, my good man, what brings you to my room?"

Spencer wiped the sweat from his forehead. "I deliver a message from Lord Hector, and you would be smart to heed it. He's a thousand times more powerful than you."

Kalen smiled and stood up, shaking his slender head. He walked over to the obstinate messenger.

"Spencer, Spencer, Spencer. Just how long do you think that silly old man will live?"

Spencer glared at him. "Go on, fool, mock him! One

day, you'll wear out your usefulness, and he will kill you."

Kalen smiled and turned back to the table. He traced his delicate hand along the edge of it, keeping his back to the sage. "Who do you think is more important, sage? You or me?"

Spencer tried to respond but felt an incredible force tightening around his neck. His hands struggled in vain to claw at it.

"Spencer, your silence shocks me. Why would he need you? I can do everything you can. You have no real magic, only knowledge. Anything you can find, or remember, or decipher, I can too. Plus, I can kill any man as easy as I'm killing you. Can you do that, Spencer?"

Spencer only gurgled as his face turned purple.

"I can even read your mind, you pathetic creature." Kalen paused for effect and then said, "So our mighty king wants me to send Pav-co a message to kill the Ecnal?" He strolled past the near-unconscious sage and waved his hand at a small crystal mirror with sides made of jagged bones with intricate carvings. He recited a brief chant and the vacant mirror began to show swirls. As the image took shape, he saw a large room laced with golden trinkets and adorned with red velvety pillows.

"Pav-co. I have an assignment for you," Kalen said before turning back at the sage. "Oops. I'm sorry, Spencer. I forgot about your little breathing problem." The elf dismissed the incantation that held the sage's throat, and he collapsed to the floor, gasping for air. Spencer rubbed his throat and stood up weakly.

A voice spoke from inside the mirror. "Tormenting the sages again?"

Kalen turned to see Pav-co's cherub visage. Jewelry pierced his face, and his bald head glistened in the candlelight.

Kalen smiled and softened his tone. "Ah, my dear friend."

Pav-co frowned. "We're not friends, elf. Why is it you disturb my tedious efforts of relaxing?" "Well, my fat little cohort, our master wants someone dead."

Pav-co winced at the words, "our master." The thief had no master and would die before he had one.

He dealt with Hector and his minions for personal gain only, a relationship that seemed to call on him more and more of late. "Find some more dangerous orphans that need slain?"

"Our motives are unimportant to you. You'll do as you're told."

Pav-co glared at him. "And if I don't?"

"Then you'll no longer receive business from Hector the Great. And if we don't deal with someone, they're not our allies. Need I explain what we do with non-allies?"

Pav-co didn't respond right away as he pondered the threat, and he decided that the king's missions were worth the inconvenience. "Name your task. It will be done."

"I thought you'd see it my way. There's a man coming into town. He's very young, maybe eighteen, and he travels with a large swordsman. The youngster wears a black robe with silver on the cuffs. The swordsman wears chain armor. We don't know their names, nor do we wish to learn them. We just want them dead."

"It might be beneficial for me to know their names."
Kalen narrowed his eyes. "Then go ask them."

Pav-co started to respond, but Kalen waved his hand to dismiss the dweamor activating the mirror. He sat back in his soft chair and thought about the specifics of the pair. They were interesting, at least. A human boy with a Necromidus was something he didn't hear about every day.

A Necromidus in itself was very rare. The complete collection of the basic necromancy incantations was very expensive, and it took years of study just to be able to read it.

He scratched his head, curious if the boy had any ability to cast the spells. If he did wield the necromancies in the book, he might be more of an ally rather than enemy. He shrugged his narrow shoulders and returned to his studies. What threat the king saw in a mere human boy was of no consequence to him. The old pink-skinned man would soon be dead, replaced by a much more decisive ruler.

"Damn that elf!" Pav-co screamed and slapped one of his many concubines in the face. She recoiled in shock from the unexpected blow. He put on his silk robe and turned back to them. "Out, out, get out! All of you!"

The concubines hurried out of the room, grabbing clothing and robes as they left. The fat thief placed on his belt and boots, then checked himself in the looking glass before sticking his head out of his chamber door.

"Kellacun!"

A nimble woman of five and a half feet tall walked over wearing a long black cloak that floated about the air as she walked. She kept her black hair tied in a knot behind her head, held by a silver hairpin that doubled for a knife, and small pouches on her belt carried various poisons and potions. She kept her steel blue eyes on him as she approached. "Yes, your fatness?"

Pav-co's face immediately flushed red. He grabbed the woman by the hair on the back of her head and pulled her within an inch of his face. She could smell the stench of his breath as he spoke. "You're lucky you are so valuable to me, bitch, or you might find yourself in a riverbed one morning." He pulled her into his chambers and locked the door.

Kellacun gingerly readjusted her hair and stretched her neck. "And how important are you to me, thief?"

Pav-co winced at the title "thief." He knew she was reminding him that without the guild, he was nothing more than a cutpurse. "Damn you wench, why are you so insolent? I pay you twice as much as I ever paid Grascon and four times more than my other thieves."

"Speaking of the fool assassin, do you know his whereabouts? I still owe him from our last encounter a few years back. I'm eager to learn who hired him for that attempt on my life." She flashed a knowing smirk as she delicately sat on his desk. The vixen crossed her shapely legs, revealing her slick black boots that depicted a red spider under the knee.

Pav-co shook his head. "I need two men killed. A young man in a cloak and a large swordsman."

Kellacun stood up and started walking to the door. "That's a job for one of your less-skilled thugs, not an artist such as myself."

Pav-co rushed to block her exit. "Not so. I need you to find out about them first, what their names are, if they're important, and what connection they have with Nalir." Kellacun's eyes lit up. "Nalir? Working for Hector again?" Pav-co nodded. "And getting a pretty penny for it, too."

Kellacun folded her arms and shifted her weight to one foot. "So why not send someone cheaper?" "Because I know nothing about the pair and I don't want to take any chances. Even with your high cost, I should make a few coins from it."

"Since the work is for the mighty king of Nalir, himself, I would hope to get a little more than the usual," Kellacun said with a wry smile.

Pav-co walked across the chamber and opened a thick book that rested on an oaken table. He didn't look up from his writing as he spoke. "You're not a freelancer, Kellacun. If you think you can make more coin on the streets, I can put you there."

Kellacun smiled devilishly. "I am the streets, Pavicious. You will do well to remember that."

She silently stared with contempt as he wrote in his charge book. She contemplated sticking the thin blade of her cutlass into his pig heart, but instead, the skilled assassin unlocked the chamber door and left.

Grascon slowly opened the iron door to his room. He'd oiled it the night before to ensure it didn't make any noise. He'd hoped that Lance's door would have external hinges but they were impacted. Nothing was ever easy.

He examined the door again, checking it for wires or other signs of traps, and he found none. Grascon wished he had. He would much rather diffuse a poison needle trap than stumble into a glyph or some other warding spell created by the mage. He wasn't sure if Lance knew how to cast such spells, but he wasn't taking any chances.

Grascon drew his dagger and reached into one of his belt pouches for a needle-like wire with a flat hook on one end. The dagger's blade was covered in black oil to avoid any glint in the dark. Pav-co had trained him well when he worked for him. Grascon had assassinated many people for the guild, but Pav- co eventually betrayed him, nearly costing his life. He bore an ugly scar in remembrance and vowed to kill Pav-co one day, but he was still too strong. Another time, he thought.

Grascon placed the small tool into the door lock and could feel it slide across the tumblers. He then inserted a wider tool just above the first. He slowly worked them around until they silently fell into place. With careful breathing, he twisted the knob slowly until he felt the resistance from the bolt being moved. Using the notches behind the knob that he'd placed the night before, he gauged how far to turn it without creating the resounding click. Finally, he pushed open the door and slipped inside like a ghost.

Grascon easily scanned the room in the darkness and saw two beds. One had a figure in it, asleep. Instead of moving straight toward the mage, he moved along the walls, measuring each step and searching for traps or alarms. He found none. Grascon couldn't believe how easy this was.

What a fool, Grascon thought as he crept toward the bed and raised his dagger over Lance's sleeping form. He would have his revenge tonight.

Jude staggered down the dark streets and narrow alleys. It had taken him a while to get his bearings after emerging from the sewer, and he avoided anyone he saw on his way back to the Blue Dragon Inn. Fortunately, it was the first clear night in a while, so he had the stars to guide him. As he walked, he studied the dwarven axe in the moonlight. The double blades gleamed and revealed runes carved into it. The edge was precision sharp, despite the many nicks in it, and though it was heavy, it seemed it should be much heavier than it was. It was also so well balanced, Jude felt it could be thrown as easy as swung. The craftsmanship of the keen dwarven blade mesmerized him. Though he favored the use of his two- handed sword, Jude entertained the idea of wielding the axe as his primary weapon.

He put the thought out of his mind for now. He needed to get back to Lance as quickly as possible. He'd been gone for a long time and Lance was undoubtedly anxious to see him. And despite Lance's eagerness to get his papers read, they needed to get out of this deadly city.

Jude lumbered into the common room of the inn. His chain armor was covered in filth. Dark red blood stained his breeches and dripped on the polished floor. It was late evening and there were only three patrons in the room. One was a poorly dressed man at the far end of the room. His greasy brown hair blanketed his head, which was face down on the table, and a flagon of thick mead was clasped in his dirty calloused hand. He was mumbling something about crops and taxes. The other two were playing a game of cards near the bar, and Jude noticed that their table's location gave them a complete view of the room. They were male and female, both in their late teens. The male was dressed in a green outfit covered by a dark cloak while the beautiful female wore a tight-fitting tunic that revealed her voluptuous breasts. She also wore a black cloak held together by a silver hairpin. Her brown hair was pulled back in a ponytail. Her revealing tunic forced Jude to take more than a passing glance. He silently cursed his lustful eyes, but decided that neither of the two were a threat, so he hurried up the stairs. As Jude rounded the corner at the top, he noticed his wet boots made little sound on the hard floor as he walked down the hall toward his room. The inn was a much sturdier establishment than he'd ever experienced.

Jude turned the doorknob and noticed it was unlocked. He couldn't believe Lance was so foolish as to leave their room unsecured. Jude slipped inside, closed the door, and walked to the unlit lamp on the small table next to his bed. His chest and shoulder stung horribly. He was in dire need of a bath, and he needed to repair his chain shirt.

Jude grabbed the flint and steel from the table and was striking them together to light the ornate lamp, when pain tore through the right side of his ribs. Cold steel had pierced his chain shirt just above his kidney. Jude thrashed out his right hand and struck something. He turned to see a small man clutching his face and tumbling back against the wall, while Lance awoke violently and sat up in bed.

Grascon recovered from the blow and rushed in to meet the giant man. Jude accepted a stab to his belly as he drew his sword; the intruder's blade was too small to fatally penetrate the mail. Jude's sword came slicing down and caught him between the neck and shoulder, cutting deep and sending him sprawling to the floor. Blood splattered across the wall and the plush rug in the center of the room. The thief clutched the wound as he writhed in the throes of death. Jude took a step toward Lance and swooned. He felt stinging pains from the minor knife wounds, causing the room to spin. His vision failed and he fell to his knees, dropping his sword in a clamor.

Lance leapt from the bed and rushed to his friend. "Jude, thank the heavens you returned when you did! Are you all right?" He placed his arm under Jude's and tried to lift him.

Jude's eyes rolled back in his head. Before losing consciousness, he said, "Poison."

Lance let his friend slump gently on the floor, and then frantically began checking the wounds to see if they were fatal. He concluded that he'd survive them, but he was unsure about the poison.

He rose to his feet and gasped in horror. The slain thief was standing in front of the door. His clothes bore a long blood-soaked tear from the collarbone to his waist, but there was no wound.

Grascon smiled. "Remember me, boy?"

Lance recognized the one-toothed grin and the scar across the man's face and knew he had to act fast, using the spell he often cast on his adoptive father to make him drop his axe. Normal mages, and even sorcerers, had to move their hands, recite chants, and sometimes use components to cast their spells. Lance had always been able to visualize the movements and chants in his head to cast them. He knew it was a unique ability, and it allowed him to use magic without others knowing.

Grascon watched in shock as the dagger shot away from his grasp and skittered across the floor, but then he chuckled. "Impressive, mage, but I don't need the knife to kill you." The assassin's face began to elongate and sprout hair. His hands grew thick fur and his fingers sported sharp black claws. His body convulsed and changed rapidly.

Lance knew he had little time. He began reciting the movements and incantations of the spell learned from the Necromidus, and as he finished, a strange energy filled him, building up and searching for release. But Lance fought it, struggling to gain control but it was too great. He felt himself losing his grip, barely aware of the half rat, half man advancing toward him. Lance grew more afraid of the magic continuing to grow within him, yet he didn't know how to release it. He fell back against the wall, unable to stand, while his vision changed to a hazy black. He shook his head as intense cold washed over him. His flesh tingled and his bones ached, and he could hear nothing but ringing in his ears. His only concern was to release the energy.

Grascon brought his claws down to slice into Lance's neck, but they barely cut his skin when his monstrous body was racked by tremendous pain. There was a great explosion but no sound was made. The black snake-like energy fired from Lance's body and ripped into Grascon's. The wererat was hurled back across the room, clutching his chest and stumbling to a sitting position.

Lance's thoughts cleared, and he was overwhelmed

with a sense of euphoria. He walked over to Grascon, feeling the energy rebuild and strengthen. He reached down, grabbed the wererat by the head, and loosed the energy again. Lance could see the weaves shoot from his fingertips into the wererat's body. He could feel the magic reaching deep into Grascon's life force, pulling at it, trying to wrench it free from his soul while he writhed in pain, crying in agony. The assassin clutched his chest and thrashed on the floor, trying in vain to escape the suffering.

Lance took his hands away and stared at the would-be assassin. Grascon lay panting on the floor, struggling for each breath. Again, Lance felt the energy build, and he loosed it on his enemy. Grascon the Nimble screamed in terror for only a moment longer before dying.

The door of the room burst open. A man and a woman rushed in with weapons drawn. The woman wielded a relatively plain short sword, save for runes along the blade, six inches up from the hilt. The sword looked strangely familiar to Lance. The man's weapon, however, had a longer, thinner blade that he'd never seen before. The hilt was made of thick wire-like silver woven around the pommel, and the blade had a sharp edge on each side.

"What's going on?" the man asked as the woman sheathed her sword and approached.

"We were attacked by this thing." Lance pointed to the body, which had changed back to human form.

Kaisha kneeled down and recognized him. She turned and signed to Ryshander. "It's Grascon. He's dead. They must have used magic to slay him, because I don't see any silver or enchanted weapons."

Lance checked Jude for signs of life and was relieved to feel the warm breath on the back of his hand as he watched Jude's chest rise and fall. "My friend was poisoned. Can you help him?"

Kaisha examined him, sticking her finger into a tiny hole in his side, then pulling back to smell the yellow fluid that stuck to it. "He'll live," she said, and then signed to Ryshander: "Jahallawa extract." Ryshander frowned.

It was a poison used to paralyze victims. It was most commonly used by assassins like Grascon to capture enemies so they could torture them to death. Ryshander wondered what the large man could have done for Grascon to risk returning to Central City.

"I'm Kaisha, and this is my partner, Ryshander." She gestured to him.

Ryshander bowed low and crossed his sword over his chest. "We heard the commotion downstairs and came up to investigate. We're glad you're okay." He pointed to Grascon. "This one here was particularly deadly."

He lifted Jude by his shoulders. "Grab his feet. Let's put him in bed."

Lance picked up Jude's filth-covered boots and helped, then covered his nose and mouth with the sleeve of his sable cloak. "Where on Terrigan has he been to be mired in such stench?"

Ryshander chuckled. "Who are you?"

"I'm Lance Ecnal, and this is my friend, Jude."

"Ecnal, as in the house of orphans?" Ryshander asked.

Kaisha's jaw dropped. "Ryshander!"

"What? I just asked him if he was from that house."

Lance smiled disarmingly. "No need to dance around the question. I'm from the orphan house of Ecnal, adopted by a woodcutter named Davohn Ecnal of Bureland."

Kaisha sat on the bed across from Jude. "But the house was eradicated by assassins from Nalir, or so I was told."

Ryshander stepped forward with mock interest. "Yeah, that's what I heard. I wouldn't go around proclaiming I was an Ecnal. Those dogs might still be lurking around, looking to snub you out." Kaisha picked up on his questioning antics. "Maybe that's what Grascon was doing."

Lance shook his head. "No, we had a history in Bureland. He stole some items for me and got caught.

He tried to get me to cover for him, but I wasn't going down with the fool. I didn't think he'd try to kill me, though. I figured he knew it was part of the risk he took when I hired him."

Kaisha and Ryshander were unconvinced. They knew Grascon when he worked for Pav-co. He was a skilled cat burglar and assassin, and he wouldn't get caught unless he was set up. But they also hadn't thought he could be killed so easily. The definite truth was that he wanted to repay Lance for something, since he was using Jahallawa extract. The poison was quite difficult to prepare and expensive to buy. It wasn't something you used on a job; it had to have been personal.

"What did he steal for you?" Ryshander asked boldly.

Kaisha's face reddened, appalled at his carelessness, but to her delight, Lance didn't seem guarded at all. "Well, I'll show you." He fetched the leather case containing the elven writing. As he picked it up, he sent small weaves into the pages, transforming them into portraits of what he envisioned his mother to look like. He handed them to Ryshander. "There are some pages missing. These are just the portraits. I was supposed to receive paperwork recorded in elven, but I'm waiting for the new thief I hired to retrieve them. I left word where I'd be staying and expect them at any time."

Ryshander skimmed through the portraits before handing them back. "She's beautiful. A lost love?"

"You could say that." Lance placed them back in the case.

Kaisha could sense Lance's growing paranoia and decided to dress the wounds of the large man to regain lost confidence. She went to the closet for clean towels to create bandages, and then poured water from a clay pitcher into a wash basin. After wetting the towels, she dabbed the wounds carefully.

To her surprise, Jude started to wake. Ryshander stared in disbelief as Jude began to speak weakly.

"Lance."

Lance rushed to his side and grasped his hand. "I'm here, my friend. You're going to be all right." Jude half-laughed. "Some protector I turned out to be."

"Just rest. You were poisoned and it'll take a while to get your strength back." Jude smiled and drifted back into a deep slumber.

While Jude and Lance spoke, Kaisha asked Ryshander in a flurry of signs, "How could he be awake?" Ryshander shrugged and signed back: "How much did he get?"

"Two full doses, though they didn't pierce as deeply as Grascon would have liked, I'm sure. But the man still should have been out for at least a few days." She glanced back to the others to make sure they weren't watching.

"It must have something to do with his size," Ryshander signed.

Lance asked, "How long will he be like this?" Ryshander stepped closer. "It depends." "Depends on what?"

Ryshander picked up Grascon's dagger to examine it, then held it up to Kaisha, who nodded and sat back down on the bed next to Jude. "Well," she said, "I'd say a week before he made a full recovery, but he seems sturdier than most. It will probably be a couple days before he can travel."

"A couple of days?" Lance said in disbelief. "I can't wait that long." "What's so important?" Ryshander asked with a touch of skepticism.

Lance shifted uneasily on the bed. It was strange that these two showed up with so much interest in them. He didn't think they were working for the magistrate, but it disturbed him that they knew Grascon. "Why the interest in me? I'm just a traveler looking for a sage." He began to envision the formation of another spell.

Ryshander looked at Kaisha and then back to Lance.

Kaisha shrugged. "I don't care, tell him."

"Tell me what?" Lance didn't have much energy left for a battle, and he was a dunce with a blade.

Ryshander grabbed the desk's chair and turned it around to sit in backwards. He cleared his throat and said, "Kaisha and I are members of the thieves' guild here in Central City. Grascon was one of our assassins a few years back. We were never sure of the details, but he'd wronged our guild leader and was marked for death, but he escaped. He was scarred on his face from the encounter, so he fled the city."

"Who's your guild leader?"

Ryshander laughed and Kaisha shook her head. "We don't speak his name to commoners." Lance made a mental note that the guild leader was male.

Ryshander continued, telling Lance how they'd been investigating the presence of dwarves in the sewer, and came across Jude dispatching two of them. Once they were convinced he was heading for the Blue Dragon Inn, they went ahead of him and were eating when he arrived. Then they heard the commotion upstairs, and the rest Lance knew.

Lance could barely contain himself at the mention of dwarves. As Ryshander finished speaking, he jumped up. "Dwarves! How many?"

Ryshander was confused by Lance's sudden interest. Perhaps they were tied together, after all. "I don't know, thirty, maybe forty."

Kaisha said. "What's the big deal about a few dwarves?"

Lance looked at her in disbelief. "You've got to be kidding me. Do you people not get out? Didn't you hear about the Torrent Manor?"

"What about it?" This was their first trip from the under-city in days.

Lance shook his head. "What, do you two live in a cave?" Then it donned on him that they probably lived in the sewers, and no doubt the guild was located there. "The Torrent Manor was attacked by an army of dwarves, and it was burned to the ground. They killed every man, woman and child there. Jude thinks they're heading here to destroy Central City."

Kaisha looked at Ryshander nervously, as he laughed aloud. "Yeah, right. There's no way ten armies of dwarves could destroy Central City."

Kaisha lightly back-handed Ryshander in the belly and said, "I'm sure that's what the people of the Torrent said."

Ryshander stopped laughing, but still emitted the occasional chuckle.

Lance's eyes filled with regret. "Jude told me of the dwarves attacking before we arrived, but I still pushed for us to come here."

"Why were you so urgent?" Kaisha asked.

"Well, I mentioned those papers that were coming; they're written in elven and I can't read them. I need to find someone who can. That's what Jude was doing when you saw him.

He was looking for a renegade sage or someone that worked under the table, so to speak."

"What makes these papers so important?" Ryshander asked.

Lance paused, unsure if he should trust the pair, but doubted that Kaisha would let Ryshander attack him. He couldn't imagine someone as beautiful as her harming anyone. "You know how all the Ecnals were being slain?"

They both nodded.

"I think these writings have something to do with it."

Ryshander and Kaisha were intrigued. Everyone in Beykla knew of the killings, but because they were orphans, no one cared to find out why.

Kaisha rose from the bed and placed a hand on Lance's shoulder. "Well, my friend, we have some pressing affairs to tend to. We'd like to return and aid you, if we could." Lance was puzzled. "Why would you help me?"

Ryshander placed Grascon's dagger in his belt. "Lance, we aren't going to lie to you. We may profit from it. You never know when a task might be worth something, but I tell you this, on a thief's honor, we'll never turn you in to the magistrate for being a surviving Ecnal. That's how we work."

"A thief's honor?" Lanced asked almost in a laugh.

Kaisha frowned at him. "Don't think us backstabbers because we live in the night. There are rules that we live by." Her warm smile lifted some of the doubts Lance harbored. As the pair were walking out the door, she said, "Plus. I can read elven."

Lance couldn't help but grin with anticipation. He couldn't wait for the devious duo to return.

Therrig walked back to examine the bodies of the two slain dwarves. He marveled at the strength it must have taken to cleave through a dwarven helm. The other body had a broken skull around the nose and eye area. It appeared as if he had been struck with a metal gauntlet shaped like a fist. He turned the body over and examined the back wound. The slash was too short to have been made by the weapon that killed the first soldier. Therrig suspected it was done by the dwarf's own axe. He studied the area for a while, noticing scuff marks in the moss-covered stone ledge leading away from the bodies.

"Come on." Therrig placed his helm on his head. The leather straps holding it in place dangled unfastened from around his dirty cheeks. The helm's bright blue mohawk bounced as he walked, and the other dwarves dared not speak. Therrig was known to be much more ruthless than Amerix. He didn't tolerate questions or general rabble. He felt ignorance was a sign of stupidity and often punished those who showed either.

The group followed him blindly through the putrid passage for almost an hour. Therrig studied the trail as he walked, noticing that there were three separate scuff marks now, and he wondered who or what was following the warrior. He expected to find two more bodies, but the trail led him to a ladder from a sewer grate. The second pair of tracks then led back the way they came, but on the other ledge. Therrig waded across the green water and followed the tracks for another hour. The rest of the group were becoming impatient after dealing with the sewers for over three hours, but it was far better than crossing blades with their wicked patrol leader.

Therrig stopped in the middle of the corridor and the others paused to watch. He'd noticed the tracks stopped for a few feet before resuming, and he wondered if there was some kind of a trap they were avoiding. He kneeled and checked the passage slowly and meticulously. Though he was unsure what he was looking for, he knew most traps had a tripwire or some kind of a pressure plate.

After examining the floor, he checked the wall. Therrig pushed and prodded on the stones, and one of them moved. He winced and prepared for whatever he'd set off, but nothing happened. He opened his eyes and examined the mossy wall more closely. With a deep breath, he reached up and depressed it again. This time, it made a grinding sound and a small door opened, revealing a long hallway with a fifteen foot ceiling. The other ten dwarves with him fanned out in case an enemy charged out.

The floor was made of polished marble and the air was fresh. Granite pillars lined the walls, and enormous tapestries hung between them.

Therrig and his soldiers carefully stepped through the doorway and crept down the hall. Their leather boots thumped softly as they moved to the far end, closer to a wooden door with an intricate carving of a beholder with its mouth open, displaying thousands of razor-sharp teeth. Therrig was torn. He felt he should return to Amerix and tell him of the hall, but he feared there might be someone inside who could alert the city of their presence. Then again, he was sure the warrior who'd escaped was working on that. But Therrig would feel cowardly if he passed up searching and destroying everything in the hall. Therrig bit his bottom lip as he thought about it for a moment. He was in the mood to spill blood, so he decided to push on. Being knowledgeable of human cultures, he was sure this type of structure was an abnormal occurrence in the sewers, so it must be of some importance. And destroying important human structures was a good thing.

Therrig looked for a door handle, but found none. After many unsuccessful attempts, he took his hammer in both hands and swung hard at the door. Pieces of wood splintered away from the carving as the hammering echoed down the halls. Again and again he struck the door, and with each massive strike, more and more of the door was chipped away. Sweat beaded on Therrig's forehead and his helm fell off with a clang, but he let it lie among the wood chunks littering the floor around him. After a few minutes, he could feel the door was about to surrender.

"Get ready, me brothers! Time for killin'!"

Pav-co heard the booming sound coming from the chamber door. He brushed his meal's crumbs from his protruding belly as he struggled to his feet. He stumbled among velvet pillows toward the door of his private quarters while half-dressed women scurried about looking for their tops.

He stuck his syrup-splattered face through the doorway and saw his wererats scurrying about, donning weapons and armor. Some had picked up bows and crossbows and were heading up the marbled stairs on the east and west side of the large room. Pav-co had never seen his men in such a state before. The booming was much clearer, and he noticed that the chamber door at the far end of the room was shuddering. Chunks of plaster and chips of marble fell away from the frame with each resounding thud.

"What's going on here?" he demanded.

No one paid him attention as they got into their positions.

One of his many concubines inside the chamber said with a soft voice, "What is it, Pavie?"

Pav-co turned and struck her in the mouth with his fist. "Shut-up, whore!" The woman shrieked and grabbed her mouth as blood streamed from a gash in her lip. Pav-co slammed the door shut and slid an iron bar across it. He stepped over the wounded woman and glanced around the room, ignoring the cries of his men from outside as he gathered his belongings. He placed anything golden into a small chest and donned a silk tunic and breeches. He didn't bother to button his shirt, and his hairy belly jiggled as he ran, dropping several golden trinkets as he hurried to the rear of the chamber. He grabbed a large silk tapestry hanging from the wall, and he grunted as he pulled it down to reveal a trap door made of polished wood and stained glass. It had a thin metal gate that was easily lifted. Inside was a platform that could be hoisted to the surface by pulling a chain. Pav-co glared at the screaming pleas of the concubines to take them with him, then abandoned them as he rose to safety.

Therrig's mighty war hammer smashed again and again into the door. Chunks of wood were broken away, revealing glimpses of the room on the other side. "As soon as I get this door down, I want ye's to attack!"

The dwarves readied themselves. They were not overly concerned with the battle at hand, but what Amerix would do when he found out they'd sacked this structure.

Therrig used his sleeve to wipe sweat from his brow as he backed away. Only small pieces of wood hung from bent hinges. The expansive room on the other side was similar to the hall, but much wider with a higher ceiling. Marble pillars stood on each side of the room and at the far end, there were stairs on each side ascending to a ledge that lined the walls. Tapestries hung between each pillar and a green carpet spanned the room across the floor's center.

Hiding behind each pillar was a man with a bow or crossbow. Arrows and bolts rained on the dwarves as they rushed inside. They silently took each hit and continued on.

Therrig calmly put his helm on and sprinted the length of the room toward the stairs. Pain shot through his leg as he ran. He looked down to see a bolt protruding from his right thigh, and without pause, he ripped the bolt out and started up the left stairway. He ducked behind the first pillar as arrows whizzed past. His leg was a little numb, which confused him. He'd been shot a hundred times and a wound never went numb before. Perhaps the injury was more serious than it appeared, but he didn't have time to ponder on it. The dwarven leader took a deep breath, ran out from around one pillar and darted to another. An arrow pierced his left forearm and another grazed his helm. He paused to gaze at the battle below. His men had nearly cleared the room, but four were dead or dying. Therrig was shocked; these were not simple dwarves. They were battle hardened and skilled fighters. These humans were definitely a spirited bunch.

While some dwarves rushed up the opposite stairway and the others began battering the door at the far end, Therrig jumped out from the pillar and charged the humans who'd been shooting at him. To his surprise, there was no one there. He glanced over the ledge to the splintered door and saw two humans running through it as fast as they could.

Therrig plucked the arrow from his forearm and marched back to the first floor. The six remaining dwarves were gathering bodies of the slain humans, which left a trail of red as they were drug to the center of the room. Therrig counted all twenty-four of the bodies with passing interest.

"They use poison, sir." A dwarf held a bolt up for Therrig to examine.

Therrig looked at it carefully. The shaft was made of wood and the head was metal. "Looks normal to me."

"The poison is in the head, sir. When the bolt is removed, the tip tears away, releasing the poison." Enraged by the dwarf pointing out an obvious fact that he felt he should have known, Therrig threw the bolt to the ground and shook his finger at him. "Ye think I don't know that?! I meant, it looks like a normal poison shaft made by the humans, ye whelp!"

The dwarf bowed and apologized. "I'm sorry, sir, I didn't mean to show disrespect. I... uh... was trying to show you that I discovered the fact. I was sure you already knew... I mean... that..."

The dwarf's attempt to appease Therrig's ego was met with a gauntleted fist to the face. The dwarf's legs swooned and he staggered back, clutching his jaw. Blood streamed from his mouth as he returned to the others who were gathering bodies.

Therrig made note of many dead females wearing scant silk outfits that revealed their soft forms.

They bore no armor or weapons. None of the dwarves reported spell casting, which led Therrig to presume they were for someone's amusement. He smiled to himself. They'd killed someone important. Amerix was going to be pleased.

"I vaguely recall the rumors about the battle of the Torrent Manor. It was won and lost by arrogance and confidence.

"The battle for the Torrent Manor was lost by the Beyklans because of their arrogance. They believed the walls of their keep were impenetrable from the outside. And in truth they were, but they were penetrable from the inside. The Beyklans failed to consider all possible forms or methods of attack, and in their arrogance, ignored the few warnings of danger when received.

"The dwarves, through confidence and superior tactics, knew of their strengths and weaknesses, and exploited each prospectively. They lacked the force or ability to siege the castle, so they struck in the dark from inside. Therefore, their confidence in their ability to see at night allowed the victory over the humans' arrogant belief that they were invincible.

"Alas, arrogance and confidence is applied to more than just battles, it can be applied within one's life. I was fortunate enough within my adventures to have never been so arrogant that it overshadowed my confidence, yet being aware of the implications of such, a claim is what keeps each in check."

- Lancalion Levendis Lampara

10 Lostos

Ryshander and Kaisha strolled into the cobblestone streets of Central City, enjoying an unusually warm morning for early October. There were a few farmers who'd spent the night in the city, rising and heading back to their farms. But for the most part, the streets were bare. Ryshander and Kaisha rounded a corner and ducked into a dark alley. In moments, their vision shifted, acclimating to the darkness. They moved silently from shadow to shadow until they reached one of the four alley sewer grates. Ryshander hoisted the heavy grill up and gave an exaggerated bow as he motioned for Kaisha to enter. She curtsied with a quiet giggle and descended. Ryshander lowered himself after her and replaced the iron cover over them.

Once in the sewers, the pair changed from cheery to dutiful. They moved with precision and grace down the black corridors, which grew lighter to a green hue with every passing moment. They'd rounded the corner that led to the entrance of Lostos when they first noticed something wrong: the secret door was open, revealing the long passage to their home. Ryshander drew his rapier and Kaisha unsheathed her short sword. They cautiously moved to the mossy wall next to it, where Ryshander listened for a moment.

"I hear nothing," he signed to Kaisha nervously.

She signed back: "What now? Should we enter?"

He shrugged. "I'm not sure. I guess we should see what's going on. I find it impossible that someone just left it open."

Kaisha nodded tensely. "Something is terribly wrong."

Ryshander peered into the passage, making sure it was

safe before walking down the hallway. Kaisha followed backwards, guarding for a rear attack. As Ryshander neared the wooden door at the end, he was shocked to find it smashed into hundreds of pieces on the floor. The splintered remains hung from bent and busted hinges.

Kaisha bumped into Ryshander as she backed down the hall and turned to see why he'd stopped. The beautiful thief gasped at the sight of the ornate door's destruction.

"I don't know if we should enter, my love," she signed to Ryshander.

He looked back the way they'd come. "One of us needs to go. I don't want you to be in danger, so stay here while I investigate. If I don't return in a short while, flee."

Kaisha shook her head in defiance. "Whatever dangers lay in wait, I'll not let you face them alone. If death comes to claim you, it'll have to go through me. I could never live my life if you weren't in it."

Ryshander smiled. He was torn between the need to protect his love, the respect to let her act as an equal, and the sheer admiration of her bravery. "Okay, my sweet Kaisha, but I'll lead. I'm better with my blade than you."

She signed back with a half-grin: "After we find out what happened to our brothers and sisters, I'll make you eat those words."

Ryshander placed caltrops on the floor near the base of the doorway, hidden among the debris in case anyone tried to sneak up from behind them. He hoped they'd cry out and alert him to their presence.

The pair advanced side by side, as equals, through the shattered door, where they witnessed the most horrible, unimaginable sight they'd ever seen. Their friends and co-workers lay dead on the marble floor. The magnificent tapestries were torn and strewn about, covered in feces and urine. There were spent bolts and arrows scattered all over the chamber. Some of their loved ones were stripped nude, their genitals removed and placed in disgusting positions. The females were exposed and appeared as if they'd been ravaged multiple times.

Kaisha hid her face in Ryshander's chest and sobbed

uncontrollably. He placed his arm around her for comfort but remained cautious.

Kaisha realized the potential danger still lingering and forced herself to regain composure. She pulled her face away and returned the blank stare of death that came from her fellow guild members. Ryshander tightened his grip on his rapier and stealthily moved to Pav-co's chamber door. It was ajar, and after looking inside, he went back to Kaisha and signed: "They've been in there. His concubines are lying on the floor. I couldn't tell if they were breathing, but they were nude like the females here."

Kaisha winced as Ryshander referred to the dead guild members as "females." He knew their names as well as she did. She thought perhaps that was his way of de-personalizing the tragedy. "There are only twenty-four bodies here," Kaisha signed, trying to mimic his way of referring to them.

"Who's missing?" Ryshander signed back.

Kaisha fought back tears. "Kellacun, Travits, and Miranhka."

Ryshander frowned. "Well, at least Miranhka escaped. I don't really care about the other two. They weren't much better than Pav-co."

Kaisha nodded and moved toward Pav-co's chamber, slipping through the cracked door with Ryshander close behind. Once inside, the scene was much the same. The concubines had been stripped, tortured and raped many times. Ryshander and Kaisha searched the entire chamber without locating Pav- co's body, yet they did find the chute and elevator used to escape.

"He abandoned everyone to die," Kaisha signed in disbelief.

Ryshander put his arm around her in comfort and then signed: "We should leave before we too, become victims of his cowardice. Let's return to the Ecnal and his swordsman. They seemed to know something about the dwarves; I bet the bearded folk were responsible for the murders."

Kaisha nodded blankly and they hastily departed the razed guild hall.

Apollisian, Alexis, Victor, and the twins were nearing the north gatehouse of Central City, tired from their fast-paced ride. Apollisian's armor was dirty and he was in dire need of a new sword. His second weapon, a short sword, was sufficient, but he longed for the smooth touch of Songsinger and was eager to reclaim it from Amerix.

During the trip, Alexis had complained constantly about needing to clean up. They were in a hurry to get to the city, however, and long periods of rest were unfeasible. But as the elf's protests wore Apollisian and Victor down, the paladin suggested that she bathe in a small pond near the road while the others prepared a meal. No time would be lost that way, and after frequent suggestions, Alexis agreed. The elf didn't like the others working while she bathed, but she liked being dirty and grimy even less. After a short rest and a quick meal, everyone was satisfied and they were back on the trail. They'd managed to make the half week journey in a mere two and a half days.

Alexis watched with great interest as they approached Central City. Human settlements amazed her. They were so compact compared to an elven village. She often wondered what it was like to be human. If she were one, she'd be dead or close to death from old age. She couldn't imagine living such a short life, how terrible it must be to die so quickly. She guessed the limited lifespan is what drove them to be so ambitious.

Cerebron appeared unimpressed by the large city. He made no comments as they neared, and showed no signs of interest. Corwin, however, was eagerly straining to see around his brother and take in all the sights and sounds. He was in awe of the giant battlements and the expansiveness of the settlement. They had spent their entire lives within the confines of the Torrent Manor. Their mother feared they'd be slain for being identical twins, but that was the least of the paladin's concerns and he knew they would be safe at the church.

The group approached the gatehouse, which consisted of two towers over thirty feet tall, made of brown stone bricks that were cut rather than molded, and they each had six murder holes, two on each story. The top battlements housed bright silk Beyklan flags that slowly tossed in the light wind, and they were manned by two armored crossbowmen wearing leather armor and metal helms that glinted in the afternoon sun. The lower guards sat between the towers on wooden chairs, and they occasionally picked someone entering the city to question. They wore austere leather armor and wielded long spears decorated with ribbons earned from orc attacks, which were becoming less frequent with each passing year. Since the orc wars half a century ago, King Theobold led a crusade across the land to eradicate most of the evil surface races. An occasional orc tribe attempted raiding the city, but afterward, they were hunted down and killed to the last creature.

Though there was no portcullis preventing entry to the city, the towers acted as a waypoint for the heavily-traveled northern roads. As Apollisian neared, he removed a gauntlet and hoisted it in the air. "Hail guard!"

One guard turned his head and stared at the man. He narrowed his weary eyes, searching for some standard that needed to be acknowledged. The other guard recognized Apollisian's symbol and bowed low. "My lord, good day to you, sir." Seeing this, the first guard also bowed.

Apollisian touched the tops of their heads. "Rise and greet me as men."

Alexis rolled her eyes, uninterested in stupid human formalities. All she wanted was to get to a room and take a real bath.

The guards stood and grasped Apollisian's hand firmly. The second guard said, "Good to see you again, my lord. I'm glad to see you survived the Torrent. We were certain you'd been lost. Where is your steed?"

Apollisian shook his head as a grim expression crossed his face. "He didn't survive, cut from under me by a dwarven demon that I shall soon send back to Hell."

"You may get your chance, my lord. We're on alert,

but scouts report nothing in all directions." The second guard noticed the first standing in awe of the paladin, and he ordered him on a task to relieve the embarrassment of his staring. "Stahlsman, go and fetch our finest warhorse for Lord Apollisian to ride while he's here."

Stahlsman leaned his spear against a wall and hurried to the stables.

"Listen to me well, watch," Apollisian said with cold seriousness. His change of tone caught the guard by surprise. "The dwarves, if they are to attack, would not march against you as any other army might."

"What do you mean?" The guard removed his brass-colored helm and scratched his sweaty head.

"They'd tunnel underneath and erupt from your innards, hitting you behind the front lines and burning any defensive retreats you might have established." He looked to the city. "I must warn your duke."

"Duke Blackhawk is not in, my lord. He's away at a meeting with King Theobold at Kalliman Castle, and he isn't due back for a few days." "Then who's here in his stead?" "Colonel Mortan Ganover."

"Then I'll go to him, post haste," Apollisian replied. "I have one other need, good sir watch." The watch bowed slightly. "Name it, my lord, and it shall be done."

Apollisian gestured to the twins on Victor's horse. "These are the only surviving members of the Torrent that I'm aware of. I need you to take them to the church of Stephanis and have them enlisted as my charges. Their names are Cerebron and Corwin."

The watch frowned as he looked at the boys. "How will anyone tell them apart?"

Apollisian chuckled. "They are as night and day. Cerebron seldom speaks and Corwin seldom keeps quiet." He pulled out a leather bag from his belt pouch. "Give these gold coins to the church. It should be more than enough to rear the children until they're old enough to fend for themselves."

The guard placed the violet and orange bag under his tunic and hooked it to his belt. "I shall see it is done as you wish, my lord."

Apollisian glanced over the bowing guard's shoulder at the first guard, who was leading a large warhorse toward them. It was a black stallion with three white spots on its flanks. It was well over eighteen hands tall, and though its chest wasn't as thick as normal warhorses, its legs were much longer and more muscular.

Stahlsman handed the black chain reins to Apollisian.

The paladin accepted them and stood in awe at the steed. "It looks unusual. Never have I seen one like it."

Alexis helped the twins dismount and led them to the first guard's position inside the battlement. She glared at Apollisian, aggravated at the human's love for animals.

"It's just a horse," she said as she walked past.

Ignoring her, Apollisian's eyes feasted on the magnificent creature. "What is he called?"

Stahlsman shrugged. "I don't know. He was in the stables when I got there. We ain't had him long, that's for sure."

Apollisian slowly stroked its neck. "Then he shall earn his name by deeds in service."

Alexis was displeased with Apollisian's decision to dump the children, but could think of no other viable choice. They couldn't take them along. Her village wouldn't accept them being human, but leaving them with a church didn't seem much better. Alexis was unsure if she was angry at the decision they were forced to make or the death she'd witnessed at the manor. Regardless, she was happy to be back on Amerix's trail. She owed him a few well-placed arrows.

She recognized the spots on the new horse's flanks. It was no doubt a type of Vendaigehn, a breed of horse from the plains of Vendaiga. It was a small city in the queendom of Aten, far to the west near the great sea. She knew the women of Aten were powerful spell casters and enslaved every male they encountered. Only elven males were tolerated, and only a few of those were allowed safe passage. Most everyone avoided that deadly country, even females from other races. Aten women were born with a gift of innate magical abilities, and were known as sorceresses. Only purebloods had the right to citizenship there. Alexis doubted the paladin knew anything of the place.

She climbed atop her horse as Apollisian mounted his. She was happy the squire remained quiet during the affair. Alexis was becoming more aggravated at his simple advances. They were nothing more than futile attempts at best, but the thought of marrying a human detested her.

The trio rode through the streets of Central City, passing many people hurrying about. Apollisian marveled at how smooth the strange horse moved, like sailing along the road on a cloud. He noticed that the general mood of the city guards was heightened, which pleased him. They were ready for an attack, unlike the soldiers of the Torrent Manor.

They passed a large round stone building that bore no windows. It had an expansive set of marble stairs that rose from the center and stopped midway at a depression.

Alexis pointed to it. "What is that?"

Apollisian glanced at it with disgust. "That's the coliseum."

"What's a coliseum?" Her grasp of the human language was still weak. Victor chuckled until her venomous frown silenced him.

Apollisian replied, "It's a terrible place where criminals and prisoners are forced to fight each other and sometimes animals or monsters, all for the amusement of the crowd."

Alexis's jaw dropped as she stared wide-eyed at the building. "Why would someone be amused by another person's death?"

Apollisian struggled with a response. "You know how your race thinks alike, seldom attacking anyone or anything unless provoked, while orcs are just the opposite?" Alexis nodded slowly as she studied the pained expression on his face.

"Well, humans aren't born with those ideals. Each is as unique as their faces, and some have hearts uglier than any face. That's why I strive, every waking hour of my existence, to seek justice for those who cannot find it on their own."

"Have you ever been to the coliseum?" Alexis asked.

Victor laughed at the thought of it.

Apollisian gave her a reassuring smile. "My dear Overmoon, if I were to ever set foot in that abhorrent place, it would be to destroy its owners and bring its walls crashing down atop the vile patrons."

Alexis smiled at his decree as they continued through the bustling streets. The trio approached a several-story building with a stable barn next to it. They left their horses at the stables and entered the building known as the Blue Dragon Inn. Alexis took in the sights and sounds of the settlement. She'd never imagined the structures would be so large. Her father had told her stories of how plentiful humans were, but she only now realized the depths of his words.

The common room was full of people eating and drinking. Some bore weapons, some were militia guardsmen, and some appeared to be farmers. The overall mood was pleasant and few paid the trio much attention.

"I'm going to find the acting magistrate and have a talk with him," Apollisian said and tossed Victor a small violet bag of coins with a bright orange "A" embroidered on the side. "Get two rooms: one for us and one for Overmoon. I expect to return sometime this evening, probably after dark, so get something to eat and have your clothes laundered." He headed out the door.

Victor turned to Alexis with a warm smile. "Do you want to get something to eat after we get our rooms and bathe?"

Alexis studied his face as he spoke. He was so young, even for human standards; she wondered if he really comprehended the ordeal they'd endured at the Torrent Manor. She wondered if he fully appreciated how lucky he was not to have burned to death when the building fell on them. "I'll meet you at your room when I'm ready. I'm dying to eat some freshly prepared food."

As they went to their rooms, Alexis eyed a young Beyklan sitting at the far end, near the wall. He had black hair and bold green eyes. He wore what appeared to be a cadacka, a ceremonial robe of mourning worn by elves when someone close to them was slain or murdered. It was worn until they found justice or were slain themselves. Anger began to flood through her, and she fought the urge to draw her sword and spill his entrails on the floor.

She took three deep breaths to calm herself and made a mental note of the man. She would look into this. If he indeed wore a true cadacka, he would give it up or be slain. Alexis forced her tired legs up the long stairway and settled into her room.

Lance had been sitting in the common room of the inn since Ryshander and Kaisha had left. He went up frequently to check on Jude, then made his way back to his table. He was excited about Kaisha's visit and hoped she could read the elven pages, but was concerned about leaving before the dwarves attacked. Jude was still in his poison-induced sleep, and Ryshander had suggested he might be unable to walk for a few days, so Lance decided to wait in the common room in case the mysterious pair returned.

From the small round table by the back wall, he had a wide view of the entire room. He watched each person as they entered, hoping with each new patron it was Kaisha and Ryshander. But as time passed into mid-morning, he concluded the couple would be gone for a while. He had no idea what they were doing, but they didn't seem like the type to waste time.

Lance was finishing his breakfast when a strikingly beautiful woman entered, accompanied by two young men not much older than Lance. The woman wore a green cloak that hung loosely over a thin suit of tightly woven chain mail. A white bow was draped over one shoulder, and she had a leather quiver loaded with long arrows with bright green fletching. Her riding boots came up to the bottom of her slender calves, and her strange belt accented her outfit poorly. It was much wider than most belts and was made of tanned leather. It had small chains woven around it, and the front buckle had a symbol or a word from a language foreign to Lance. She was much shorter than most women, four and a half feet, at best.

One of the men wore a suit of violet padded leather armor with a bright orange religious symbol sewn on the front. He had striking features and held himself with an air of superiority. He appeared to be intimidated by the woman, but the more Lance watched, he decided he was smitten, instead. He handed the other man what looked like a coin bag and left the building.

The woman purchased a room from the innkeeper and was walking toward the stairs when she paused, looking Lance in the eye. She stared for a moment as if contemplating something, and then her expression turned to shock before starting up the stairs. Lance felt the need to follow her, but decided against it. Jude hadn't eaten yet, and the woman looked unsafe.

After he'd finished eating, Lance went to his room carrying a bowl of steaming-hot vegetable soup, a loaf of bread, and a hock of mutton for Jude. He struggled to open the door with his foot without spilling or dropping anything, and once inside, he placed the soup on the table next to his sleeping friend. Lance reached over and gently shook Jude's shoulder, who slowly opened his eyes and turned over.

"I brought you some soup, little bear."

Jude's weak arms strained to lift his body upright, propping himself up on his elbow. "May the gods curse you and your childish mockeries."

Lance laughed and dipped a spoon into the bowl, allowing the soup to pool into it before offering the large man a sip.

Jude frowned and growled low. "Get your damned hand away from my mouth, or you'll draw back a bloody nub."

Lance tossed the spoon into the bowl. A bit of soup splashed onto Jude and the table.

Jude wiped it from his cheek. "I'll remember these

moments the next time an assassin looms over you."

Lance snickered at the threat and began to study the Necromidus.

Jude dipped the bread into the soup and hungrily stuffed it into his mouth. He then took a bite of the juicy mutton and chewed the soggy concoction. "Mmmh. Vis es goomb." He swallowed and then stuffed another oversized portion into his mouth, savoring each delicious bite. A few heaping spoonfuls later, the soup and mutton were gone. Jude snapped the bone in half and picked at his teeth with the splintered end. Despite the teasing, the swordsman was happy to have a friend who stood by him.

Jude slowly rose from the bed and stumbled to his gear that Lance had neatly stacked against the wall. His massive sword was leaned against the closet where his laundered clothes hung. Jude fumbled through his dirty leather pack and removed a whetstone. He struggled to lift the sword and staggered back to bed. He plopped down and tried to catch his breath. "I had no idea there were poisons that could do this without killing you."

Lance replied without looking up from his reading, "Ryshander and Kaisha said a normal man would be unconscious for days, and wouldn't be able to move for weeks. They were surprised by your great constitution. I, on the other hand, was surprised that the feeble concoction felled you at all. You must be getting weak in your old age."

"Come over here, mage, and let me get my hands around your scrawny neck. I'll show you how weak I am."

Lance smiled and returned his concentration to his studies.

Jude glared at Lance a while longer before scraping his whetstone against the sword, making a shrill scratching sound.

Lance winced. "What on Terrigan are you trying to do?"

Ignoring him, Jude rubbed the blade a second and third time. Lance fumed as he tried to block out the annoying noise, but after a few minutes more, he slammed the book shut. He got up, snatched his cloak from the hook in the closet and headed for the door.

"What?" Jude held his arms out wide, grinning ear to ear. "I'm going downstairs." Lance slammed the door shut. Jude laughed for a good while.

Therrig and his six dwarves marched triumphantly through the sewer corridors toward the command room, nursing the minor injuries suffered in the fight. They carried the bodies of the four slain plus the two they'd found dead, so they could be laid to rest in a proper dwarven ceremony.

Commander Fehzban saw the patrol approaching. He despised Therrig but tolerated his presence because Amerix considered him valuable. "Therrig Alistair Delastan! Where have you been? You were supposed to find the missing dwarves, not go gallivanting throughout the sewers!"

Therrig ignored the aging cleric's comment and slammed his shoulder into him as he brushed by.

Commander Fehzban recovered and started after the disrespectful thug. "How dare you insult me?!" Therrig turned quickly and swung his hammer; its head whistled and slammed into the commander's breastplate. There was a great thunder clap from the blow as blue bolts of energy ripped into the stunned cleric.

Fehzban stumbled back onto his rear and then struggled to stand.

"It is you who insults me, Commander." Therrig shook a stubby finger at him. "You forget, I'm not one of your lackeys. I obey no Stoneheart!" He spit on the ground near Fehzban and continued marching toward Amerix's headquarters.

After attempting unsuccessfully to get to his feet, even with the help of his men, Commander Fehzban resigned to sit until his strength returned.

"My lord! My lord!" A dwarf yelled as he ran into Amerix's tent.

The dwarven general looked up from his complete map of the under-city laid out before him on a block of stone. He'd marked western grates from which to emerge when they attacked the surface. "What is it?"

The dwarf paused to catch his breath. "Therrig has returned. He lost four soldiers, he found the two missing patrol members dead, and now he fights Commander Fehzban!"

Amerix's face grew red. "He what?!" He pushed by the dwarf and saw Therrig coming toward him with a furious purpose, his deadly hammer in hand. Twenty dwarves followed. Amerix stopped in front of the group. He'd made it abundantly clear that though Therrig may dislike the commander, he would not tolerate any more disobeyed orders.

"Therrig," Amerix shouted. "Where in the nine hells have ye been? I demand yer report!"

Therrig narrowed his eyes. "I found the missing patrol. They were slain by a group of humans. One fled to the surface, the others retreated to some kind of church located down here. We stormed the structure and killed all of the inhabitants. There were–"

He was cut off by Amerix's booming voice. "Ye what?! Who gave ye permission to engage the humans?"

"No one, I took it upon myself to–"

"That's right! No one gave you the authority to risk the lives of our brothers, and our mission." Therrig's fist grew tighter around his hammer. He was growing stronger every day, and the thought of taking orders from some old has-been was taxing his restraint. "It was a successful–"

"It was nothing but foolish!" Amerix screamed. "And furthermore, ye insult your commander in front of his own soldiers, and worse than that, ye have committed a treasonous assault against him!"

"He is no commander of mine!" Therrig's tone grew bolder with each passing moment. "And Leska and her mission be damned! Durion would not have us sulking around in these foul sewers. We would be defeating our enemies, not cowering below them like roaches!"

The crowd of dwarves gasped at the blasphemous words. Even Commander Fehzban couldn't believe Therrig had spoken such atrocities.

Amerix moved quickly. He grabbed Therrig's hammer and at the same time, he struck him in the face with his gauntleted fist. Amerix kept him from recovering by punching him a second time in the ribs, where his armor was linked together by soft leather. Using Therrig's shifted weight, the general twisted the hammer up and along the back of Therrig's arm, forcing the young dwarf to the ground. Therrig's chin struck the hard sewer floor. Amerix tossed the hammer away, placed one hand around Therrig's throat and used the other to grab his leather shoulder strap, then held him aloft.

"Ye are hereby removed from rank, title, and clan. Ye are no longer a Stoneheart. Ye had better cling to the Stormhammer name, for it is as dead to ye as ye are to me. Ye will forever be the renegade survivor of clan Stormhammer." Amerix tossed the dazed dwarf to the ground.

Therrig hit the stone floor hard and slid on his back. His beard was soaked in blood from his nose and mouth as he sat up and looked around for his hammer. He noticed it was behind the general and doubted that he'd survive a risk to retrieve it. Therrig stood and lifted his chin defiantly. No one could believe what they'd witnessed. They knew Amerix was a skilled fighter, but to have dispatched a ruthless killer like Therrig so easily; it amazed even Commander Fehzban, who'd served under Amerix since he came to clan Stoneheart.

"Give him a pack and enough supplies for one week," Amerix shouted. "Remove his armor and weapons so that he may not make war."

The dwarves rushed to Therrig and stripped him down to a dirty brown loin cloth. Therrig didn't resist, keeping his deadly gaze fixed on the steel blue eyes of Amerix.

"You cannot do this to me, Amerix," Therrig said. "I will have my revenge. I'll savor the thought of it as long as I draw breath."

"Ye are right Therrig," Amerix said softly. "I cannot do this to ye. No one could. Only a pitiful coward such as ye, could have done it to yerself." He turned to leave.

"Don't you dare turn your back on me, Amerix Alistair Stormhammer! Just like you turned your back on clan Stormhammer the day the dark dwarves attacked." Amerix continued to walk away without response.

"I will have my vengeance in blood!" Therrig's voice trailed away as he was escorted to the caverns, away from the army, away from Stoneheart, and away from Amerix.

Though the young dwarf was gone, the truths he shouted echoed in the old general's tortured heart.

"Family. Did Amerix turn his back on his by ousting the wicked Therrig? My mother would have said the old general owed it to Therrig to find out why he committed the evil acts. But, I argue that some people just don't want to be helped. They are content in their dark hearts. My mother was the goddess of mercy. Her empathy often blinded her to the real motivations behind me. Actions do not make men; their hearts do. Tragedies could be seen as sunlight. If you have a heart of butter, the sunlight will melt it until it goes away, allowing you to form a different shape. But if your heart is clay, the sun will harden it and mold it that way forever. It matters little if you understand why they're evil. The fact that they are is unchanging. I loved my mother, but it frustrates me that despite her unfathomable wisdom, she lacked the serenity to grasp this truth."

- Lancalion Levendis Lampara

11
The Plea of Apollisian

Apollisian crossed the cobblestone street from the Blue Dragon Inn to the city civic building. At four stories high and over three hundred feet long with a large round dome in the center, it was more like a work of art than a functioning dwelling for governing bodies. It was made of a dark gray stone, polished smooth around the doors and windows. The dome was highly decorated with precious metals and detailed designs. The main level was on the second floor, and an expansive staircase led up to four large pillars on a balcony area sporting huge double doors. Many well-groomed people came and went, carrying various papers and books.

Apollisian confidently entered and strode down its marble halls. Inside, people milled about their daily tasks. The entire floor reeked of perfumes and scented soaps. His armored boots clanged against the polished floor, and he felt out of place with his unshaven face and soiled traveling appearance. All eyes watched him with obvious scrutiny.

"Good day, sir," he said to a robed man who was speaking with someone dressed in a green silk tunic.

"I was wondering who might be in charge of the city while Duke Blackhawk is away on business."

The pair looked Apollisian up and down and scrunched their noses in disgust. The one with the tunic walked away while the robed figure dusted off his sleeve, as if the paladin had somehow contaminated it by standing too close to him. "Why would the acting duke waste his time with you?"

Apollisian struggled with restraint. He took a deep breath and spoke again. "Good sir, I care not to dabble with the silly answers to your prejudiced queries. I only require the knowledge of the acting duke's stateroom. If you don't wish to show me, so be it. But I'll remember your name, and call on you to explain to the duke when he returns."

The robed man appeared unimpressed but pointed to a stateroom down the hall. Apollisian said nothing as he headed toward the chamber.

He marveled at the blind arrogance of the officials as he walked, passing several offices with men hard at work, shuffling papers and filing files. He entered the large room and stood by a hefty wooden chair located just inside the door in front of an oak desk. The room was large with thick oaken edges covered in ornate carvings. Bright colors – mostly reds and yellows – covered wall tapestries, desk cloths, and any other items that could bolster such emblems.

A man with gray hair and thin spectacles looked up from his paperwork at the imposing figure standing before him. "Can I help you with something?"

Apollisian looked down at the aged politician and exhaled slowly. "Good day to you, sir. I am Apollisian Bargoe of Westvon Keep. We have much to discuss."

Ryshander and Kaisha navigated the city streets, moving from shop to shop. The day was cool, much cooler than the previous one, with the kiss of autumn in the air. They'd pawned off a few items to line their pockets with gold coins. They noticed how the city militia was on alert, and were beginning to believe Lance's story about the dwarves, or at least some of it. Kaisha suspected the dwarves were responsible for the slaughter at Lostos, and their leaving behind Pav-co's golden trinkets that littered his chamber floor further proved the fact. Had the dwarves plundered the guild hall, it would seem they were not there for war. Armies have no need for gold, only food, weapons and armor.

Ryshander surmised that if the dwarves could conquer Lostos, a strongly-defended guild hall that stood for fifty years, they'd have little trouble wreaking havoc in the city. The pair decided to gather as many supplies and gold as they could before fleeing. They had spent most of the day shopping, having purchased many supplies, including some fine clothing and traveling gear. Now, the evening sun was rapidly waning and the shopkeepers were closing their doors early.

They walked down the dusty side streets of the market. Ryshander played with a brass-lined wooden spyglass he'd purchased while Kaisha wore a gold necklace and three gold rings, stolen while the greedy shopkeeper focused on Ryshander's fat purse. They looked more like a wealthy couple than skilled thieves as they walked hand in hand. They gazed into each others' eyes and became lost in a moment that was theirs to share, one that was so intense, only two souls equally entwined by the shackles of love could fathom its greatness. The couple frequently shared these intimate looks and often laughed when others had no idea what they said to one another without speaking.

A scream tore into the fabric of their reverie. It ripped through the darkening alleys and echoed off the buildings. Ryshander placed a hand on his rapier, hidden under his new silk cloak, and Kaisha did the same with her short sword. They were near the west side of town and were planning to leave through the east gate, across the Dawson River. Ryshander strained his eyes and shifted to night vision. He could no longer make out specific colors more than a few feet away, but he could see farther and more detailed in the night than the best humans.

Kaisha focused her eyes and shifted her vision, also. All around them, they could hear strange voices and sounds from the darker areas of the streets and alleys. Kaisha turned her head to movement she'd picked up directly behind them, westward. She made out dozens of small, stocky silhouettes rapidly moving in the shadows, and she struggled to speak through the lump in her throat, "Dwarves."

Ryshander grabbed her hand and they ran east as fast as their legs could carry them, toward the Dawson River, toward freedom.

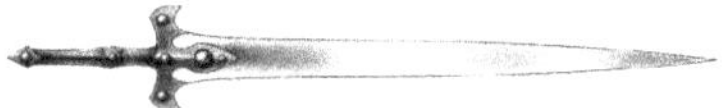

Lance sat in his posh room with Jude, reading the Necromidus to learn another spell. The ancient text often amazed him. Its strange symbols, arcane writings, and diagrams talked to him sometimes. Though they never actually spoke, it seemed to Lance that they had a message meant only for him. Occasionally, he took a break to think about how he could twist or change the weaves of a dweamor to better fit his needs.

Jude had finished sharpening his sword and was napping again. He'd regained some of his strength, but was still unable to wield the blade properly, and he had a difficult time keeping his breath when performing the simplest of tasks.

As it grew darker, Lance wondered what was keeping Ryshander and Kaisha. He planned to depart in the early morning but wanted to remain until Kaisha deciphered his papers for him. He'd endured an encounter with the Bureland militia, the journey to Central City, and an attempt on his life by a wererat assassin. All Lance wanted was to get the script read and return to his adoptive father, Davohn, who he hoped wasn't too angry at the letter he put on his bed when he left.

Lance heard an odd commotion outside the window and looked down to the street. He could see men with weapons running west and townsfolk fleeing east. Lance strained to see into the alleys and thought he noticed small shapes moving about.

"Jude," Lance called out while continuing to stare into the near darkness. After receiving no response, he grabbed the swordsman by the shoulder and shook him. "Jude, wake up."

Jude opened his tired eyes and sat up, pleased at how much easier it was than earlier that day. "What is it?" He yawned and stretched.

Lance moved back to the window and peered outside. "I'm not sure. There's something going on outside, a lot of people running east and the city guards heading toward the north alleys."

Jude got up, slowly went to the window, and looked down over Lance's shoulder. A bright light flared up near a building east of them.

"Torches?" Lance asked.

Jude moved from the window and started donning his chain shirt and equipment. "Fire."

Lance continued to watch out the window. "What do you think started it?" He spied a group of short stocky silhouettes emerging from the alley with weapons.

"Dwarves!" they said in unison.

Apollisian sat outside the office of Duke Blackhawk for most of the day. The acting duke, Colonel Ganover, had chastised him for such a foolish notion as dwarves attacking, so Apollisian demanded divine sovereignty, an executive form of defense that any paladin in the kingdom of Beykla could enact. It gave the paladin the authority to lead a city militia until either the king or one of his generals arrived to relieve him. By Beyklan law, the local magistrate had until dusk of that day to relinquish authority of the militia to the paladin. Colonel Ganover told him to wait outside the office and he would present the forms by dusk. So Apollisian sat on a hard oaken bench and had waited for almost seven hours when he first heard the commotion.

He rose from the bench and walked stiffly to the front double doors of the civic hall. Peering out into the darkness, he noticed a group of excited militia guards running west while citizens fled from their homes in a panic. He drew his short sword, stepped to the balcony area and stood between the pillars, focusing his eyes at flames that were sprouting up the sides of a small building just east of the

Blue Dragon Inn. The young paladin's heart began to race. He placed the tip of his sword between his feet and closed his eyes, concentrating his thoughts on the core of his soul. He scanned the area, his subconscious filtering through the crowd, searching the inner depths of all that was near him. His soul touched on the vile blackness of evil intent once, then again, then many times.

Apollisian awoke from his brief trance and rushed across the street to get Victor and Alexis. His worst fear had come to pass. The dwarves had arrived.

"General, what attack are we going to use?" Commander Fehzban asked as he entered Amerix's tent.

The old general continued about his work without answering. He had to explain everything to Fehzban, which annoyed him. When Amerix finished the task at hand, he turned to him. "Aye, Commander, ye will take two hundred of yer men, and emerge from the eastern sewer grates as planned."

Commander Fehzban was visibly shaken. "I thought we agreed that a massive attack from the east was the best strategy."

Amerix stroked his black, silver-streaked beard. "Aye, 'twas a good one. I'll give ye that. But methinks such an attack is better served as a diversionary scheme. Ye and yer men will emerge from the east grates first and set buildings aflame with the leftover oil from the Torrent Manor. Then, after ye run out of oil, attack and kill every human ye see. As ye are doing that, me and the rest of the army will begin a mighty sweep from the west grates and annihilate the humans." He offered a proud smile.

Commander Fehzban nodded, took the scroll detailing the emergence points, and headed to round up his men. He knew that disagreeing with Amerix was futile, and he did lead a successful battle at the Torrent Manor.

Amerix spent the next few hours organizing the move of his army to the many west grates running north and south of the city. He briefed each commander and gave them rallying points in the city. Amerix planned to use the sewer passages as communicating lines while the battle progressed. That way, messengers couldn't be killed or intercepted as they moved about. He wanted the military units to be attacked first; there were too many civilians to spend valuable strategic time slaying them. They could be dealt with after the city was well within their grasp. It was dusk when Amerix received reports that there were several fires on the east side of town. The attack had begun.

Apollisian burst through the common room doors of the Blue Dragon Inn. There were a few patrons drinking and eating who turned to look. Some had moved to the windows to peer out at the commotion, but showed little concern about the fires. Apollisian stretched out his arms to get the crowd's interest. He stood as a formidable figure with his plate mail glistening in the setting sun and his silk cape flapping in the breeze from the door. He paused before speaking: "Listen to me, good people of Central City..."

Very few patrons paid attention.

Apollisian went on, anyway. "Outside, the same dwarven army that attacked the Torrent Manor runs rampant through your streets, killing all they see and setting buildings ablaze."

That proclamation gained everyone's focus.

"Dwarves!" one man cried out. "What should we do?"

"Flee for your very lives!" Apollisian yelled. "Their numbers are in the fives of thousands, and they won't rest until every man, woman and child lay dead and burning!"

The crowd was set alive. Some ran screaming for the door, while others went to windows to validate the paladin's claims.

Apollisian ran up the stairs. He didn't know where Alexis and Victor were staying, so he called out for them. Many opened their doors and stuck their heads out to see who was screaming in the halls. Apollisian merely yelled, "Dwarves!" and moved on. Most closed their doors without comprehending the claim. Apollisian reached the third floor of the large inn when he recognized his young squire, who'd already donned his armor and was making his way toward him.

"Victor!" Apollisian called out.

"Stephanis be praised!" Victor rushed to Apollisian's side. "We feared you'd already been caught in the fighting." He bowed low to his lord's feet.

Apollisian shook his head and urged Victor to rise. "Not yet, though I'm eager to find the demon responsible for this bedlam."

"Alexis and I were planning on keeping the east road clear for innocents to escape," Victor proclaimed proudly. "With you here, it just might work. We counted only three or four score of dwarves. The rest must be attacking from another direction. Alexis thought to cover us from the roof, and you and I might slay any advancing enemies that might try to harm those fleeing."

Apollisian said nothing as he turned and headed back downstairs to the street. There were a lot of people to help escape.

Jude and Lance had finished placing on their gear when they heard the shout of "dwarves" coming from the hall. The voice sounded urgent and somewhat panicked.

"What should we do?" Lance asked.

"Flee, obviously!" Jude opened the door and checked the hallway, making sure there were no dwarves in the building.

"Of course." Lance placed the Necromidus in his backpack and slid it over one shoulder. "But, where? We don't know what direction they're attacking from."

Jude paused in the hall. People rushed by as they learned of the news, dropping belongings as they ran down the posh corridor. He turned back to Lance and said,

"Let's go to the roof. Perhaps we can see where they're attacking from and then head in the opposite direction."

Lance agreed and they were soon rushing upstairs past fleeing patrons. They reached the flat rooftop door, made of wood with metal bands crossing it horizontally. The door's lock had been smashed and it was standing open. Jude drew his sword and stepped out into the darkness. He was still recovering but had enough strength to wield his weapon for short stints of time. He glanced around the rooftop, scanning for signs of a struggle. On the north side, he could make out a small form leaning over the edge, firing arrows down to the street. He started to charge, but then realized that though the form was short, it was too slender to be a dwarf.

Lance came panting up the stairs and they made their way to the south side of the building, away from the mysterious shooter.

Jude pointed his finger westward. "You can see several buildings aflame. They must be coming from there."

Lance tugged at Jude's arm, pulling him back toward the open door as he regained his breath. "Then we go east."

The figure on the north side of the building turned and spoke with a feminine voice. "Flee to the East.

We're going to fight their lines and set up an avenue for retreat. Hurry!"

Lance started to say more. He wanted to find out who she was and what correlation she had with the dwarves, but this time it was Jude who pulled him into the stairwell.

"I think that's the woman I saw earlier," Lance said as he ran.

Jude didn't answer as he started down the stairs. He took two to three steps with each stride as he hurried toward the ground floor. Lance had a difficult time keeping up.

As they neared the common room, they heard the sound of steel ringing on steel. Jude peered around the corner. To his horror, there were three dwarves already in the room and many townsfolk lay dead.

"Only one way out," Jude whispered to his friend.

Lance nodded and gritted his teeth. This was going to be his first real battle.

Ryshander and Kaisha rushed along the cobblestone streets, hearing screams of terror and agony behind them as the wave of dwarves advanced through the west side of the city. The distant sounds of clashing steel echoed through the night and ricocheted off of burning buildings. Guardsmen shouted commands and calls of warning as they tried to organize some semblance of defense in the murky blanket of confusion.

Fires blazed in every direction now, but Ryshander felt that east was still their best chance for escape.

The Dawson River ran alongside the eastern edge of the city, and they could swim to safety if necessary.

The sounds of battle closed in around them as they made their way around the meandering alleys toward the Blue Dragon Inn. They could see it a few hundred feet away, and beyond that was the great stone bridge that crossed the Dawson River. Dwarven invaders battled militia lines that were forming as they tried to funnel people down the street and across the bridge. A small man in violet padded leather armor stood over a few dwarves he'd slain while another man wearing full plate armor was on the other side of the street wielding a short sword. They appeared to be commanding a score of militiamen as they stood against a tidal wave of dwarves. The shadows of the human defenders danced across the road from the raging fires that flared up from surrounding buildings.

Ryshander and Kaisha rushed past the militia, following the crowd that hurried toward the bridge. Villagers were already fanning out into the forest on the other side of the river. Some continued down the road while others stood in disbelief at the siege of their beloved city. Some wept at the horrific sight, others shouted angrily, but none dared to cross back into town.

Kaisha stopped dead in her tracks and kept her iron

grip on Ryshander's arm, jerking him back violently. He turned to see her at the edge of the stone bridge, gazing at the tremendous battle unfolding before them. Multitudes of people rushed by, clumsily bumping into them as they scurried to safety. Screams from other villagers prompted them to continue.

"Come on!" Ryshander tugged at Kaisha's hand but she resisted.

Ryshander moved behind her and wrapped his arms around her waist. He started to lift her, but she forced his arms away and screamed, "No!"

Ryshander stood in shock. She turned to face him, and he noticed that her eyes were red and puffy with tears streaming down her face.

"We cannot flee," Kaisha said softly. Another person bumped into her as he went screaming by.

Ryshander gently grasped her arm and moved to the edge of the bridge, out of the frantic townsfolk's way. "What do you suppose we do? The dwarves are many, and we are only two."

Kaisha pointed to the man in plate armor, and then to the man in the violet padded leather armor. "So are they."

"But, my love," Ryshander pleaded.

Kaisha placed her finger over his lips as she pursed hers and made a hushing sound. "I understand how you feel, but I cannot let those two strangers battle the dwarves alone. Those bastards killed our friends and family. They destroyed our home and took our livelihood." She doubled up her fists at her sides. Her normally soft demeanor was replaced with the hardness for battle. "I'll not let that go unanswered!"

Ryshander lowered his shoulders. He loved Kaisha with all his heart, but sometimes she was foolhardy. Why would she want to risk herself for something already lost? Lostos was gone. Their friends were gone. Getting killed in a meaningless battle would do nothing.

He hung his head low and shook it slowly, then drew his shining silver rapier and pulled his cloak back. Kaisha gave him a long passionate kiss. Her hands delved deep into his thick hair and she seemed oblivious to the death around her as she drank in his lips. Once finished, she pulled away and gazed into Ryshander's eyes. They shared a moment of utter silence. They heard no screams, no sounds of battle, no crackling of fire. There was only their love.

Ryshander smiled uncertainly and Kaisha drew her short sword. The pair started back across the bridge into the battle for Central City.

Jude rushed down the flight of stairs and into the common room. On the floor were five dead bodies: three farmers and two bar wenches. All had suffered horrible slashing wounds and lay in a pool of blood. Another bar maid was being pulled down behind the counter by a short hairy arm. Near the front door, two axe-wielding dwarves in chain mail fought a group of four militiamen, who were bleeding from several wounds while the dwarves laughed and mocked them.

Jude hurried across the room with a booming roar. The dwarves turned to see his massive two-handed blade crashing down. The blade laid a deep gash across the first dwarf's chest, then embedded itself in the floor. Bright red blood spurted from the wound as the invader screamed and collapsed.

Still weak from the poison, Jude was unable to work his weapon free. The second dwarf smiled eagerly and started to slice in at the exposed ribs of the large man, but before he could swing, the tip of a thin spearhead erupted from his chest. The stunned dwarf clutched awkwardly at the fatal wound from the militiaman's spear. His axe fell to the ground as he gurgled in protest.

Jude had enough time to wrench his sword free and swung the mammoth blade in a circular motion, striking the dwarf in the neck. The dull sound of steel striking bone rang out just before his head tumbled through the air.

Lance rushed to the woman behind the bar. She was

bleeding from her eye and her nose appeared to be broken. The dwarf was huddled over her, oblivious to the battle his fellow soldiers were losing. He had a handful of her hair and was pulling her head back as he kissed and bit at her neck. His left hand fumbled with his leather belt to loosen his breeches.

Lance imagined the motions of the spell he'd cast on the wererat, Grascon. The magical energy swirled inside of him, raging to peak in mere moments. The speed in which the spell came surprised Lance. He reached down, grasped the dwarf by the back of the neck, and loosed the magic that danced along his fingers. The black energy snaked from Lance's hand and invaded the dwarf's stout body. The bearded foe lurched and arched his back in pain as the necromancy ripped at his life force, tearing it from his body while his arms and hands recoiled in rigor from the intense pain surging through him. The dwarf's teeth clenched so tight, they cracked and popped. Lance felt the magic rebuilding instantly. It didn't call to be loosed like before. Though he could feel its lust, he had more control this time.

The dwarf screamed in agony as Lance released the magic a second time. The tendrils entered, forcing his eyes to roll back in his head. The soldier moaned and drool dripped from his mouth as his soul was shredded. Within seconds, the dwarven soldier lay dead.

Lance glanced around the common room. He noticed Jude had dispatched the other two dwarves and was beginning to barricade the door with tables and benches that the militia pulled over to him. The young mage looked back down at the woman he'd saved. She was half naked, covering her exposed breasts with her arms. She shook uncontrollably and rocked back and forth in shock.

"What does it look like outside?" Lance asked as he continued to stare at the woman. He wanted to say something to console her but was unsure what he could possibly do to help.

Jude moved to the window, peered out, and said with a sarcastic smirk, "Looks dark to me, Lance." He then placed a heavy table against the glass.

One of the militiamen nursed a deep gash in his right shoulder. "Where did all the dwarves come from?" The others mumbled similar questions as they fanned out to drag more tables for the doors and windows.

"The sewers." Jude wiped blood from his sword on a dead dwarf.

The wounded militiaman struggled to grasp the claim. "How did hundreds of dwarves get into the sewers undetected?"

"Thousands," Lance corrected as he poked his head into the kitchen.

The men pulling the tables stopped mid-stride. "What?" "Thousands," Jude repeated.

The wounded man sunk to the floor and stared at the far wall of the common room.

Another said, "It can't be."

Jude ignored him to finish barring the door. Lance ducked into the kitchen as Jude placed his heavy pack on a table and walked toward the bar.

"What are you looking for, Lance?" Jude asked.

"How do you know this?" the wounded man asked.

Jude walked toward the kitchen door to see what Lance was up to. As he approached it, Lance came out holding a brown cloak and said, "Just checking to see if there was a back door they might come through. There isn't." He leaned down and placed the cloak around the shivering woman. She recoiled at his touch, but he put it around her, anyway.

Sluggish from the quick battle, Jude walked over to the window and peered behind the table in front of it. He noticed many dwarves dead in the street with arrows protruding from their bodies, embedded up to the bright green fletching. There were two men in the street: one wore plate armor that was covered in blood. The other had a few minor wounds, but was also covered in splattered blood.

"Lance!" Jude called excitedly.

Lance ran to his hulking friend. "What is it?"

"Those two men are fighting to keep an avenue for escape open for the townsfolk, but the dwarves are rapidly shutting it off. If we're to escape, we need to leave now."

"We must help those men," the wounded militiaman said.

Jude turned and laughed. "This city is lost. Your only chance is to flee." He gathered up his pack and slid it over his shoulder.

Lance pulled up the woman from behind the bar by her arm. She'd wrapped the cloak around her waist, but she gave no other clues of realizing what was going on around her.

One militiaman called out, "You may not want to help, but we'll not let those brave men hold the line alone." Another stood and agreed.

Jude exhaled in defeat as, Lance, the woman, and the four militiamen entered the battlefield.

"What is evil? I mean, can it really be defined in a concrete term? Is it a way of life, a thought process, or merely a title given to those who lack the majority view? Is thievery evil? And if so, what defines it? Is not a salesman who deceives the masses about the quality of his product stealing? Are not the lords of the land stealing when they demand taxes?

"Is hanging a horse thief not evil? Why not, because it is law? What if the law said that if you do not worship this god, we will burn you at the stake? Who is the evil one? Too many times, evil is nothing more than a word used by the powers that be to manipulate the masses. The Beyklans had committed evil acts when they tried to oppress Clan Stoneheart, yet their own people viewed the dwarves as a wicked lot. But were they attacking, or merely defending?

"Evil is not as clear as one would like to convince others it is. Evil is little more than a blanket term used to cover the truth."

- Lancalion Levendis Lampara

12 Unlikely Heroes

Apollisian burst into the street from the Blue Dragon Inn with Victor on his heels. "I'll stand on the north side of the road. You stay on this side so Overmoon's arrows can help keep an axe from your gullet." He crossed the street and drew his short sword, then waited for the first enemy to show while Victor mimicked the paladin with his long sword.

Three dwarves came from an alleyway with an empty oil keg that they'd dumped on the civic building, and they noticed the paladin ushering townsfolk to cross the stone bridge. The dwarf holding the keg tossed it down and drew his axe. Then all three let out a battle cry and charged.

Apollisian steadied himself and set his feet to receive them. The first dwarf came with a high axe strike. Apollisian sidestepped and stuck out his foot to trip him. As the stumbling attacker went sprawling by, Apollisian ducked low under the second dwarf's slice, then rammed his sword through the chain mail, lodging it deep into the dwarf's stomach. The attacker gurgled as blood spilled from his mouth, dripping onto the paladin's helmet and shoulder. With the sword rooted deeply in the dying dwarf, Apollisian let go in time to grab the third dwarf's arm as he swung his axe.

The paladin's muscles strained as he shifted the momentum of the dwarf to spin behind him. The first enemy had recovered from the fall and was getting to his feet when he was hit by the body of the third. Both tumbled to the ground as Apollisian wrenched his sword free from the dead dwarf's belly, then twirled the blade in preparation for their next attack.

The dwarves glanced at one another before charging, and Apollisian brought up his shield to block the first strike. The dwarf's superior blade sliced into it, and the strength of the blow ripped it from his grasp. While the dwarf tugged frantically to free his axe from the shield, Apollisian jabbed the short sword just under his nose. The blade protruded from the back of his head.

The third dwarf brought his wicked axe toward the paladin's exposed shoulder. Knowing he couldn't move in time to intercept the blow, Apollisian prepared for its shock. Instead, he was hit in the face with a splash of sticky blood. He looked up to see the final dwarf with an arrow piercing his skull. The tip stuck out from between his eyes and his beard was already soaked with blood. Apollisian wasted no time as he rose to his feet, picked up his shield, and hurried back to the street at an endless wave of dwarves from the West. He would thank Overmoon with a firm handshake for that well-placed arrow, if they survived.

The light from the burning buildings waved their red reflections off of Victor's shiny mail. He motioned for patrons to flee toward the river whenever they exited the inn. Most didn't need instructions on where to run; they simply followed the crowd.

The dwarves soon discovered that he was directing humans away from the attack, so four of them charged from the west road, wearing heavy chain armor that bounced as they ran. To Victor, the armor looked more like silver cloth shirts than chain mail, but he'd heard of their immaculate crafting abilities.

An arrow from Overmoon struck the lead dwarf in the left knee. The shaft made a hollow thud as it pierced through his leg and lodged into the street. The dwarf dropped his axe to grab at his leg, while the other three held their shields aloft to deflect further arrow attacks. Victor brought his long sword down, knocking the lead dwarf to the ground with a deep gash across his chest.

The second dwarf swung his axe horizontally, hitting Victor in the right hip. He cried out as the weight of the blade tore through his armor, cutting into his pelvis. The force of the blow knocked him from his feet as the third dwarf's axe sliced the air where the squire had been standing.

Victor weakly rolled to his feet with his sword set in a defensive position. The pain from his hip clouded his mind, but he ignored it and brought the blade down in an overhead strike, hitting the dwarf who had just missed him. The dwarf recoiled and dropped his axe to the road, then fell dead from another of Overmoon's arrows.

Victor noticed Apollisian battling dwarves on the other side of the road. He wanted to run over to help but knew he was to keep his side of the street clear. The squire glanced down at his stinging wound. He tested his range of movement to check its severity. After deciding that he could still work on it safely, he backed against the wall of the inn. More dwarves were coming from the West, and he could hear movement inside the common room, along with a woman's scream. He struggled to keep from rushing into the inn. He could hear fighting and the woman crying for help, but he knew if he left the roadway, many more would die, possibly even Apollisian. Tears streamed down his face as he listened to the woman's pleas. Then a sickening bulge rose to his throat when he heard her no more.

Alexis stood next to a small ledge lining the rooftop of the Blue Dragon Inn. She set down her leather backpack and strung her white ashen longbow. The weapon had served her ever since she learned to fashion it as a child. The elf princess made many modifications as she aged, making the powerful bow accurate, as well. She tested the air and knelt down to ensure her silhouette went unseen from the ground as the sun fell under the horizon.

Alexis hoped she was high enough from the streets that the invaders would have trouble seeing her. She hadn't considered that at the Torrent Manor and had no intention of making the mistake again.

Alexis had a clear view of both sides of the road and a few alleys. She had well over sixty arrows to rain down on the bearded soldiers, and she'd hung a grappling hook and rope on the side of the wall for escape when the time came. Two men had come to the roof as she was shooting dwarves. She'd told them to flee and it seemed the pair had listened.

Despite her good position, Alexis was terrified at the sight laid out before her. It was like the slaughter at the Torrent Manor all over again, except at a much grander scale. As far as she could see, there were fires rising up at the foundations of the city buildings. The militia would organize a defense, but the dwarves would then rise out of a sewer grate to cut the attempt in half. She watched helplessly as the onslaught slowly made its way east, toward her and her companions.

Alexis notched an arrow and brought the shaft back to the corner of her mouth. She slowly inhaled the scent of the bow string and the fletching of the arrow as she held her shot, waiting for the right time to loose it. She held her breath for a half-second, and then started to exhale, releasing the shaft. Before the arrow struck its mark, she had pulled another from her quiver and began to draw it back.

Despite her efforts to cover them, Apollisian and Victor were getting wounded time and time again.

Whenever she helped one, the other would be overrun. And to make things worse, the inn had been set on fire. The flickers of firelight made it difficult to pick anything up in her dark spectrum of vision, and she often held her shot, unsure if something was a foe or merely a shadow.

Alexis was running out of arrows and slowed her shots, saving them for the most opportune times.

She paused and took hold of the grappling hook to ensure its iron claws were set.

Lance and Jude burst from the common room doors and ran down the crowded street by the light of raging fires. Jude took the lead while Lance led the woman by her arm as best as he could toward the Dawson River Bridge. The lines that the militia had set up were broken, causing townsfolk to flee in different directions.

Three dwarves with thick hammers and heavy axes rushed out from behind a small wooden guardhouse near the bridge. Jude skidded to a halt and drew his sword, oblivious to the dwarves pursuing them from the rear.

Lance faced the four behind them, who in turn slowed their charge, taunting him with gruff voices. The young mage glanced nervously at the bar maid, who was cowering behind him as if he was the most powerful wizard in the realms. Lance gulped and wished he had someone to cower behind.

Jude charged in and swung his sword down, hitting the first dwarf in the shoulder. The force of the blow carried the blade down to the dwarf's waist, nearly splitting him in two. Blood and entrails spilled out as his two counterparts lunged in at the giant man. Jude sidestepped a strike and shot out his foot, awkwardly catching the dwarf in the face. The invader grabbed his bloodied, broken nose and staggered back. Before Jude's thick leg finished the kick, he suffered a wicked axe cut across his thigh. He growled in pain and answered with his two-handed sword, cleanly severing the attacker's head. As the bearded cranium bounced down the road, it was kicked inadvertently by fleeing townsfolk. The third dwarf ran away clutching his bloody nose.

Lance envisioned his spell, forming a simple weave of transparent energy around the hand of the first enemy. The axe shot from the dwarf's grasp and went hurling through the air.

The dwarves screamed out a spell casting warning to one another as two of them roughly pulled the woman away by her arm and hair. Their eyes held an unbridled lust for murder, and they giggled at her horrific screams.

Something deep inside of Lance was set afire. He was suddenly more concerned with the welfare of the woman than for himself. He didn't know her, her family, or even her name, but something was loosed from the young mage that he'd never felt before.

Lance rushed after the kidnappers only to be blindsided by another dwarven soldier who had joined the fray. Searing hot pain in his left shoulder silenced the world around him; his body went weightless. He no longer heard the sounds of battle, the screams, or the crackling fires around him. He was no longer scared or angry. What little peripheral vision Lance had, was in slow motion. He was at peace with himself in a semi-conscious state, until he was violently jostled as he tumbled on the ground. When his body finally came to a stop, he could hear the battle around him again. He smelled the thick pitch from the fires. Everything sped back up as his eyes readjusted to reality. Lance could hear screams from the men, women, and children who were mercilessly cut down in the street. As he struggled to stand, he felt the intense pain from his fresh wound. Lance raised his head and was surprised to find he was lying on the ground. Blood soaked his robe and matted his black hair. He couldn't raise his left arm and had trouble sitting upright. People ignored him as they screamed past, trying to get across the bridge. He looked up and saw the dwarf who'd blindsided him, coming at him with a bloody axe. Lance tried to form a spell but couldn't get the jumbled thoughts out of his head. All he could do was watch helplessly as the attacker approached.

The dwarf raised his axe and brought it streaking down at Lance's head. Lance closed his eyes and prepared for the killing blow.

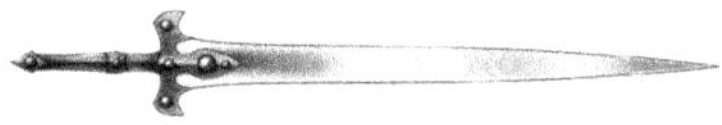

Ryshander and Kaisha rushed back to the city streets as a score of civilians ran past. They could see many dwarves who had broken the militia lines and were wreaking havoc.

"I'll go to the north side of the road and see if I can help the man in plate armor," Ryshander said.

Kaisha nodded and motioned for him to kiss her. Ryshander did so and smiled, then disappeared into the mass of townsfolk. She watched him go before turning her attention to the hysteria around her. Two dwarves were dragging a woman into an alley, so Kaisha rushed to the entrance and set herself against a building's stone wall. She stood motionless, listening to the dwarves' heavy panting and excited voices, as well as the woman's muffled screams for help. The rogue stepped silently into the alley's shadows and saw one of the dwarves on top of the woman, forcing her legs apart, while the other pulled his belt free and dropped his breeches to his ankles.

Kaisha struggled to ignore the woman's screams. She could tell the dwarf's fingers were probing between her legs, but she was unable to help without exposing her presence too early. As she inched closer, the stench of the dwarves grew stronger. The wererat thief deftly maneuvered behind the dwarf that waited his turn. She reached around and grabbed his beard with her left hand, while her right drew her blade across his neck, slicing both air and blood ways. The dwarf clutched at the wound while Kaisha kicked the back of his knee, forcing him to the ground. He rolled over on his back as blood spurted like a fountain. The other dwarf jumped away from the woman, snatched up his axe, and stood in a defensive posture as he tried to hoist his breeches.

Kaisha dipped in with a low slash into his unprotected groin. The dwarf dropped his axe to clasp his hands between his legs, screaming and rolling around on the ground.

While the dwarf twitched in the damp alley, screaming in pain, Kaisha pulled the woman to safety. The thief thought about killing the second dwarf, but due to the nature of his injury, she felt life would now be worse than death.

Apollisian suffered from more wounds than he could count and his plate mail was scuffed, dented, and bloody. His muscles screamed for a moment of rest, but a horde of murderous dwarves surrounded him. They must have finally recognized him from the Torrent Manor. They kept their distance and Apollisian slowly forced his way toward the bridge. He could see Victor battling enemies on the other side of the road, but he was unable to tell how his squire fared.

As Apollisian glanced around, he saw that most buildings were ablaze and the fighting seemed to be lessoning. He knew that if he faced Amerix in his weakened state, he'd surely die. Though none of his injuries were fatal, they slowed his movements and reactions. But he still found his steel eyes searching for the demon general to end his existence.

He noticed the dwarves near the bridge focusing their attention on a new foe. Steel ringing against steel echoed through the streets. This new ally wore a black cloak and wielded a silver rapier as he danced and glided through the ranks like a circus performer.

The man adroitly forced his way through the dwarven lines and burst into Apollisian's circle. He was winded, but bore no injury that the paladin could see.

"Ryshander Delastan, at your service, good sir knight," Ryshander said through labored breaths, dipping low out of respect while keeping a wary eye on the dwarves around them.

Apollisian eyed the amazing man up and down. Dwarven blades had slashed his clothes to tatters, so they looked as though they might fall away at any minute. He wore dark green breeches under his cloak, and his rapier had a thick wire hilt that spiraled around and ended at the pommel.

"Well met, Ryshander Delastan. I'm Apollisian Bargoe, defender of Westvon and champion of Stephanis." He brought his bloody short sword to his chest in salute.

"How are you not wounded, my good man?"

"Well, I have certain enchantments that make their blades next to useless against me." Ryshander struggled to keep his face from twitching nervously. In truth, wererats could only be harmed by magical and silver blades, and so far, none of the dwarves that he'd faced wielded either.

"Shall we go, good sir?" Ryshander said with a sly grin. "It seems we've worn out our welcome, and you look a little tired."

Apollisian nodded. He didn't appreciate the way this man made light of the senseless slaughter of thousands of people, but it wasn't the time to argue about moral sensibility. "Wait, we need to cross the street for Victor."

"My partner, Kaisha, is on that side. She'll get him." Ryshander waded into the east flank of dwarves and began his slash and dance once more.

Apollisian launched himself into the horde with renewed vigor and followed his new acquaintance toward the Dawson River Bridge.

"General! General!" the panting messenger screamed as he rounded the corner of the grinder. Amerix turned his head and climbed down from the ladder to face him. The general stood battle-ready, adorned from head to toe in his ancient plate armor. Ram horns curved around the scarred helmet and iron spikes protruded from the dwarven runes across the top. His steel shield was strapped to his arm, and he carried his magnificent axe in his right hand as he towered over the others.

"What is it, messenger?" Amerix asked. The battle was going well. His army had suffered more casualties than expected, but overall, the campaign was a wide success.

"They have the human champion cornered, the one from the Torrent." The messenger propped his hands on his knees, fighting for breath.

"What champion?" Amerix's posture straightened and he became more interested.

"The one you slayed at the Torrent Manor and knocked into the fire. He lives somehow."

Amerix scowled and stroked his silver and black beard. How the human survived the fire, he didn't know, but he was determined to kill him again. The old general grabbed the messenger by his chain armor and pulled him closer. "Where is he?"

"He's at the east side of town near the bridge. He's wounded but too skilled for us to overcome him, so Commander Fehzban ordered us to surround him until you got there."

Amerix started down the corridor with the messenger in tow. "Where's the elf and human whelp that run with him? If the champion survived the fire, it's feasible that the other nuisances survived, as well."

"The elf is on the roof of some building by the bridge," the messenger said. "She rained arrows down, keeping us at bay for some time, but she slowed her shots enough that we set fire to the building. We think she's running out of arrows." He took labored breaths as he scurried behind, trying to keep up with Amerix's furious pace. "The human boy is surrounded on the other side of the street."

Amerix remained silent, marching as fast as his stocky legs would carry him to the eastern grate.

Lance was too dizzy to move so he closed his weary eyes. He laid wounded and bleeding, waiting for the dwarven blade to slice him in two, but all he heard was a shrill ring of steel on steel. He opened his eyes to see Jude's mammoth sword rising back from deflecting the strike.

"Get up Lance!" Jude screamed as he blocked another swing.

Lance ignored the pain in his shoulder and struggled to his feet. His arm hung limp as he stepped back, scanning the streets for the woman in the brown cloak. A feeling of profound loss crept over him, fearing she'd suffer a fate worse than death.

Jude deflected another blow, sending the dwarf's axe wide, and stepped close to pound him in the face with his sword's pommel. The dwarf clutched his broken nose and staggered back as blood poured down his chin. Jude pressed in with a horizontal slice, but to his surprise, the dwarf recovered quickly, ducking under and slashing a gash into Jude's already-wounded leg. Jude howled and stumbled to his left. The dwarf followed his momentum and struck again from the right. The swordsman managed to bring his heavy blade up in time to block, but the force of the blow knocked him to the ground.

The dwarf attacked furiously and Jude weakly lifted his sword to intercept. As his would-be murderer raised the axe over his head, however, it shot from his grasp and flew through the air, landing far away.

Jude kicked up with his good leg and crushed the dwarf's nose further. The dwarf stepped back, holding his face as Jude forced himself to stand, then sliced his blade through the air and into the invader's side. The dwarf tumbled to the ground, clutching a gaping wound in his ribs. He stared wide- eyed at his own entrails just before he died.

"Come!" Jude said as he limped through the crowd toward the bridge.

Lance followed reluctantly, constantly looking back in hopes of stealing a glance of the woman he'd lost.

Kaisha fought her way west a few hundred feet. There were not as many dwarves on the south side of the road as the north, and when she could sneak by, she did. When she reached the Blue Dragon Inn, she noticed a bloodied man in violet leather armor. She could tell he was wounded, but most of the blood was from the dead dwarves around him. The man was unknown to her, but the sight of him standing alone against such a horde to help townsfolk to safety inspired her. Kaisha rushed in with her sword blazing. She slashed any dwarf that challenged her, cutting them down quickly. Soon, the invaders were stepping back to assess the new enemy who seemed impervious to their weapons.

"Come on, this way!" Kaisha yelled.

Victor looked back toward the soft yet commanding voice, and was shocked to see a beautiful woman standing before him. She wielded a short sword and wore a black cloak covered in slash marks.

Kaisha used a finger to move a lock of hair behind her ear, then held her blade in a threatening manner, daring the dwarves to press another attack.

Victor didn't hesitate and backed toward her, covering the rear as she fought a path eastward. Soon, they were out of the dwarven ranks and in a full sprint toward the Dawson River Bridge.

Alexis climbed down from the flaming building and eased herself into a narrow, debris-filled alley. Apollisian and Victor were making their way to the east bridge and she knew she had to take a discreet route. She placed her quiver over her shoulder and secured the bottom strap to her belt to keep it from turning over when she ran. She slid her bow over the other shoulder and drew her long sword. As she was making her way down the alley, she heard voices in front of her, so she ducked against a wall and peered into the darkness. Dwarven forms were coming from a sewer grate ahead. Hoping to avoid a confrontation, she doubled back toward the street. As she rounded the corner, however, more dwarves appeared. Surprised, the bearded soldiers cried out at the sight of her. Alexis slashed out and caught one in the shoulder. The dwarf howled and dropped back as another swung forward at her right side. She ducked the axe and stabbed low, but at the same time took a vicious slice across her back. She ignored the pain and backed up, parrying another strike. She fought her attackers from both directions, wounding several of them, but her strength soon failed and she lost the grip on her sword. The weapon clanged to the alley floor as she was overcome by her enemies. Alexis took a wicked slash across the midsection that cut through her elven chain armor and into her belly. She felt sick and doubled over, clutching her wounded stomach.

The dwarves called out and heckled her as they kicked and beat her. She fought back as best she could, but soon knew only darkness.

Apollisian and Ryshander were in a full run toward the wide vine-covered bridge that spanned the Dawson River. A hundred yards away, Ryshander spied an unusually large dwarf adorned in full plate armor, wielding an axe and a great metal shield. His long silver-streaked black beard jostled in the breeze as he stood between the wererat and his goal.

"One more, then we'll be home free," Ryshander announced as he and Apollisian slowed to a walk.

Apollisian strained his eyes but couldn't see far into the darkness.

As they neared the dwarf, Ryshander arrogantly flicked his thin rapier around, taunting him as he chuckled. "You're an awful big dwarf." The irony of the statement was not lost on his ears.

When Apollisian heard Ryshander's words, his heart sank. He knew of only one big dwarf: Amerix.

"No!" he screamed and raced forward as the man who'd helped him escape clashed with the renegade general.

Amerix emerged from the eastern-most sewer grate with several of his officers and sent them on other menial tasks. He slowly inhaled the wonderful smell of death and battle that hung in the air. His ears swallowed every jovial ring of steel against steel, and he relished each human scream that echoed in the crisp autumn night. He could see a few humans still fleeing across the bridge, but his eyes were scanning for a particular foe. The ancient general cracked a half grin when he saw the bloody paladin being led by a lone human with no armor. Amerix stepped in front of the strange human and watched the fool confidently stride up to him, saying something in his disgusting language and chuckling to himself. It made no difference to Amerix. The thin weak-looking man wielded a small sword that he doubted would pierce his skin, let alone his thick plate armor. Amerix didn't understand what the man said; he only understood two languages: the dwarven language and the language of war.

Ryshander paired off what he thought to be a good distance to attack the dwarf, but before he could react, Amerix moved with lightning speed, swinging out with his axe and jabbing Ryshander in the face with its tip. The sharp serrated shaft ripped a deep gash across Ryshander's nose and tore the corner of his eye. Ryshander howled in pain and shock because the weapon had actually hurt him. Holding his bloody eye, Ryshander lunged in with his rapier. His small sword slashed through the air, but to his surprise, the blade hit nothing while a horrific pain ripped through his ribs as the axe tore a large hole in his side. Ryshander's legs buckled under him and he tumbled to the ground.

He struggled to see the next strike coming down through his left eye. He managed to deflect the blow, but the heavy axe shattered his blade and cut into the wererat's hip. There was a flash of brilliant yellow light as the enchantment on Ryshander's shattered rapier escaped into the night.

Amerix smiled as he prepared to kill the arrogant human, when he noticed movement in the corner of his eye. He instinctively ducked a strike from his left. His shield took a portion of the blow and deflected it wide. He pulled his axe free, swinging it blindly toward the new attacker. Amerix felt his keen blade bite into the enemy's shoulder, then squared off and smiled a yellow-toothed grin. The champion of Torrent was his at last.

Apollisian ignored the minor wound and circled, drawing Amerix away from the downed thief.

Ryshander sat up weakly, amazed as the two champions squared off in the city street, dimly lit from the fires. There was apparently a past between the two. The rogue surveyed his injuries and realized he was in serious trouble. His wounds would kill him if he moved much, so he sat back and watched the epic battle unfold, hoping Apollisian would emerge the victor.

"How many times must I kill ye?" Amerix growled, knowing the paladin could speak his tongue.

"Know this, evil Amerix," Apollisian said through gritted teeth, "when I kill you, you will remain dead." He feinted in, drawing the dwarf's shield down, then struck high.

Amerix deflected with his axe and lunged forward with his shield, but Apollisian had moved and the shield hit only air.

The battle raged on, neither combatant gaining an upper hand, and each sporting more than a dozen minor wounds from the fight. Amerix's mind wandered as he fought the champion paladin. He struggled to understand why the human called him evil. He wondered if it was a context error he may have made in the dwarven language, but he didn't think so. The ancient general was amazed that the human had the gall to think him evil. It was the Beyklans who were the evil ones. They'd persecuted his people and caused the death of his beloved wife and child. Had they not imposed the embargo on goods to Andoria during the civil war, his family would have received the necessary medicines needed to treat their illnesses. Instead, they received nothing and died. His family was slain as a direct result of the Beyklans' greed.

Apollisian attacked and moved, repeating the movements as he maneuvered closer to the bridge and away from Ryshander. Amerix followed the paladin blindly, striking hard and fast.

Lance stood at the base of the bridge and looked over the side. It spanned a deep chasm that the Dawson River had formed from centuries of erosion. The cliff face was sheer and well over a hundred feet high. The many docks at the base of the cliff were well lit by torches, and Lance could see where the city was constructing a larger dock with a retractable platform to raise and lower goods. There were a few townsfolk climbing into the small boats to escape.

Jude limped along the bridge, occasionally glancing back at the militia's battle line. The bridge was fifty feet wide and the sides were covered in green moss that dangled over the edge and hung down. In the center of the bridge were two ten-foot-high battlements that a few militia guardsmen had manned in case the dwarves followed townsfolk across.

Lance paused and gently pressed his hand on his wounded shoulder. The pain was excruciating and caused him to swoon.

Jude pulled his pack from his shoulder and dropped it next to the stone rail. "We're a safe enough distance away." He leaned against the rail, pulled some cloth strips from his pack and examined Lance's injury. The axe wound had severed tendons and bit halfway into the bone.

Lance winced as Jude tightly tied the bandages around his arm and shoulder. "Well what's it look like, leech?"

Jude half-smiled at the title. "Leech" was another term for doctor. "Well, it's not good. I've seen similar wounds in swordsmen, and they'd never wield a sword again with that arm. I've even seen some lose the arm."

Lance studied his friend's face. He noticed deep remorse in his eyes, and knew Jude believed the worst. He looked away and tried to think of solutions, wondering if there were any healing spells in the Necromidus. Every spell he'd reviewed so far was for war, which was most likely all that the tome contained. Evil mages were not known to study healing magic. Lance could purchase healing from a church, but they lacked enough gold.

Jude pulled the knot tight and saw Ryshander with a man in plate armor, squaring off against the biggest dwarf Jude had ever seen.

"What do you see Jude?" Lance asked.

"It's that thief we met in our room." Jude never took his eyes from the impending battle.

"Kaisha?"

"No, the other one."

They watched as the thief fell, and Lance screamed, "That dwarf just cut him down!"

Jude limped a few steps back toward the city. "Look, he lives; the other warrior stepped into the fray." He drew his two-handed sword.

"What do you think you're doing?" Lance asked weakly as he slumped against the rail.

"The same thing you were doing when you ran after that girl the dwarves grabbed."

"The same thing I did?" Lance groaned as he fought to his feet to follow his friend. "You mean getting your fool self cut down?"

Jude half-smiled. "No, growing a conscience."

Lance grinned through the pain from his shoulder and envisioned the motions of a spell in his mind.

"We have very poor timing at developing these things."

Victor fought his way through the crowd to the base of the bridge, where he saw Apollisian battling the dwarf that he recognized as the renegade general, Amerix. As he neared the fight, he lunged in with his long sword, swinging it wildly at the dwarf.

Amerix easily caught the blow with his shield, ducking away from Apollisian and swinging his double-bladed axe low at Victor. The squire was amazed at the speed and fluidity of the attack. Frantically swinging his long sword, Victor managed to deflect most of the blow, but the axe still laid a deep cut across his calf.

"Victor, get back!" Apollisian screamed as he pressed his attack.

"I'll not let you face this demon alone." Victor limped a few steps away.

Apollisian didn't respond, focusing his strikes to Amerix's right side to deter his attention away from the squire.

Amerix recognized the ruse and shifted his movements, forcing the paladin where he wanted him while cracking a wicked smile. "I can dispatch yer whelp at me leisure."

Apollisian's heart raced, knowing it was true. "He's not your foe, Amerix." He grunted as he deflected a fierce blow from Amerix's axe.

"Nay are ye," Amerix responded. "But ye refuse to let me get the justice my people deserve, so for that ye must die."

Victor guessed the paladin was trying to distract the demon dwarf, so he pressed his attack. Victor leaned most of his weight forward into his thrust. Amerix quickly sidestepped and attacked Apollisian high so that Victor's wild stab went just under his swing. He clapped his shield arm down on the squire's blade, pinning it against his body. The renegade general twisted and swung at the paladin while ramming the edge of his shield into the squire's exposed hand. Victor shrieked and let go of his long sword.

Amerix raised his shield arm slightly to allow the sword to fall, then ducked a strike from Apollisian.

As Victor backed away and drew his short sword, his gaze shifted to a young woman helping the man away that Amerix had cut down earlier.

"Ye see, human scum," Amerix bellowed, motioning to the squire's blade on the ground. "That is all the mercy ye will get from me. Turn away and let me have me justice, or ye and yer whelp will die."

Apollisian's stomach was queasy. He couldn't leave, and he couldn't let Amerix slay the innocents of Central City. "Victor, go help the militia! I've got the dwarf."

Victor ignored the command, knowing that Apollisian would die to protect him, and he wouldn't let that happen. One good thrust and the evil dwarf would be no more. The squire watched the strikes and feints of the champions and waited before lunging in with his sword, catching Amerix under the shoulder plate.

Amerix howled as the short sword ran deep into his shoulder, and his steel blue eyes fixed on the squire. He cocked his shield arm back and thrust it with all his strength at the paladin. The shield hit Apollisian, knocking him off balance while the general shoved forward to push him down.

Apollisian adjusted quickly and rolled with the blow, stabbing upwards under the shield and piercing the dwarf's breast plate. He couldn't believe a skilled warrior such as Amerix had made such a mistake, but it was in the next instant that the paladin knew it was he who had erred.

As Apollisian's sword came stabbing in, Amerix accepted the blow with grim determination, and after it hit the mark, Amerix turned and laid a deep slice along the back of Victor's shoulder.

Victor cried out and dropped his blade, clutching the crippling wound. Apollisian watched in helpless horror as he struggled to get to his feet in time, yet knowing in his heart he would not.

Amerix feinted low and Victor, misunderstanding the ploy, moved his leg and dropped his arms.

Amerix shifted his weight and brought the double-bladed axe down from above, easily slicing through the leather armor. Blood streamed from the wound as Victor stumbled backward.

Again, Amerix swung his axe in an arc, catching Victor in the neck. The squire was dead before his body hit the ground.

Jude ran through the fleeing crowd as fast as his

wounded leg would carry him, limping over bodies of dead humans and dwarves alike. Lance hurried after him, keeping an eye on the front lines in case more dwarves managed to force their way through. The militia was holding for now, but there were only a few hundred fighting, and Lance knew they would soon be overcome by sheer numbers alone.

Amerix attacked with such ferocity that the air whistled with each deadly strike. Apollisian had suffered a severe gash across his right leg, and he could feel his toes going numb. The paladin knew his leg was soon to follow and he tried to lead the dwarf onto the bridge.

When Jude reached the pair, he swung in with an overhand slash at the general. Amerix raised his shield and deflected the blow, then whipped his axe across his body to knock away a thrust from the paladin.

"Get away! You don't know his skill," Apollisian called out as he tried to maneuver between the dwarf and the large man.

Jude said nothing, but backed away as Amerix glared at him.

"Tell yer friend to come closer," Amerix said with a yellow-toothed grin. "I'll cut him down like I did yer whelp."

Apollisian backed onto the bridge, launching several feints and thrusts as they took their battle over the Dawson River.

The renegade general taunted him. "Lead me were ye will, human. I'll cut ye down wherever ye flee." Apollisian fought his way to the rail, knowing he had little time to defeat the dwarf, who seemed to gain strength as the fight raged on. His strikes were becoming more focused and precise, and he had an easier time defending the paladin's ailing attacks.

Jude watched from a few yards away, honoring the man's request to stay back. He recognized the dwarf's skill and knew it was far superior to his own, but he remained close in case the armored man fell. Jude was unsure how long he could last against such a foe, but he would not let the man die.

It was soon obvious that the battle was coming to an end. The warrior's attacks were becoming labored and weak. He threw fewer strikes and his defenses were getting sloppy.

Jude glanced over at Lance, who was watching from the base of the bridge. The dwarven soldiers were making a push and the militia was falling back. On the far side, almost all of the fleeing townsfolk were out of sight and a few of the militia were futilely firing arrows at the dwarven front lines.

Jude took a deep breath and unsnapped the leather strap holding the rope and grappling hook that hung at his waist. He ran to the edge, swung the hook over the rail and pulled up fiercely. Its thin teeth bit into the underside of the bridge and the rope groaned as Jude strained, setting it deep into the moss and stone. He then tied the rope around his waist and pulled it taut.

Apollisian cried out as the dwarf's axe ripped across his shoulder and splattered blood on the bridge's rail. His short sword tumbled over the edge, dropped a hundred feet, and splashed into the swift river. Seeing the human champion near defeat, Amerix swung his axe down again. Apollisian tried to avoid the blow, but it tore a gash in his armor and bit into his lower back. He fell to his knees with blood pooling under him.

Amerix then kicked him in the mouth with his metal shin plate, knocking him on his back. Apollisian stared up for what seemed like an eternity, at the thousands of stars visible for fleeting moments through the black smoke. He struggled with the thought of dying. He could heal himself in mere minutes, but not before the dwarf finished him off. He wondered what was taking so long. The kick had left him stunned and every sound around him was muffled. Was he already dead, but his soul hadn't left his body yet? Apollisian tried to raise his head and managed to lift his chin a few inches. There was a strange woman kneeling over him with long brown hair and beautiful eyes.

He smiled as best he could. The woman said something to him but he was unable to make it out. Behind her stood a bizarre young man in a black cloak with silver trim and elven runes on it. The man had a vicious wound in his shoulder and his arm hung limp. Despite his youth, he had a wise, ageless look in his eyes. His hair was wild and unkempt, held in place by dirt and sweat from the battle.

Apollisian figured he was still alive. He tried to gauge where the dwarf had gone, but the strain was too much for him and he'd lost too much blood. The paladin watched helplessly as the two people slowly drifted from view as he slid into darkness.

Jude double-checked the rope and took a deep breath. He watched the paladin's sword get knocked over the edge of the bridge, and in a swift series of attacks, the dwarf cut the paladin down and kicked him in the face. Jude winced as blood splattered from the man's shattered jaw. The dwarf stepped over the downed man and raised his axe for the killing blow.

Jude rushed across the bridge, ignoring the pain in his leg as he forced his muscles to trudge on. As he gained speed, he lowered his broad shoulders and outstretched his arms. He growled as his tired legs shot his body like a catapult into the stout dwarf, catching him around the neck and shoulders as the force of the blow carried them both into the rail. Jude hit the stone ledge and his momentum carried him over it. He desperately clung to the dwarf's beard with his left hand, and he hooked his right arm around to grab his shoulder plate.

Amerix struggled against the weight of the huge man. His back hit the moss-covered rail and his feet lifted from the ground. His shield arm tugged at the iron grip on his beard while his right arm released the axe to cling by his fingertips to the rail's edge. The enchanted weapon fell to the stone bridge with a loud clang.

"Throw him over!" Jude screamed.

Amerix twisted and with brute strength, forced Jude's hand from his shoulder plating. He then turned his stomach to the rail and clutched Jude's wrist. His iron muscles contracted as he hoisted Jude up one- handed, relieving the strain on his beard.

Kaisha ran up behind the dwarf, grabbed his legs and rammed her shoulder into his buttocks, launching him over the edge. She watched as Jude and the dwarf tumbled head over heels through the air as they fell toward the dark depths of the Dawson River. Jude fell thirty feet and was jerked violently as the rope went taut.

The dwarf hit the river and disappeared in a white splash.

Jude clenched his teeth, grabbing at his rope-burned waist and sore ribs. "I thank you, my lady. Now if you could somehow hoist me up."

Kaisha pulled while Lance helped with his good arm. When Jude slowly climbed over the rail, he untied the rope and bundled it up, placing it back on his belt.

"We've got to hurry," Lance said. "The dwarves have pushed the militia to the bridge. We haven't much time."

Cries of anguish from the militia echoed in the night as they tried in vain to hold the front line.

Kaisha helped the wounded Ryshander to his feet. He was badly injured, but she'd dressed his wounds and he was well enough to travel. The pair stared long and hard at the burning city. The flames from the buildings now lit the western sky. It had been their home for so long, and now it was in ruins. Kaisha tried not to think of the thousands still trapped in the city, fighting for their lives.

"How are we going to move him?" Jude motioned weakly to Apollisian. Lance looked around. Ryshander was too injured to move anyone, and Jude's leg hindered him. Lance couldn't even move his arm. It was then that they heard a trumpet sound and heavy horses running toward them.

"More dwarves?" Kaisha's voice cracked with fear.

Jude limped by her and stared to the eastern road with

a hopeful smile. "I don't think dwarves ride horses."

Lance stepped forward, clutching his wounded shoulder. "Then who?"

Just then, a score of mounted lancers emerged from the night and onto the bridge. They wore brilliant brass-colored plate armor with flowing, red silk capes. Their hoof beats thundered on the stone floor as they charged.

"Get against the rails!" Jude yelled.

All three moved next to Apollisian. Kaisha knelt and tended to him as the others watched in awe of the riders. They wore large helms sprouting red plumes, which bounced around their shoulders. Their capes danced in the rushing wind behind them, and their horses were barded in bright plate armor that hung over their heads and flanks. The first horseman had the Beyklan flag attached to the end of his lance.

Another trumpet sounded and the remaining militiamen who held the bridge parted. The dwarves rushed in, thinking they'd broken the resistance. The first dwarf looked up as a lance lodged into his chest, and the rest fled when they saw the blood-soaked banner of Beykla erupt from his back.

Militiamen let out a heartfelt cheer as hundreds of horsemen charged across the bridge. They raised their wounded and bloody arms in triumph. Jude, Lance, Kaisha and Ryshander watched as hundreds more armored men began to march across the bridge. They displayed the Beyklan banner, and some bore a blue banner with the depiction of a yellow battlement.

"The banner of Westvon Keep," Kaisha whispered.

Lance turned to look at her. She was staring into the black of night. A few moments later, the banner came into view, carried on the end of a pike.

"How can you see so well?" Lance asked.

Kaisha blushed but said nothing, tending to the fallen paladin instead.

Lance frowned, trying to solve the riddle.

"Didn't you hear the trumpets?" Ryshander said, stepping forward. "Those are the Westvon trumpets.

Had you never heard them before?"

Lance stammered. "I'm from Bureland. I've never been to Westvon."

"We should go there sometime," Ryshander said, "to thank them for saving our city." He knelt beside Kaisha. When Lance turned back to watch the soldiers march by, Ryshander signed to her: "You need to be more careful, my love. We're not in the company of our brothers and sisters. There are things we unconsciously do that they cannot. We don't know how they'd react to our bloodlines."

Kaisha nodded and lifted the paladin upright. She dabbed his head with a rag while Ryshander looked around at the ragged group. Lance was a mystery. He wore a strange robe and claimed to be a wizard, yet he bore no spell components. He was barely a man, yet he seemed so able and fearless in seeking out his own agenda. Ryshander knew nothing about his writings needing deciphered, but when the time arose, the mage put himself in harm's way to protect a woman he'd never met. Jude, the giant of a man, seemed to care for nothing but the safety of his friend. Yet, he too risked his life to save the strange warrior who battled the large dwarf. What a bizarre group of unlikely heroes they were.

Ryshander smiled warmly at beautiful Kaisha. She felt his eyes on her and returned his loving gaze, smiling as she rose to stand by his side. Ryshander placed a gentle arm around her waist as the pair watched the army establish a hold at the eastern edge of town. For the soldiers of Beykla, the battle for

Central City was far from over. The dwarves' fighting prowess was double the militia's, so it took hours to drive them back to the underground caverns that spawned them. By dawn, the city had been saved.

"What is a hero? I often struggled with this title given by men to other men. It earns its benefactor no wealth, land, or advantage. In fact, it often makes the bearer a target for cowards who resent the courage they can never possess.

"Then I ask, what makes a coward? Is a man who flees from battle a coward? Some say 'yes,' but what if he fled out of wisdom? Is fleeing from fear a cowardice act, or is fleeing as a whole? I believe that allowing fear to overcome you insomuch you run in terror is cowardice. A man who flees with the knowledge that he cannot have victory in battle is wise. Though in truth, I've learned that men cannot make cowards and heroes by labels. You either already are a hero, or a coward, merely undiscovered. It takes a crisis to find which. A man can never know what he is until he's been tested.

"But the mantle of a hero is a grave one indeed. Most say it is not a title that you can give yourself. I believe it revolves around some unwritten edict based on the sense of honor. But can a man without honor be a hero? Again, I say 'yes.' Being a hero is not someone else's perception of your deeds, but an inner force that compels people to act unselfishly. An orc raiding a village could be a hero, even if he's slaying innocent women and children. If a comrade of his is surrounded by the defenders of the village and the orc charges into the face of certain doom to free him, I believe he could be called a hero. Certainly not by the villagers' standards, but placing his life on the line for a friend is heroic. I believe most men fall between the lines of cowards and heroes, never excelling beyond one or the other. "Most men would disagree with me, but I've never been like other men, which is the single largest compliment the human race could afford me."

- Lancalion Levendis Lampara

Epilogue

The old general looked at the downed paladin and decided not to slay him. He was not Amerix's enemy. He was a champion of justice. Though Amerix thought him confused, his intentions were honorable. Amerix raised his axe above his head to give thanks to Durion, the mountain god, when he was struck in the side by a tremendous blow. He felt the weight forcing him over the railing of the bridge. Amerix reacted instantly, twisting his body and struggling with all his strength to keep from being forced over the mossy edge. His armor on his back squeaked as it rubbed against the cold railing. Something had a hold of his beard and was twisting his head to the side, while strong fingers tugged at his right shoulder. Amerix strained his muscles and let out a roar, then turned his body to face down over the edge. He stared into the eyes of the large human who'd attacked him earlier. Amerix reached down and snatched the wrist of the swordsman. With one arm, he hoisted the human closer and smiled at his astonishment of the feat. The old general noticed the human was anchored by a rope tied around his waist, and he reached down to cut it, when he felt someone grab his legs, then a shoulder hit him in the rump. Before he could react, Amerix tumbled over the bridge and zipped by the dangling human. He tried to reach out for the man, but he tumbled past. Amerix knew he didn't have much time before he hit the swift waters of the river below. He used the knife in his hand to cut the laces of his armor as he plummeted. He cut the side straps and then his leggings, waiting until impact to cut the rest, hoping the armor would take the brunt of the blow from striking water after such a high fall.

Amerix hit the river with a tremendous clap. The air was forced from his lungs and he felt himself sinking rapidly. He thought about letting the ancient armor pull him to the bottom of his watery grave. He'd lived a long life, longer than any dwarf should have. Dwarves normally died of old age by the time they reached their four hundredth year of life, but somehow the general kept living. He wasn't young by any standards, but he still had more vigor than dwarves two hundred years his junior.

As he slowly sunk, Amerix struggled with losing the armor. It was not only a symbol of the Alistair's, Amerix's family, but of the last remaining members of clan Stormhammer. It'd been handed down from generation to generation, some three thousand years. He gazed off into the black depths at an image that called to him, floating closer with an outstretched hand. It was a dwarven woman with white skin, adorned in silk robes. She had bright blue eyes and was clad in fine jewelry made of gold and precious gems. Her long straight hair danced in the murky depths as she watched the old general. Next to her stood a much younger dwarf, shorter than Amerix but taller than most dwarves. He wore sparkling chain armor that bore the symbol of Stormhammer. Amerix strained his eyes and recognized the pair to be Seraneen and Torgalt, his wife and son. He smiled and outstretched his bloodied hand. Amerix felt a wave of warmth fall over his body, despite being at the bottom of the icy river. His heart soared and he felt a sense of completeness that he'd not felt since their deaths. He was glad to be dying, to be reunited with them, but they didn't take his hand. Seraneen smiled and shook her head slowly. Her thin brown hair waved in the water.

Torgalt stuck his chest out proudly. "I wear not the plate armor of Stormhammer, yet would ye deny me family's honor?"

Amerix unconsciously shook his head. The sound of his only son's voice made him want to weep.

"Then why, Father, do you deny yourself that same honor?"

Amerix watched the pair fade away, then he violently roared in despair as he tried in vain to grab them. Suddenly, his lungs screamed for air and he realized that he was on the muddy floor of the Dawson River, being bounced and drug along by the strong undercurrents. Amerix ripped his armor off and with a mighty thrust from the river floor, his thick legs launched him toward the surface under a cloud of silt. He kicked and paddled as he fought the currents. He felt his limbs going weak, his lungs burned, and his mind was tingling from the lack of oxygen. The renegade general stared at the black water above him as he frantically searched for the surface. Just when he thought he wouldn't last any longer, he erupted from the river's deadly grasp to feel the crisp autumn night and smell the muddy odor of the water. He looked around, searching for the bridge but saw nothing. He floated down the river, exhausted. In a few minutes, he reached an area with a slower current and slowly paddled to the sandy bank, but he didn't bother crawling ashore. Instead, he lay exhausted on the small beach. Amerix's thick padded underclothing clung to his wet body as he mulled over his underwater encounter, ignoring the battle just before.

Amerix had been in thousands of battles before. Near death experiences were nothing new to the old renegade. He wondered if it was real or a hallucination from the lack of oxygen. Before he thought out any answers, he drifted off into a deep sleep. He'd survived once again when any other dwarf would have perished. Would death ever claim him, or would it merely mock him, teasing him until he was feeble and crippled, begging for it rather than fighting it as he'd done for over four hundred fifty years?

The adventure continues in
The Trial of Innocence
from newbabelbooks.com

and coming soon to Troll Lord Games
trolllord.com

Aboe- (a-bow) Kingdom on the southernmost peninsula of Terrigan. The kingdom has little or no army, but does not fear being conquered due to the great mountain reaches that surround its borders. It is wealthy and home to merchants and pirates alike. Of all the kingdoms in Terrigan, it is the most racially diverse with humans, dwarves, and elves holding political offices.

Aclia- (uh-clee-uh) Black-skinned dark angel. She is the most warrior-like.

Adoria- (A-door-ee-ah) Kingdom just west of Beykla. It waged a bloody civil war against its western half, Andoria.

Alexis Alexandria Overmoon- (a-lex-us / al-ecks-zan-dree-uh / Over moon) Daughter heir of King Christopher Calamon Overmoon. She travels with Apollisian Bargoe, trying to learn the ways of justice to aid her when she becomes queen.

Amerix Alistair Stormhammer- (am-er-icks / ali-stair / storm ham-er) Dwarven general of clan Stoneheart, formerly of clan Stormhammer. His clan was wiped out before him, when he was a young man, by dark dwarves and a white dragon. He fled with a few survivors and was welcomed into clan Stoneheart where he excelled in the art of war.

Amyrillion- Arch devil of pain.

Andoria- (an-door-ee-ah) Formally western Adoria, this kingdom's brief history came when it declared its independence from Adoria. It waged an eight-month-long war with Adoria, but was eventually re- conquered.

Androdius- (an-drode-ee-us) The great black dragon imprisoned in the swamp west of Aquabar.

Angelique- Greyshalk wife of Petrovisk

Apollisian Bargoe- (A-paul-issi-in / bar-go) Paladin of justice who was sent from his order in Westvon Keep to oversee the negotiations between humans and the dwarves from clan Stoneheart, in an attempt to derail a conflict, when he was caught in the middle of the war.

Aquabar- (awk-wuh-bar) Capitol of Aten. Lies near the great swamp and the Mountains of Meara.

Arluda- (are-loo-duh) Blue mistress and friend of Delania.

Artamanake- (art-man-uh-key) Dark dwarven general.

Aten- (A-ten) Queendom to the far west that is ran solely by women. Males of any race are considered inferior and are immediately made into slaves or killed at birth. Only a choice few males are kept alive for reproduction purposes only. The women of Aten are adept sorceresses and keep a rigid society of backstabbing and political maneuvering.

Artez Undermoon- (Are-tez) Captain of the Undermoon Darayal Legion.

Athodrin- (Uh-thod-drin) Soulless beings created by gods. Demons and angels are some of these. Ayden- (A-den) Powerful salomin who used Therrig to gain control of a large clan of Dark Dwarves. Barbetin- (bar-bet-in) Also known as the "Lake of the Damned." It is the lake in the Abyss where damned souls are thrown to be tortured for eternity by the demons swimming among it.

Beovi- (bee-o-vi) Subterranean fish living in the deepest freshwater caverns of the underworld. They are a delicacy to dwarves, dark dwarves, dark elves and other subterranean races. These fish can grow to unlimited size, depending on the lake or river in which they live.

Berylys-Quieness- (Berry-liss Kwee-uh-ness) Great white dragon. She disappeared and is rumored to be dead.

Beykla- (bay-kla) Human kingdom on the northeastern corner of Terrigan. The kingdom is well-to-do, militantly powerful, and well-patrolled. It has never, in its long history, been conquered.

Blue Dragon Inn- Inn in Central City that is closest to the Dawson River and the Dawson River bridge, where Lance, Kaisha, Ryshander, and Apollisian battled the dwarven horde until the king arrived with reinforcements.

Bordeck- (bore-dek) Dwarven torture device made of iron. It is shaped like a mask with many spikes on the inside, to be placed on the victim while a thick iron bar is fastened to two long screws on each side. The bar is then cranked upwards under the chin until it forces the lower jaw into the victim's upper jaw very slowly. The teeth pop and shatter, crushing the jaw and eventually causing death.

Borkin- (bore-kin) Small wooden device that is inserted into the mouth and keeps the wearer from closing his/her jaws.

Bureland- (bur-land) Small hamlet in the southern part of Beykla where Lance spent most of his childhood and early adult life with his adoptive father, Davohn.

Breedikai- (bree-da-kii) Original gods, or gods

that were created. They have no soul and most dwell in Merioulus.

Brother of the Sword- Term given by the Darayal Legion to their legionnaires-in-training.

Broyed- (broid) Male incubus dark angel.

Bykalicus- (Bye-kal-eh-kus) Powerful arch demon who controls much of the Abyss.

Cadacka- (ka-doc-uh) Black ceremonial robe worn by elves when they mourning a lost loved one. Most elves never remove the cloak once it is donned.

Calours- (ka-loo-ers) Non-sedimentary rocks found in the underworld. Subterranean races, mostly species of dwarves, use them to heat and cook meat on.

Calito, Battle of- (kuh-lee-toe) Battle which took place in Adoria near the town of Dolzan. Adorian knights fought against an evil necromancer named Randolph Forelinger, who commanded over a thousand undead soldiers.

Carcarass- (kar-kar-us) Training school which raises and trains Aten-born pureblood males to be slaves as they age.

Casen- (kay-sin) Name applied to animals that grow giant in size. Named after the halfling wizard Nermal Casen who accidentally created them.

Cathena- (Ka-theen-uh) Falconeer greyshalk daughter of Petrovisk.

Central City- City south of the Dawson Stronghold in the center of the Beyklan nation.

Cerebron- (sare-eeb-ren) Human boy saved by

Apollisian from the dwarven onslaught at the Torrent Manor.

Cheural- (Share-uhl) Gadgeteer greyshalk daughter of Petrovisk.

Christopher Calamon Overmoon- (Kris-toe-fur / Kal-a-mon / O-ver-moon) High king of the Minok Vale.

Congarn's Orchard- (kon-garn) Large orchard by Bureland where Lance would often steal apples and pears as a child.

Copel Nin- (cope-ul nin) Fat keeper of the gladiator slaves in Central City's arena. Copel was once a gladiator champion but was severely injured, ending his career as a fighter. He was hired by the Duke to be the keeper of the slaves. Copel always worked hard at the job but as he aged, his injury and time took its toll, preventing his ability to stay in shape. He soon became fat, but he enjoyed his job at the arena as he longed for the days to hear the roar of the crowd once more.

Council of the Wise- Consists of ten elders who sit on the governing seat at the Minok Vale, though not all ten are usually present at meetings, there has to be at least six to hold a vote.

Cranetium- (krane-tee-um) Official title given to an elven high mage. The title means little to other elves, save for the wizards and sorcerers of their Vales.

Crowalta- (Crow-all-tah) Mother of the black sept, controls the Gearian.

Cutstone- Clan that makes its home under the Lalin Plateau in Southern Beykla.

Dadramedion- (day-drom-uh-dee-in) Powerful arch

demon and enemy to Bykalicus.

Dall-kal-Mour- (doll-kal-moo-ur) Title given to blood-born men from Aten. They are the only males who are allowed to reproduce. They are expensive slaves and only the highest ranking or wealthy own them. It is a status symbol for Mother's or heads of septs to own more than one, since they will never give birth.

Dalton Thornfist- (doll-ton) Dwarven king who died from an illness and left the clan to a young Tharxton Stoneheart.

Dalzon- (dal-zohn) Small city in the northwestern side of Adoria.

Darayal Legion- (dar-ray-all) One hundred of the finest elite elven rangers that patrol the Minok Vale in pairs. They are skilled swordsmen who wield a weapon in each hand during battle. They are as feared as they are awed.

Darious Theobold- (dare-ee-us / They-bold) Eleven-year-old son of King Theobold.

Dark Dwarves- Dwarves who live solely in the underworld. They have pupil-less eyes that have adapted over time to see in the dark by detecting heat patterns. They hate bright light as it is painful for them, and have turned to wicked and evil ways as a society.

Dargruden- (dar-grude-in) Dal-kal-mour that runs the Gearian.

Darkhand- One of the priests who participated in the DeNaucght.

Darren Brightson, Duke- (Dare-in / bright-sun) Duke of the Adorian lands just to the east of the northeastern border of Aten. Governs over the small hamlet of Lostom.

Darrion-Quieness- (dare-ee-on / kwee-eh-ness) Great white dragon. Oldest of all white dragons and most powerful. His lair is in the mountains of Nalir, but he roams all over the realms. He often leads lesser races against their enemies, and takes the majority of the treasure after the victory. His last major campaign was in aid of the dark dwarves against the dwarven clan Stormhammer.

David Hentridge, Master- (hint-ridge) Leader of a small mercenaries guild disguised as a farm, just south of Central City. King Theobold uses them to hunt and kill orcs, so the public remains unaware of the actual amount of green-skinned beasts still living in his kingdom.

Davohn Ecnal- (da-von) Adoptive father of Lance. He is a woodcutter who made his home in Bureland and found Lance when he was six years old. He raised him as his son until Lance left at the age of seventeen.

Dawson River- Largest river that runs in Terrigan. It stretches from the Sea of Balfour, north of Beykla, through the southern kingdom of Aboe.

Dawson Stronghold- Capital of Beykla, this port city is the largest hub in the Bay of Balfour.

Delania- (duh-lane-ee-uh) Beautiful succubus that dwells in the Abyss.

Delker- (Dell-kur) Wizard bent on creating an alliance between powerful allies across Terrigan who are interested in defeating established kingdoms.

Demphinshile- (Dim-fin-shy-ul) Dark elf city deep in the under-mountain.

DeNaucght- (day-nok-tuh) Ritual performed by

goodly priests to raise a dead person back to life.

Dicermadon- (die-sir-ma-don) God of gods. Dicermadon plots with demons to kill the son of a goddess, drawing the wrath of the gods that he governs.

Diltz Quest- (Dilts) Ceremony in which Dal-kal-mours, Aten full-blooded males, compete in a gladiator-style competition to be selected as a mate for the queen.

Dolgo seeds- (dole-go) Tasty nuts found on the steepest slopes of the highest mountain. Considered a delicacy by all dwarves and mountain people.

Dome of the Rock- Ancient dwarven temple that was supposedly built by Durion. The temple is rumored to be atop the Lalin Plateau.

Donathuku- (Don-uh-thue-koo) Arch devil of terror.

Donjurik- (Don-szhur-ick) Small thin greyshalk sword. Rarely used in combat. Primarily ceremonial.

Donk- Aten word for the penis. It is an insulting word in their culture and is associated with weakness and stupidity.

Doogan Raymer- (doo-gun / ray-muhr) Northern noble from Dawson. Doogan is a conniving tactician who has made his estates through double dealing and backstabbing. He shows his family tree as being distantly related to the king, and hopes to one day return his house to the throne.

Dorcastig- (door-cast-ig) Tall muscled priest of Rha-Cordan. Follows under Resin.

Durion- (der-ee-in) Dwarven mountain god.

Dregan City- (dree-gan) Home of the clan Stormhammer before it was wiped out by the dark dwarves and a white dragon.

Drunda- (drun-duh) The god that orcs follow. It is unknown if he actually exists, or even if he is male.

Earth Oath- Oath an elf makes, and will give his/her life trying to uphold.

Eckwon- (Eck-qwon) Trinidy's warhorse when he was alive.

Ecnal- (eck-null) Surname given to all orphans of Beykla before they were all killed by unknown assassins.

Edgar Sorenson- (ed-ger / sore-in-son) Powerful cleric of Surshy, advisor and close friend to King Theobold.

Edsil Strongbow- (Ed-zuhl) Darayal captain of the Strongbow vale.

Ehleeshuh- (Uh-leash-uh) White unicorn.

Elder Bartoke- (bar-toke) Elder of the Minok Vale, member of the Council of the Wise, and keeper of the sealed passings.

Elder Darmond- (dar-mond) Elder of the Minok Vale, member of the Council of the Wise, and keeper of the passings.

Elder Humas- (hue-mass) Elder of the Minok Vale, member of the Council of the Wise, and keeper of the passings.

Elder Varmintan- (Var-mint-ton) Elder of the Minok Vale, member of the Council of the Wise, and keeper of the passings.

Eldred, City of- (Ale-dread) Small town that brews their own specific ale not revered by most other Beyklan towns.

Elecksixs- (Uh-lecks-ick) Succubus leader of the dark angels.

Erik Stromson- (strahm-son) General of the Beyklan Western army and hero of the orc wars.

Eucladower Strongbow- Oldest elder of the Minok Council of the Wise and keeper of the passings.

Eulic Overmoon- (yew-lick) Darayal Legionnaire and cousin to Alexis Overmoon.

Famen's Tree- (fay-mens) Large tree three miles east of the Dawson River bridge. The tree was named after Jeddis Famen, a Central City militia leader who held off an orc attack. After the battle, he led a group of militiamen after the fleeing orcs and managed to slay one of the orc leaders. He nailed the orc's head to the tree with a spike as a message to any other orcs. That was the last orc battle against Central City during the orc wars. The people believed the orcs were afraid of him, but in truth they were massing to finish the elves at the Minok Vale.

Fehzban Algor Stoneheart- (fez-ben / al-gore) Commander and loyal follower of General Amerix Stormhammer. Was tried and convicted of treason after the Torrent Manor and Central City campaigns.

Fifvel- (fife-vul) Barkeeper and owner of the Blue Dragon Inn in Central City.

Fig root- Strongbow root that is dried and soaked in spirits.

Flunt- God of fire, and one of the four elemental gods.

Freedom Festival- Holiday celebrated in Beykla to commemorate the end of the twenty-year-long orc wars.

Funis- (Fu-niss) Strong straight line of waxed bowstring at the draw of all Proudarrow bows from the Darayal Legion. This device allows them to shoot several arrows at once with deadly precision.

Galla noodles- (Ga-la) Thin noodles often prepared with butter.

Garlibane- (gar-lee-bane) High mage and elder of the Minok Vale, member of the Council of the Wise.

Gearian- (Gear-ee-in) Collection of incorrigible sudas who exist for the sole purpose of raping and killing women in Aten convicted of the most serious crimes. The women are stripped of their power and thrown into a pit. Above, spectators laugh as the women are raped repeatedly over many days until they are dead.

General Laricin West- (lair-iss-in) Late general for the northern Beyklan army who was responsible for scattering the orc horde in the battle later referred to as The Quigen. General Laricin and his men fought to the last man, keeping the orc horde from wiping out what was left of the elven resistance.

General Thatcher- (Thach-er) Southern general of the Beyklan army who embraced the southern Beyklan nobles when they announced their independence.

Glaszric- (ga-laz-er-ick) Half-orc bouncer at the Blue Dragon Inn in Central City.

Gorsan- (gore-sahn) Dwarven brewmaster who is a distant relative to Fehzban. Gorsan lives in Dolzan and sells dwarven ales to the locals.

Grascon the nimble- (grass-con) Wererat thief who Lance double-crossed in Bureland. The thief bears a horrible scar from nose to ear, received from an encounter stemming from his leaving the thieves guild in Central City.

Gregory Herwain- (her-wane) Southern noble who is Chairmen of Affairs in southern Beykla. He is the leader of House Herwain that is well known for saying much and doing little. He hosts the monthly meetings of the southern nobles in the city of Motivas at the House of Affairs.

Greyshalk- Tall furry humanoids with strong beliefs in family, tribe, and warfare.

Grimolikin Hill, Battle of- (Grim-mole-uh-kin) Battle where greyshalks were forced from their land by the Beyklans during the orc wars. The Beyklans were actually trying to route several tribes of kriel that were helping the orcs.

Grinder- Main passageways in the sewers under Central City, used by the wererat thieves guild.

Gweits- (ga-weets) Tiny insect-like demons that dwell on the rocky floor of the Abyss. They feed on flesh, and burrow under skin with their horrific claws and hooks.

Harbor Mountain- Large city-state on the Dalgun island of Aboe.

Heart of the Rock- A gemstone mounted on a gold ring, said to have magical properties that can prevent the wearer from being harmed by dragon's breath.

Hector DeScoran- (heck-tor / day-skore-an) Evil warrior wizard and king of Nalir. Believes Lance was prophesized to destroy his kingdom and will stop at nothing until the boy is dead.

Henrious- (Hen-ree-us) Ex-Diltz quest gladiator and Dal-kal-mour that helps Tonya of the white and the freedom movement.

Hiramem- (her-uh-mem) Old female sorceress who lives in Aten. She often works for Ramasiel in the red tower and has a limited ability at foretelling. She often uses old chicken bones, stones and other small objects that she tosses about on a board with elven skin stretched over it. She is from Beykla, originally. She grew up in Sineuvia.

Hourid Thigguard- (hor-id / thig-guard) Master of arms and father of Mylaneia.

Ian Silverman- (E-uhn) Human knight under Duke Darren Brightstar. Fought in the battle of Calito. Has two sons, Ian Silverman the second and Myer Silverman. Both are adventurers and Ian does not agree with their lifestyle.

Ickten Norris- (ick-ton) Ranger who works for the Hentridge farm south of Central City. He is an expert tracker and skilled swordsman. His favored enemies are orcs.

Illilander Trees- (ill-lee-land-er) Largest trees in the realms. Over five hundred feet tall.

Inn of Aldon- Bureland's only inn, where Lance grew up.

Iratus- (Eye-rat-us) A rare form of a personality that has the ability to gain great strength from anger.

Jahallawa extract- (ja-hall-uh-wah) Sap from the Jahallawa plant which is extremely toxic if injected into the body. It leaves the victim paralyzed for hours and can take weeks to fully recover.

Jon Klement- Arch mage of central Beyklan army.

Jordan Gersian- (jor-dun / Ger-see-in) Southern nobleman who is leading a plot to pull southern Beykla away from the North.

Jude- (Jewd) Mercenary swordsman from Bureland. He sold his sword to fight brigands, polecats and other minor enemies of Bureland. He is also Lance's best friend.

Jurnda Undermoon- (Jern-duh) Dark elf legionnaire who fights with two axes. Big brother to Artez.

Kai-Harkia- (Kay-hark-ee-uh) Mountain kingdom northwest of Beykla. Its people are dark-skinned, dark-haired, heavy-chested, nomadic swordsmen. They seldom form static villages, though some do exist.

Kaisha- (Kay-sha) Wererat thief guild member from Central City.

Kalen Al-Kalidius- (kay-lin / al-kal-id-ee-us) Grey elf, ex-stepson of King Overmoon of the Minok Vale. Kalen turned to the shadow and hungers for power, hoping to take the throne of Nalir when Hector dies.

Kalistirsts- (kal-eh-stirsts) Underground mole people with no eyes. They live in the underworld.

Kalliman Theobold- (kall-eh-man) King of Beykla.

Kalliman Castle- (kall-eh-man) Castle and home of King Kalliman Theobold.

Kar- An orc war party; excursion leader.

Kareeg Hut- (kuh-reeg) Nobleman who owned more

land than any other noble in Beykla. His lands in the North extended from just south of the Torrent Manor to the western border of Beykla, and east to the Dawson River, then up to Dawson. His brother was a captain stationed at the Torrent Manor when it fell, and he hates the dwarves more than any other Beyklan.

Katrinal- (Ka-trine-uhl) Greyshalk daughter of Petrovisk.

Katykop- (Kate-ee-cop) Abyssal for mischievous/ feline.

Kellacun- (kell-eh-kun) Wererat assassin who worked for the guild in Central City before it was destroyed. Now she works for Kalen in an attempt to kill Lance.

Kestish- (kest-ish) Commander and loyal follower of General Amerix Stormhammer. Commander Kestish vanished after the battle of Central City, and is believed dead.

Kendalerairy Overmoon- (Ken-doll-ler-air-ee) Captain of the Overmoon Darayal Legion.

Kerstap- (Kur-stap) Mighty curved two-handed greyshalk sword.

King Minostak- (Min-oh-stack) Greyshalk king.

Kings, Game of- Game similar to chess.

Kingsford City- Largest city in Terrigan. Capitol of Ladathon.

Kornicus- (corn-uh-cus) Demon imp servant of Delania.

Korrin Hentridge- (core-in / hint-ridge) Twelve-year-old son of Master David Hentridge.

Kreegan Malone- (Kree-gun) Acting duke of Central city when Dolin Blackhawk is away. Kuma- (Koo-muh) Blade attached to the end of the Strongbow's bows for melee fighting. Kriel- (Kree-uhl) Small, thin greyshalks with dark, spotted fur. Hyena-like.

Ladathon- (lad-uh-thon) Southern country, south of Tyrine, where mysterious animals live in a thick jungle. Kingsford City is its capitol.

Ladathonian Warhorse- (lad-uh-thone-ee-un) A breed of war horse from Ladathon that stands nearly eighteen hands high and weighs nearly three thousand pounds.

Lalin Plateau- (lay-lin) Large plateau in the middle of southern Beykla, covered by lush forest. It is nearly impossible to scale its thousand-foot-high sheer rock walls. Stories tell of ancient ruins at the top, but few have climbed to its summit to validate the claims. What makes the plateau so unique is the Dawson river runs through the inside of it in a great river cave.

Lancalion Levendis Lampara- (lance-uh-lion / lev-un-dis / lamb-par-uh) Birth name given to Lance Ecnal.

Lance Ecnal- Adopted son of Davohn Ecnal. Lance's birth name is Lancalion Levendis Lampara. His natural mother was Panoleen, the goddess of mercy. Lance is prophesized to bring plague and death on the world, though he sees himself as nothing more than an orphan trying to discover his past.

Larunthus- (Lar-unth-this) God of the hunt.

Leska- (les-kuh) The earth mother goddess, one of the four elemental gods. She reigns over all living things.

Lirlithe- (lear-lith) Short-haired mischievous dark angel with curved horns.

Loke-tah- (loke-ta) Orc word equivalent to comrade, used by orcs in reference to another who is liked as a friend. Though the orcish language does not have a single word for friend, it has over a dozen for enemy.

Lostom- (loss-tom) Small hamlet on the border of Aten and Adoria.

Lostos- (low-stoes) Name for the underground complex of the Severed Heart guild of wererats in Central City.

Lukerey- (lou-kear-ee) God of luck and mischief.

Lunarian- (lou-nar-ee-in) Enchanted wells that priestly elves, or other good forest creatures, bless by the powers of Leska to rejuvenate and heal one another.

Lyndall- (lin-doll) Gladiator champion in Central City. A skilled swordsman who had fought over 240 fights.

Malwinar- (mal-win-are) Elven mage apprentice of Garlibane.

Markus- (Mark-us) Suda in Ramasiel's tower, and Reena's secret lover.

Marlana- (Mar-lane-uh) Backstabbing mistress of the blue sept who conspired with Ramasiel to overthrow the mother of the blue sept in order to control a second vote in the senate.

Marzahna- (marr-zohn-uh) Mother of the yellow sept who was banished for wanting to marry. She built a smaller tower on the border of Aten in the hamlet of Lostom.

Mary of the Yellow Robe- Mistress of the banished yellow mother, Marzahna.

Matoon- (muh-toon) Aquatic elf city in the sea of Balfour.

Merioulus- (mare-ee-oh-you-lus) City of the gods. Set on a form of the astral plane.

Mersaat- (mare-sat) Great blue dragon who lives in the desert of Tyrine. A scroll was stolen from his lair by a hapless thief. The scroll was sold several times until it ended up at the great library in Kingsford City, where Ladathon scholars identified the text as draconian. What made the scroll unique was it was written in humanoid size (few humans know draconic). It gave credibility that there is a secret sept of priests who worship the great serpents, but it led others to believe that once the beasts fully mature, they gain the ability to transform into a manlike creature. All of these theories have yet to be proven.

Mershaulk- (mur-shalk) God of serpents, some believe the god does not exist and is only worshipped by a cult known as the Sept of Serpents. Mershaulk is also the term referred to men who go into berserker rage in battle. The rage is so intense, the men feel no pain, can continue to battle long after their body has died, and have a hard time differing friend from foe on the battlefield. Mershaulks are as feared as they are respected as warriors, though they never fight with comrades, as a Mershaulk often claims the lives of those around him.

Midagord Milence Stormhammer- Amerix Stormhammer's deceased father.

Minok Vale- (my-nock) Name of the elven sovereignty set in Beykla.

Miranhka- (mere-aunk-uh) Wererat thief who managed to survive the dwarven assault on Central City and escape.

Mordrik- (more-drick) Dark elf mercenary who resided in the under-mountain. Amerix Stormhammer hunted and killed his band one by one for killing a Kalistirst friend of his.

Morilla- (more-ill-uh) Town seamstress in Bureland. She was a good friend of Davohn and Lance.

Mortan Ganover- First lieutenant of Duke Dolin Blackhawk, and acting mayor when the Duke is gone. He is considered responsible for the slaughter at Central City by the dwarves due to his inability to act on the paladin Apollisian's recommendations.

Mortigalus- (Mor-tuh-gal-us) Arch devil of gluttony and torture.

Motivas- (moe-ta-vis) Southernmost city in Beykla, built on a large brick foundation that is rumored to be ruins of an ancient civilization.

Mountain Heart- Home city of clan Stoneheart, located in the Pyberian Mountains.

Mount Steeple- The largest mountain on Terrigan, and rumored to hold the roadway to Merioulus as its peak cannot be seen due to a permanent veil of clouds.

Mowaka- (moe-walk-uh) Camouflage cloak-like blanket that elven archers, and sometimes rangers, use to spy on their enemies.

Myer Silverman- (my-er) Son of Ian Silverman of Lostom.

Mylaneia Thigguard- (my-lane-ya / thig-guard) Young daughter of Hourid Thigguard, and courtier of Tharxton Stoneheart.

Myson Strongbow- (mice-in) Darayal Legionnaire who faced Trinidy, the death knight. Myson was the first death in what was later to be named the Dead War.

Nalir- (nall-er) A militantly powerful southern empire made primarily of swamps and quagmires. They worship most of the evil gods.

Navlashier- (nav-luh-sheer) Elven city in Vidora.

Necromidus- (neck-rom-eh-dus) A collection of the first four tiers of necromancy spells.

Optis Midigan- (op-tis / mid-eh-gun) Young servant of Hector DeScoran and follower of Soran Songstream.

Orantal Proudarrow- (or-an-tall) Commander of the Darayal Legion and protector of the Minok Vale, friend of Elder Eucladower.

Osimar- (Ossy-mar) City on Dalgun Island that makes the best wine in all the realms – most expensive.

Oswald Thorrin- (oz-wald / Thor-in) Captain of the Royal Beyklan Guard and bounty hunter, though he only collects on lawful bounties set by the magistrates.

Panoleen- (pan-oh-leen) Goddess of mercy who was banished from the heavens.

Pav-co- (pahv-coe) Fat wererat guild leader in Central City.

Petrovisk- (Pet-roe-visk) Old greyshalk champion

from the orc wars.

Plaatu- (Pla-two) Kalistirst friend of Amerix.

Plains of Vendaiga- (vin-day-guh) Large grasslands in southern Aten, home of the Vendaigehn steeds, the fastest horses on Terrigan.

Pockweln- (pahk-welln) Right hand supporter of Resin Darkhand, high priest of Rha-Cordan.

Pyberian Mountains- (pie-beer-ee-an) Mountain range in the northwest corner of Beykla, near Adoria.

Quadry Proudarrow- (Quad-ree) Darayal Legionnaire of the Minok Vale.

Quigen- (kwi-jin) Elven word for sacrifice. Most widely known as the battlefield's name where General Laricin West scattered the orcish horde by fighting until every man in his army fell in the Serrin Plains.

Ramasiel- (ram-uh-zeal) One of the three mothers of the red sept in Aten. She is a powerful sorceress and a political power in Aquabar.

Randolph Forlinger- (ran-doff / four-ling-er) Powerful necromancer who was defeated and slain at the battle of Calito.

Raynard Cliffs- (ray-nard) Large group of cliffs that extend the entire north border of Nalir.

Reagle, The- A fancy clothing store in Aquabar. It does not make any article of clothing that could be used in an intimate way to make the women more attractive. Atenians believe that men have no right to be attracted to them, and the act should be gratifying to the woman only.

Reena- (ree-nuh) Third sorceress, also called third sister, of the red sept in Aten. Second only to Ramasiel herself.

Resin Darkhand- (rez-in) High priest of Nalir, worshiper of Rha-Cordan and advisor to Hector DeScoran.

Rha-Cordan- (rah-kor-don) God of death and dying. Not inherently evil, he reigns over the placement of souls when they enter the afterlife. He has been known to be incredibly vengeful to those who prolong their lives through magical means.

Ryshander- (rye-shan-der) Wererat thief who left Central City with Kaisha after the dwarves destroyed their guild.

Salomin- (Sall-oh-min) Subterranean humanoid species with powerful mind controlling abilities.

Samarkel- (Suh-mark-uhl) Large frog-like demon in the Abyss.

Sea of Balfour- (bal-four) Sea north of Beykla. Ancient lore tells of it once being dry ground and home of an ancient kingdom known as Balfour.

Serrin Plains- (sare-in) Dangerous, expansive grassland south of the Minok Vale where most of the evil races thriving in Beykla dwell.

Sespie Twinner- (ses-pee / twin-er) Young woman from Bureland who had been practicing medicine with Morilla and learned her healing ability while helping injured soldiers during the orc wars.

Severed Heart- The unofficial name of the wererat thieves guild in the sewers of Central City.

Sha-Shor'Nai- (sha-shore-nigh) God of the sun and light.

Shanorian- (Sha-nore-ee-uhn) General of devils.

Sierra Blackhawk- Duke Dolin Blackhawk's granddaughter.

Silas Proudarrow- (sigh-less) Darayal Legionnaire of the Minok Vale.

Slargcar- (sa-larg-car) Orc chief of tribe Glargcar.

Soran Songstream- (sore-in) High sage and practicing wizard in the kingdom of Nalir. Stahlsman- (stalls-man) City guard who works at the north gate of Central City. Stephanis- (stuh-fawn-is) God of Justice.

Stieny Gittledorph- (stie-knee / get-tull-dorf) Halfling thief who became mixed up with the dragon Darrion-Quieness.

Stormghast- The great stone doors that seal Mountain Heart from the dark, uncharted reaches of the under-mountain.

Suda- (sue-duh) Title given to all non-eunuch slaves in Aten. A suda is looked at as a lower form of man by the tuda, or eunuch.

Surelda Al-Kalidius- (sir-el-da / al-kuh-lid-ee-us) Ex-wife of King Overmoon and mother of Kalen Al-Kalidius.

Surshy- (sir-she) Goddess of water, and one of the four elemental gods.

Symas- (sim-uhs) Bead-like ornaments hung from the ends of braids in the Darayal Legionnaires' varmin. Symas are given for meritorious acts of bravery, ranging from leather, as the least, to gold, being the greatest.

Tallnok- (tal-knock) Young wizard who works for the Hentridge farm south of Central City. Occasionally hires himself out for specific jobs.

Talwin- (tall-win) Young apprentice war wizard who joined the western Beyklan army instead of staying with the mage guild in Dawson.

Tamra Hentridge- The daughter of Master David Hentridge.

Targavian Hollen Stoneheart- (tar-gave-ee-in / hall-in) New general promoted by Tharxton after the betrayal of Amerix and his officers.

Terrace Folly- (ter-is / fall-ee) Small hamlet southeast of Central City.

Terrigan- (ter-eh-gun) Name of the continent where all known civilizations exist.

Tharxton Stoneheart- (tharx-ton) Young king of clan Stoneheart and political rival with Amerix Alistair Stormhammer.

Therrig Alistair Delastan- (ther-ig / al-eh-stair / del-eh-stan) Illegitimate son of Amerix Alistair Stormhammer. Therrig is living proof of Amerix and Therrig's mother's infidelity.

Thomas Smith (Arwar)- (are-wahr) Blacksmith who worked at the Torrent Manor before Amerix attacked. He was head of the liaison between the two peoples, and he learned dwarven from his many dwarven friends at Mountain Heart before retiring back to Poria.

Tonya- Former mother of the white tower who staged

her death so she could anonymously lead the freedom movement of Aten.

Torrent Manor- Small keep northwest of Central City that was built specifically for enforcing the trade embargo on the dwarves dwelling in the Pyberian Mountains, and on the Adorians in the civil war.

Tracy Ross- Young girl who lives with her family at the Junction, near the Torrent Manor.

Travits- (trav-itz) Wererat thief and guild member of the Severed Heart guild in Central City.

Trinidy- (trin-eh-dee) Dead paladin of Dicermadon who was raised from the dead by evil priests of Rha-Cordan, creating the first death knight.

Trishal- (Trish-uhl) Multi-armed female demon with a human torso and a snake body.

Tuda- (too-duh) Title given to all eunuch slaves in Aten.

Tyrine- (tie-reen) Kingdom south west of Beykla.

Valga- (val-guh) Vlargcar's mother, who was slain after she fled the ruthless orc village to protect her son from the tribe. They believed since Vlargcar was abnormally large and his eyes were blue instead of yellow, she had been consorting with evil gods.

Valley of Mist- Lush green valley below the entrance to Mountain Heart in the Pyberian Mountains.

Varmin- (var-men) Long braided hairstyle worn by Darayal Legionnaires.

Vendaigehn- (vin-day-gun) Type of horse from the

plains of Vendaiga. They are marked with white spots on their flanks, and are taller than most horses with longer, thinner legs. Legend says that Vendaigehn steeds are the offspring of a Pegasus and a unicorn, though it has never been proven.

Victor DeVulge- (day-vul-juh) Squire of Apollisian Bargoe.

Vidora- (vie-door-uh) Wild, uncivilized kingdom southwest of Tyrine that is mostly inhabited by elves.

Vinr- (Vin-er) Greyshalk word for friend.

Vlargcar- (va-larg-car) Orc whelp saved by Amerix when he and his mother were ordered killed by their tribe.

Vrescan Alistair Delastan- Therrig's father who was killed fighting side by side with Midagord Stormhammer in defense of Dregan City.

Walter Thigpen- Middle-aged royal guard crossbowman and longtime friend of Captain Oswald Thorrin.

Westvon Keep- (west-van) Large keep and hamlet to the East in Beykla, on the banks of the Dawson River.

Whisten- (wiss-ton) God of air, and one of the four elemental gods.

Yahna- (ya-nuh) City in the heavens where mortal souls, blessed by their gods, dwell.

Yohr-Acht- (your-awk-tuh) Great green dragon who makes his lair atop the Lalin Plateau.

About the Author

Shane Moore grew up on a farm in rural Illinois. An only child that was six miles from his nearest peer, Shane often created wild tales of heroes and villains during his many trips into the deep woods that surrounded his rural home.

Shane was accelerated in his class and started his senior year of high school at age sixteen. After graduating and getting a waiver for his age, Shane joined the United States Navy to pay for college. He participated in campaigns; "Provide Hope" and "Secure Democracy" during the Yugoslavian civil war. Shane received several naval awards and citations and was one of the highest trained members of his ship.

After getting out of the service, Shane began college. He was soon hired by the Carlinville Police Department, beginning his multiple venue police career. Shane retired as a detective for the Gillespie Police Department after serving twelve years. His police career was quite notable with awards for bravery and with one life saving medal. He was named Officer of the Year in 2005.

A lesser known truth about Shane is that he played eight years of semi pro football with the Central Illinois Cougars. Shane is the team's all-time tackle leader and holds the record for most special teams tackles in a season and the most tackles in a game. Shane received many awards including Defensive Player of the Year in 2005.

January 14th, 2008. Shane retires from his police career to be a professional novelist.

Mr. Moore resides in Central Illinois with his son, Dakota.

Go to www.Zod001.com and Join for Free!

www.ingramcontent.com/pod-product-compliance
Lightning Source LLC
LaVergne TN
LVHW010608100826
845148LV00014B/2891

* 9 7 8 1 6 3 1 9 6 0 1 8 5 *